"Our new arrangeme[nt]... such good neighbors... toward her father and away from the appeal of Hafual's broad chest.

"Elene has captured the situation perfectly." Hafual's lips brushed the top of her head, causing a curl of heat within her.

She lifted her eyes to his and tumbled into the deep pools. When had they become so deep a blue?

"Glad you approve...dear."

He brushed his lips against hers again. Longer this time. And the curl of heat swooped and circled about her insides, making her knees weak. She splayed her hands against his chest to keep from falling.

"Why?" she whispered.

"To get the point across," he murmured against her ear.

The hall resounded to people stamping their feet in approval and cheering. A surge of triumph went through her. No one had guessed that the performance wasn't for real.

Author Note

To Wed a Viking Warrior is the story of Elene, the youngest sister of Baelle Heale, Mercia, and finishes the Vows and Vikings trilogy. I adored exploring how each individual sister confronts the upheaval which the Viking invasion of Britain brought and how, despite the odds, she manages to find love on her own terms.

The first book is *A Deal with Her Rebel Viking* (Ansithe, the middle sister's story) and the second is *Betrothed to the Enemy Viking* (Cynehild, the eldest's story). They can be read as stand-alones but certain threads and characters do run through the trilogy. I really hope you enjoy reading them as much as I enjoyed writing them.

As ever, thank you for being one of my readers. If you'd like to get in touch, I love getting comments from readers and can be reached at michelle@michellestyles.co.uk, through my publisher or on Facebook or Twitter, @michellelstyles.

MICHELLE STYLES

To Wed a Viking
Warrior

HARLEQUIN
HISTORICAL

HARLEQUIN®
HISTORICAL™

Recycling programs
for this product may
not exist in your area.

ISBN-13: 978-1-335-40771-9

To Wed a Viking Warrior

Copyright © 2022 by Michelle Styles

This edition published by arrangement with Harlequin Books S.A.

For questions and comments about the quality of this book,
please contact us at CustomerService@Harlequin.com.

Harlequin Enterprises ULC
22 Adelaide St. West, 41st Floor
Toronto, Ontario M5H 4E3, Canada
www.Harlequin.com

Printed in U.S.A.

Born and raised near San Francisco, California, **Michelle Styles** currently lives near Hadrian's Wall with her husband and a menagerie of pets in an Edwardian bungalow with a large and somewhat overgrown garden. An avid reader, she became hooked on historical romances after discovering Georgette Heyer, Anya Seton and Victoria Holt. Her website is michellestyles.co.uk and she's on Twitter and Facebook.

Books by Michelle Styles

Harlequin Historical

Vows and Vikings

Sons of Sigurd

Visit the Author Profile page
at Harlequin.com for more titles.

For my aunt,
Cynthia Ruttan.

Chapter One

September 875
Between the estates of Baelle Heale and Wulfhere's
Clearing, Forest of Arden, West Mercia
(Near modern-day Solihull, West Midlands, England)

No hero riding over the hill was going to save her or indeed her father's manor of Baelle Heale. She had to do it alone. Until quite recently, Elene, the youngest daughter of ealdorman Wulfgar of Baelle Heale, had held out hope for the man she'd considered the love of her life, but she had learned the hard way that men made honeyed promises which they promptly forgot. From here on out, she depended only on her wits to make the future she wanted instead of wishing for love.

'Mine and no one else.'

Elene marched on along the track at the edge of a water meadow with fierce determined steps, carrying the sack of clothes and other belongings she'd hurriedly gathered together before the cockerels started crowing this morning.

Intellectually she knew she must marry someone

who was acceptable to the Mercian King to secure these lands which her family had held since time began. King Ceolwulf had been quite clear in his most recent proclamation—Northmen must make loyalty oaths to hold land in Mercia. Neither of her brothers-in-law with their holdings in the North-controlled Five Boroughs and who were Northern *jaarls* with large war bands would swear fealty to a foreign king like Ceolwulf. Not when the bulk of their holdings was in the Dane-law. Their first loyalty had to be towards their own people rather than towards her cantankerous father.

Her nephew was far too young to hold the lands in his own right. Besides, her nephew was now in the Five Boroughs with her eldest sister, Cynehild. She had gone to lay her late husband's sword where his ancestors were buried and ended up marrying Kal Randrson, the Danish warlord who now controlled those lands. Kal had adopted the boy and there was talk about him inheriting his father's old lands when the time came.

Baelle Heale required a warrior loyal to Mercia and its people. Her father had impressed that point on her after she had learned of the Great Betrayal. She had finally given in to Nerian the Wessex warrior to whom she'd gifted her heart's entreaties and lain with him in the hayloft the last time he'd visited, thinking he would go straight to her father and formally make an offer for her hand in marriage. She had found the coupling vaguely unsatisfactory and painful, but he appeared to enjoy it. However, within the month, he'd married one of the wealthiest heiresses in Wessex. Until that happened, she'd considered herself the prize, rather than the handy spare.

Despite the setback, she'd always thought she'd be

given a choice of acceptable men to marry when the time came, rather than having one single candidate foisted on her.

That was until yesterday. She'd overheard the steward and his new wife talking about her betrothal to Lord Pybba of Etone as if it were a fact, not some fantastical nightmare proposition conjured by an overindulgence of mead.

She glanced down at Bugge, her wolfhound, who padded along at her side in the early autumn mist, with a faintly worried expression on her face. 'I can do this, can't I? I can stop this mad idea on my own, rather than needing my sisters to rescue me like some errant child who has become stuck in the smokehouse when the door accidentally shuts. I need time to clear my head and not to panic like some chicken who refuses to go into the henhouse.'

A small shiver went through her. She'd hated enclosed spaces ever after that. Her middle sister, Ansithe, had apologised afterwards, bringing her a bit of honeycomb to make amends, claiming that it had been unintentional, but she had not been the one who'd banged on the door until her fists bled. 'I make my own future. And I'm not spoilt or wilful like the steward told his wife. I had my reasons for refusing those other warriors…a reason which no longer exists.'

Bugge gave her hand another nudge as if to forestall another bout of tears. She was beyond crying, gnashing her teeth and wailing about lost years waiting for a man who'd married another. Until yesterday, she had been ready to live properly, starting with a planned visit to court in the autumn. She might not be as young as she once was, but she retained a good figure, golden hair and was an heiress to lands.

Flutter-brained as the steward's wife called her? She begged to differ.

'After my father experiences the sheer horror of Lord Pybba's arrogance, he will throw him off Baelle Heale lands, rather than insisting he becomes his latest son-in-law. I intend to make this happen, Bugge. Somehow.'

Elene lifted the hem of her gown, trying to keep it clear of the early morning dew which speckled the water meadow like teardrops. The last thing she wanted was to arrive at her destination mud splattered and bedraggled, not when she wanted an enormous favour. A few days of residing there, close enough to return if the situation warranted it, but away from any machinations which could lead to an accidental betrothal, or worse, a wedding.

'Lady Elene? Far too early for you to be about, particularly without an escort. Or is it that you still enjoy taking risks?' Lord Hafual of Wulfhere's Clearing loomed out of the mist, his features set in a fearsome frown. And one of the last people she wanted or expected to encounter. He was supposed to be many miles away attending to the king's business. The success of her current scheme depended on it.

Her feet skittered to a stop on a rock covered in wet leaves and moss. Thinking it was a game, Bugge ran behind her, woofed and pushed her over, causing her right ankle to buckle. She tumbled hard onto the ground, spilling the contents of the bundle she carried. She swore softly under her breath. Today was rapidly turning into a disaster. 'I… I… Oh, help…'

'Are you injured, my lady? The rocks can be slippery at this time of year.' His tone implied he expected her to be, that he would help her but doing so would inconvenience him greatly.

'Allow me to catch my breath.' Elene rotated her right ankle and tried to ignore the sudden shooting pain.

Hafual had once been part of the Great Heathen Horde, one of the Northmen who had invaded Mercia like a summer storm, driving all before them and eventually forcing a sort of peace where the western half of Mercia and all of East Anglia had been ceded to the Northern invaders.

Shortly after Ansithe, her middle sister, married her Northman, Moir Mimirson, Hafual had saved the new king of Mercia's life—King Ceolwulf—when they were hunting stags during that summer of the peace negotiations, and Ceolwulf offered him a position at the Northern court as the chief bodyguard. Moir released Hafual from his oath, telling him that the king's favour would make his fortune. After pledging eternal fealty to Mercia, Hafual had been rewarded with Wulfhere's Clearing, whose lands ran to the east of Baelle Heale. He'd proved an able lord. However, since his wife's tragic death, he spent his time at court or away on the king's business, leaving his half-sister to look after the estate and his young son.

When she was satisfied that her ankle was merely twisted, rather than broken, Elene tilted her chin upwards and extended her hand, opting for a languid drawl. 'Lord Hafual. I didn't realise you had returned. How...how perfectly delightful for all concerned.'

Hafual's scowl increased. 'I was unaware you needed to be informed of my movements.'

'Gossip is like gorse—always in season.' Elene gritted her teeth and allowed her hand to drop. She would have to find another place to hide while she figured out her future. Hafual would not permit an unwed lady like her to remain at his hall, not when he was in residence. Ever since his wife's death, Hafual had refused to allow women except for his sister and the servants into his hall.

'Are you saying that someone has gossiped about us? Together? As a couple?' His face settled into hard granite planes of unrelenting disapproval. 'Who dared to spread *that* rumour?'

'Not that sort of rumour.' Elene swallowed hard. Her and Lord Hafual? Everyone knew he had no time for any romance. Not now. Not ever. His heart lay buried with his wife, according to his half-sister. 'I mean none that I know about...people always mention arrivals.'

'I see. What will *people* say about you and I meeting like this? And in this fashion? Or do you always greet strange warriors like this these days?'

She followed his ice-cold gaze and saw that her skirt had rucked up so that her calf was showing. Bare and naked against the moss. She rapidly smoothed her skirt down before attempting to rise. A sudden pain shot through her ankle. She cautiously flexed her foot. She would be able to walk on it, slowly. She'd return to Baelle Heale and find another way. Her mouth tasted the ash of destroyed dreams. 'Nothing. No one will know.'

He gave a peremptory nod. 'Good. And your business on this pathway if I might be so bold as to ask?'

'I was…on my way to visit your sister.' She tried for a brilliant smile, the sort which told the receiver to move along as there was nothing to see or ponder. 'Honest. No harm done. Slight twisting of my ankle. Not that it is worth mentioning.'

He raised a brow. 'Asida made no mention of your impending visit. Is the bundle you carry a gift for her? Some wonderous custom of the Mercians perchance? Your generosity continues to astound but my sister is in no need of cast-offs and charity.'

She gritted her teeth, ignoring the sardonic tone of his voice, and hurriedly gathered the items together again. Lord Hafual's scorn was the last thing she required today of all days.

'I wanted to be prepared in case something happened and I had to stay. The rain can be dreadful at this time of year. I meant no disrespect to you or your family,' At his incredulous expression, she added, 'Purely a precaution…on account of the weather.'

His expression became even more forbidding. 'You are taking precautions, I see, even though my sister has no idea you plan to become our guest. A lengthy stay?'

She opted for a shrug. There was no way he could be aware of the potential for unwanted betrothals. 'Why would I want that?'

He watched her with eyes which reminded her of her father's goshawk—cold and alert to the slightest movement. 'Do you seek to bring trouble to my estate, my lady?'

'Trouble?' Elene hastily shook her head. 'The last thing I want to bring is trouble to anyone.'

'You intended to stay under my roof without letting your father know. People might say I kidnapped you or somehow enticed you against your will. Gossip as you pointed out is evergreen.'

'Your return means my visit will be shorter. Kidnapping, of all the fantastical notions.' Her voice was higher and more breathless than she liked. She swallowed hard and tried again. The last thing she required was his ire. 'Your son will be delighted with your return.'

His mouth became a hard line. 'My son hid behind my sister's skirts when I arrived late last night. Delight was the last thing on his mind. Or did I mistake the famous Mercian sense of humour again?'

'At least you are aware Mercians have a sense of humour.'

'The love of practical jokes can be hard to miss. Both here and at court. So, I laugh and pretend to get the joke. Being a Mercian, one must always get the joke.'

No mistaking his sarcasm this time. And she knew that when he first was at Baelle Heale, the assistant pig-keeper had played a trick on him, something which could have made things far worse for everyone if the leader of the Northmen had not discovered the trick.

'I will take your word about what happens at court. My duties at Baelle Heale mean I'm often absent.' That and the last time she was there, she'd managed to trip and spill a tankard of ale on the queen. Her father had suggested that she might want to have a period of absence.

'My joy at your faith in me is unbounded.'

Elene plucked at the scissors which hung next to her eating knife on her belt. Hafual had this way of always making her feel like she was a girl with a dirty face, rather than a grown woman. As if she was the girl who fainted at the sight of blood, instead of being the woman who had assisted the priest in his last three operations, including one trepanning. 'Family legend is that at about your son's age I screamed until I was sick when my father returned.'

If anything, the ice in his eyes grew colder. 'Family legends have a way of growing in the retelling. But thank you again for those unasked-for crumbs of attempted comfort. I will ponder them and hold them in my mind as a beacon.'

'I was trying to be kind.'

'Kindness is what brought you to this place? I see.'

Elene gritted her teeth. The sudden sickening sense that he knew about her predicament and expected her to behave impulsively rather than thinking things sensibly through filled her.

'One could inquire the same of you. Why are you headed towards Baelle Heale instead of staying with your son and setting your hall to rights, Hafual? Your sister recently told me there are some things which only the lord can decide.' She gave a tiny smile. 'We agreed to disagree on the matter.'

He inclined his head, making the tiny droplets of mist which were caught in his hair shine like diamonds. 'A certain matter has come to my attention. Like a boil, it needs to be lanced.'

She winced as her own blithe ignorance about her father's scheme was laid bare. 'The proposed visit and potential betrothal offer from Pybba. You consider it detrimental to the neighbourhood. Well, so do I!'

'Pybba and I are less than friends. Rumour circulated at court he is seeking a new alliance after his wife died of a fever. I was unaware the scheme went as far as an actual betrothal.' His gaze could freeze a puddle on a summer's day. She wondered that she even for a heartbeat considered him approachable. 'Even faced with that, I did not expect you to be running away.'

'Running away is not what I'm doing. I need time to come up with a plan.'

'I expected you to wait until transport could be arranged,' he continued as if she had not spoken. 'But you were always the most impetuous of the three sisters. Accept my apologies for the miscalculation, but we can recover from it. Help is at hand as you require rescuing.'

Elene balled her fists. 'Why does everyone think I need rescuing? I am a fully grown woman. Everything will be under control by the time Lord Pybba arrives.'

He lifted a maddening brow and a faint dimple appeared in his cheek as if she somehow existed for his amusement. 'But you are running, my lady, however much you want to deny it. You even tripped and hurt your ankle in your haste. Or do you make a habit of such things?'

'You startled me. And if you are referring to my last sojourn at court, I caught the hem of my gown.' Someone had stuck her foot out, but Elene knew Hafual would discount the notion like her sisters had.

He bowed as if they were at court instead of on a muddy path. 'I merely wish to point out your actions have consequences for everyone in the general neighbourhood. This business with Pybba affects more than you. Think beyond the end of your nose as one of your sisters would undoubtably say to you if either were standing in my place.'

'How can visiting with your sister have conse-quences?' She tightened her hold on Bugge's iron collar. Consider what one of her sisters would say? She had spent her entire life considering that and she doubted she was better off for it.

'You have no idea of my current relationship with Pybba or if thwarting his scheme is something I wish to be involved in. You seek to bend my sister to your will without any regard towards what might be best for her. I see you seek to be like the queen and her ladies—concerned with their own thoughts instead of other matters.'

She rolled her eyes heavenwards. May St Etheldra and all the other saints preserve her. Heaven forfend that she act to save her future rather than waiting to be rescued. And it was far from selfish to wish to en-sure her own safety and that of her people. Deep in her heart, she knew, despite what the steward proclaimed, any alliance with Pybba would be the ruin of Baelle Heale rather than the saving of it.

'Have you made an alliance with that obnoxious show-off Lord Pybba?' she said in her sweetest honey-soaked voice, the one which her sisters had learned to fear. 'Will wonders ever cease?'

A muscle jumped in his cheek. 'Ever since the spring campaign against the Hwicce war bands who were burning farms on the border, Pybba has waged undeclared war against me, seeking to undermine my influence with the king. He hopes to open a new front through ensnaring you and your father.'

His overly superior tone grated on her nerves. As if the sole reason for Pybba's actions centred around him rather than Baelle Heale's prosperity or the influence her family enjoyed. Elene swallowed her first retort and continued in a sweetened tone accompanied by much batting of her lashes. 'Pybba would be a mistake for Baelle Heale in any capacity. My father, however, needs to learn this lesson for himself and without my interference. I want to give him time to ensure it is thoroughly digested and then spat out in revulsion. I anticipate given the characters involved, Pybba need not trouble the neighbourhood for long.'

A muscle jumped in his cheek as if he were trying to suppress a laugh. 'Pybba of Etone takes offence easily and your father's temper can be short. The combination could be combustible in the correct circumstances. But, my lady, these sorts of conflagrations can have unexpected consequences.'

She tucked a strand of hair behind her ear and attempted to maintain a sense of dignity rather than slipping back into the sort of reckless behaviour she used to exhibit. That first summer when Hafual, Moir and Ansithe rescued Nerian and her from the outlaws, she had been giddy and overexcitable. 'You believe I possess the grasp of nuance and subtlety of a dancing bear. I would beg to differ.'

'Who said that?'

'The steward and his wife… I overheard them speaking about the betrothal and what they needed to do to ensure I went along with it.' She didn't bother to hide her bitterness. 'Apparently, it would not take much—a bauble or a new gown. I'm easily distractible. After all, my father is not exactly overwhelmed with offers due to my faux pas with the queen.'

A tiny smile tugged at his features, softening them and transforming him back into the gentle warrior she had first known and liked, back before his wife had had her accident and died. 'Your father's steward is blind or has lost his wits if he thinks that. You and your sisters are stubborn and have more cunning than most warriors. I still bear scars from my first encounter with you all.'

'Ecgbert recently married a woman from Etone. He's besotted with her and parrots all her words as if wisdom from on high.' Elene shook her head. 'I suspect promises of advancement have been made if the betrothal is secured. You know how ambitious Ecgbert is. Before Cynehild left to lay her husband's late sword in the Dane-law country, Ecgbert had even considered my eldest sister might marry him.'

His mouth twisted to a harsh expression. 'When the scales fall, they really do fall.'

'The proposed betrothal is to be sprung on me as an accomplished fact. The woman thought it the best way to get me to agree.' She shook her head. 'As if!'

'They truly have misjudged you.' He held out his hand palm upwards and several raindrops splashed down. 'The heavens are about to open and even women who are most definitely not…what did you say—distractible—should keep dry. You can explain everything once we get to my hall, and we will discuss a suitable way forward.'

She opened her mouth to explain that she and she alone would decide her future but at his forbidding expression, she decided against it. 'Bugge dislikes the damp,' she said instead.

A deep blue spark showed in his eyes. 'Then your dog has settled the matter. You accept my help. Give me that bundle you carry'.

She remained where she was. 'Do I have a choice?'

'Always a choice with me.' He gave a half-shrug. 'But I've never understood why a woman might like to carry a heavy burden alone.'

Elene hugged the bundle tighter to her chest. 'Because I prefer to?'

'Reason enough.' He bowed. 'I merely wanted to be helpful.'

She ignored his hand. 'I don't need rescuing. I make my own way. I want to make that perfectly clear.'

'For now.'

She firmed her mouth. She didn't need her sisters coming to her rescue or anyone else. What she needed was time for her father to realise what a mistake Lord Pybba would be. Except for some reason the tightness in her chest eased with the tall Northman walking beside her. 'For ever.'

'I will take your words under advisement. You have the unfortunate habit, Lady Elene, of needing rescuing at inconvenient times.'

'That no longer happens. I've learned my lessons.' She mentally crossed her fingers. 'My scheme to prevent Pybba from taking over Baelle Heale will work. The finer detail needs adjusting and hopefully your sister…' She paused and glanced up into his forbidding features. 'And now you will ensure I have the benefit of both your collected wisdom.'

Chapter Two

The instant Hafual saw his half-sister emerge from his hall, he knew he'd made a tactical error. Bringing Lady Elene to Wulfhere's Clearing invited input from his sister on how he should conduct his life. Whereas keeping parts of his life in separate iron-bound trunks like he'd done ever since Svala died rather than permitting things to overlap and mingle meant he stayed in control.

The distinct twinkle in her eye and the faint upwards twitch of her mouth into that superior expression she sometimes wore showed Asida clearly had made plans, something which involved him and Lady Elene. He silently cursed.

If he failed to prevent her, Asida would be volunteering him to do something which he had no intention of doing like offering to be the stand-in bridegroom until the storm blew over. Other ways around the conundrum of Pybba's ambition existed without the burden of marrying again. Her earlier suggestion, followed with a half-teasing remark about Narfi needing a proper mother, drove him out the door before breakfast. Now she smiled and mouthed, 'Runes,' at him.

Ever since they were children, she'd informed him he must do such and such because she had cast the runes and had the Sight like her mother. He'd always scoffed as a young man but unfortunately she was often proved right.

Marrying anyone to provide Narfi with a mother or any other reason that Asida cared to come up with wasn't going to happen. He owed Svala's memory and the failure of their marriage that much.

'Lady Elene has arrived. Good. I made extra pottage as I doubt you have eaten, lady.' She gestured towards the hall. 'Hafual will see to it that you are well fed. He has some uses like providing a good table.'

'A good table is one of life's pleasures.' Lady Elene's laugh sounded like a clear bell as if life held some goodness instead of being the series of trials that he knew it was.

'Has Narfi said good morning to the cows?' Hafual said in a brusque tone, determined to retain some sort of control of the situation. Keeping them apart would prevent Asida from carrying out any scheme. 'You know how much he likes to greet them.'

Asida fluttered her lashes. 'We are greeting our guest.'

'The cows, Asida.'

Asida remained standing in the doorway with Narfi balanced on her hip. It annoyed him that Narfi burbled happily to Lady Elene, holding his hands out to her while his son's response to him had been to stick his thumb into his mouth and regard him with those un-blinking eyes of his, eyes which reminded him more and more of Svala. The unblinking eyes and the moon-shaped scar on his temple, the one he'd acquired the day his mother died.

'Narfi cares nothing for cows, brother. This morning or ever.'

'Asida, I do know something of my son. Cows are his favourite.' At least he hoped they were. Before he'd left for court, Narfi had taken great delight in making mooing noises. He was certain of it. Asida was the one misremembering, not him. 'Please.'

'Narfi and I are going to the barns. He loves seeing the *horses* in the early morning,' Asida said, tickling Narfi under his chin. His son merely stuck his thumb in his mouth and watched him with those eyes.

'Horses.' Hafual gritted his teeth. Of course. 'My error.'

'You and Lady Elene must speak.' Asida lowered her voice as she passed him. 'Alone without me complicating things. She has come here for a clear purpose. I predicted such a thing would happen before you departed this morning.'

'You think I remain in ignorance about you and your predictions?' Hafual asked, lacing his tone with heavy sarcasm. 'Are you angling for a return to the North and our half-brother's rule? If so, be honest and go.'

He waited, knowing that the last thing Asida wanted was a return to the North and their half-brother's rule. She might find his son difficult, but she feared their half-brother and his drunken threats to kill her if she set foot on his land again due to her prediction that he'd one day meet a violent end.

Asida shifted Narfi to her other hip. 'Hardly a prediction, but rather a fact like Lady Elene requiring breakfast.'

'Sister, your talents never cease to surprise me. Can you inform us on how long she intends to stay?'

'My gift of sight fails on that.' Asida's skirts twitched as she strode over to the barns with Narfi in her arms.

'Your sister can't really tell the future, can she?' Lady Elene gave another of her laughs, and that tight place in his chest eased.

He noticed the length of her lashes and the way her eyes crinkled and then wondered why he was noticing. He made a point of never noticing things like that, not now that Svala was dead. All that belonged in a place that he'd buried deep within his brain and never visited.

He silently cursed his sister for her earlier hints about his need to be human and remarry.

He shrugged and ushered Lady Elene into the hall. 'My sister knows that I found Lord Pybba a particular trial this summer. Nothing more. She keeps her nose out of my court business as she calls it.'

A small frown appeared between Lady Elene's brows. 'Oh, I see. She was teasing you.'

'Sisters are sent to try their siblings.'

'I have two older ones, you know.'

In the uncomfortable silence which followed, Hafual was aware of the deficiencies in his hall which Lady Elene must see—the mishappen back wall made of wattle and daub which had not set as well as he had planned, the way the fire was off-centre and how old the rushes were on the floor because Asida had been busy with other things. Far better than the house he'd grown up in but not on the same scale as the grandeur of Baelle Heale.

Lady Elene sat down on the intricately carved bench which ran along the back wall with a thump and leant her head back against the rough wall. Her dog settled at her feet, laying her head on her paws but watchfully guarding. The perfect picture of a fine Mercian lady who expected pampering. He had met enough of those at court, and he had no intention of putting his estate in jeopardy for another.

'What are *your* plans, Lady Elene, beyond a calculated disappearance designed to cause your father to dispatch Ecgbert to one of your sisters, and thus removing one of main instigators of the match?' Hafual asked. 'Your father will not send both Ecgbert and his wife, so the problem will remain, and you won't be there to supervise. Or will you suddenly reappear?'

Lady Elene's generous mouth took on a stubborn cast. 'I keep hoping the entire nightmare vanishes like the smoke going up through the roof once my father experiences the full force of Lord Pybba's obnoxious demands. The fire is too hot, the pillows not soft enough, the sparring is being done incorrectly.'

'What excuse have you given for your current absence? Precisely and without prevarication.'

'I left word for Father Oswald. I need time for prayerful contemplation.' Lady Elene pressed her palms into her eyes, the embodiment of injured innocence. 'I've turned it over and over in my mind. It is why I thought finding a reason to stay here for a few days would be a good one, except you are back now...'

'I received the lands as a boon after saving the king's life that summer we first met. They are my home now.'

'You've rarely visited since your wife's death.'

The mention of Svala caused a dull ache in Hafual's chest, not the searing raw pain from when he first found her lifeless body. He no longer looked for her to be lying beside him when he opened his eyes or had the awful words they'd uttered to each other ringing in his ears or had the guilt choking his throat that he should have done more to prevent her rushing out that day.

'The prosperity of these lands depends on my service to the king,' he said, pushing away all remembrances of his failings. 'Should I jeopardise my claim when my sister claims to be capable of managing the estate?'

'Pybba is supposed to be one of the king's closest companions, according to Ecgbert. My father has lost favour in recent years as his two eldest daughters have married Northmen rather than loyal Mercians.'

Hafual struggled to keep his temper. 'Does Ecgbert have a problem with this estate? He should speak to me or my sister before rushing to petition the king.'

Lady Elene's cheeks turned a rosy pink. 'I'm always doing that—speaking in haste. As far as I know, my father has no trouble with you or your sister. He is always very twinkly after your sister has visited. I merely wanted to explain the why of Pybba, according to Ecgbert.'

'I know who he is and what he stands for.' Hafual bit out each syllable to prevent any misunderstanding. The last thing he required was someone like Lady Elene explaining the nuances of Mercian politics to him as if he were ignorant due to his birthplace.

He turned away and stirred the fire vigorously until the sparks flew up, making the fire burst into life, rather than giving full vent to his ire. He knew how

Pybba had tried to undermine him and his authority along the western border of Mercia when they dealt with the incursion from the Hwicce. However, he'd lacked the positive proof of Pybba's involvement which King Ceolwulf required.

He'd even tried to engineer a fight with the man several times over the summer to settle the issue, but Pybba had always found a way to avoid a head-to-head confrontation. But Hafual intended to have a confrontation over the Yuletide season or possibly when he returned to court. Their dispute was not supposed to touch Wulfhere's Clearing or his family. He watched the flames for several breaths and felt the anger ease. The situation was far from Lady Elene's making. She was one of the innocents caught up in the tangle.

'Thankfully, the king is not entirely his creature. Yet. Ever, if I have my way,' he said in a calmer tone.

'Are you seeking to destroy him? Is that why you are willing to assist me?'

Hafual watched the flames flash and die. There was no point in spilling his troubles. His shoulders were broad enough to carry the weight. He'd learned the hard way to keep parts of his life completely separate. 'My reasoning has little bearing on this matter. My actions do.'

Lady Elene glanced over her shoulder. 'Will Asida and your son be long? Surely, I can wait until they return.' She peeked up at him with heavily fringed eyes, the sort of eyes a man could lose his way in.

Hafual pinched the bridge of his nose. She intended to get Asida on her side of the argument. And he suspected Asida would be in favour of Lady Elene's scheme, particularly as she did not understand the situation at court or what he'd hoped to achieve with his new venture to Frankia, provided the king agreed to it.

'I would say you were too upset to eat yesterday after learning the news, and skipped breakfast, slipping out before most everyone was awake. Hard to think straight when your stomach grumbles.' He gestured towards the cooking hearth with its pot of bubbling porridge. 'My sister has left everything in readiness, my lady. Rest your ankle. Eat. Then we'll decide on the appropriate action. Not King Ceolwulf's court but your belly will soon be full.'

'It is not what I meant. I can...that is to say... I am hardly a fine imperious lady like those you meet at court who have no thoughts in their skulls except about their gown.' Lady Elene held out a tiny hand with long tapered fingers. 'Hardly that, Hafual. We are old friends. Pray let us behave like that and not stand on ceremony.'

Hafual concentrated on ladling out the porridge and ignored the hand. Old friends. Lady Elene's words dripped of insincere flattery. And Asida would use it against him if he had been the less than perfect host.

'You turned your ankle and hobbled. I must insist I wait on you.' He inclined his head. 'Unless you'd rather not seek help from a former man of the North.'

Her bottom lip had become the colour of a spring dawn. He frowned. He had no business noticing the tint of her mouth. Lady Elene was a lady with expectations of a fine marriage. And marriage was the last thing he should offer her. She deserved better than him.

'When I was growing up, it was always "Elene can't do this or that because she is too young." Now I dislike

being waited on, particularly when there is no need.'
She made a move to rise.

'Listen to your host.' He handed her the steaming
bowl of porridge. Their hands briefly touched. An unexpected warm pulse went up his arm and he nearly
dropped the bowl before she had tight hold of it. He
rapidly retreated.

'I dislike being troublesome.'

'You could have fooled me.'

Her face tried to be stern but broke out in a wreath
of smiles. 'You speak a form of truth. I don't mean to
be troublesome.'

'You are not a good patient, my lady, are you?' he
asked into the quiet.

'I'm far better at healing people and tending my me-
dicinal herb garden even if my father says it is not the
proper thing for a lady to be interested in. He would far
rather I was like my eldest sister, Cynehild, and solely
concerned with the spinning, weaving and cooking.
Possibly why—' She settled back on the bench and
examined her bowl.

The firelight caught the burnished gold in her hair,
and he wondered if it would be soft to the touch. Hafual pinched the bridge of his nose. Lack of sleep and
Asida whispering that the time had come to remarry
were the reasons for these unexpected jolts of attraction. Nothing to do with Elene, personally.

'Your rivalry with your sisters has no bearing on
the present matter.'

Lady Elene put the bowl down with a crash. 'My
father has lost patience with me. I've refused too many
men for too many spurious reasons, the steward's wife
said. But I had my reasons. I want to marry a man who

will respect me. I thought I'd found one who was worth waiting for…but I was wrong.'

'We need not speak of the man. Some things were not meant to be.' Hafual concentrated on eating his porridge. The man in question, Nerian of Wessex, had been a close friend once, but the friendship cooled after Hafual was awarded these lands. That first summer, though, he'd witnessed the blossoming of their young love and had known about Nerian's need to acquire a suitable estate in order to provide for his intended bride. It had surprised him when nothing came of it, and Nerian married another lady earlier this year. 'The man made promises to a young woman which he failed to keep. It has happened since time began.'

'My father remarked the other day that I was getting old and withered.'

Hafual glanced up and saw the full force of Lady Elene's dewy skin, eyes like the North Sea on a summer's day and the way the firelight gilded her hair. The warm jolt returned and curled about his insides. 'Your father's eyesight grows dim if he thinks that. You would outshine the ladies at court.'

She ducked her head. 'Is that what you suggest? Going to court? Asking the king for help? Throwing myself on the queen's mercy?'

The opening he'd been waiting for. Elene would follow his advice and the problem would be solved. 'We will go to your sisters. Neither will refuse you.'

'You and me? Together?'

'Yes. Now.' He stood up and held out his hand. 'Surely you must see sense, Lady Elene, now that your belly is full and you can think logically. Your best course of action rests with your sisters and their husbands.'

Best course of action. Elene blinked rapidly and tried to come up with something which might be worthwhile. The well-appointed room with its cosy fire, carved pillars and general air of friendliness and belonging swam in front of her eyes.

The offer was unexpectedly generous, much more than she deserved.

Each sister would have a different solution. Cynehild, the oldest, would suggest something diplomatic like staying with her for ever in the Five Boroughs, while Ansithe would recommend direct action like kicking Pybba where it hurt and taking the consequences. But it would mean once again the baby sister sought her big sisters' help. She'd stopped doing that now that she was grown.

No, she had to find her own solution to the dilemma without leaning on either of her sisters or their husbands.

She lifted her chin and stared directly into Hafual's deep blue eyes with their shifting shadows. His face was more weather-beaten from what she recalled and the lines about his mouth held a certain harshness, something which had only appeared after his wife's tragic death. She needed a plausible reason. 'I can't have my little friend thinking ill of me for taking his father away so soon.'

'My son's thoughts on the matter are of no concern to you. Stop finding excuses and tell me what you want to do.' He ticked the options off on his fingers. 'No sisters. No court. Where do you wish to go?'

She put up her hand, preventing Hafual from speaking. 'Please do not mention convents either. Even though they are the time-honoured way to avoid an unwanted marriage, I lack a sincere vocation and my father knows it.'

'Would he disinherit you and your sisters? Name Pybba as his heir? You must be prepared for the worst, my lady, if you follow your inclination. Are you willing to accept the consequences of fighting for your future?'

Elene pressed her lips together. Hafual had found the flaw in her scheme. Her father could do that, particularly if Ecgbert the steward and his wife urged him on. Ecgbert had always encouraged her father's worst excesses in times of crisis.

Elene forced her lips into a smile and stood. Instantly Bugge moved to her side and nudged her hand with her nose. Elene put her hand on Bugge's collar and knew she was doing the grown-up thing, the right thing and the only thing.

'Speaking to you has made me see that hiding away will cause more problems than it solves.' She titled her head upwards, met his frowning gaze directly and refused to flinch. 'I stand squarely on my feet, rather than leaning on my sisters or their husbands. I thank you for that confidence. There is no need to see me out. I will fight for my future.'

His eyes became shards of blue ice. 'My sister will be pleased that I proved to be some little use. Send word if you change your mind about going to your sisters.'

'Your advice means more than you can know but my mind is made up. I can be stubborn that way.' She waited for his answering smile but the frown on his face increased. 'My father directed me to prepare a feast for Lord Pybba as he has sent word—he will be arriving on the morrow. I will discover a way to make my father lose his temper with him.' She lifted her chin upwards and met his blue gaze full on. 'If my father thinks I will tumble into Pybba's arms because I suffered a disappointment in love, he is gravely mistaken. All that has done is made me more determined to have the sort of husband I want rather than one foisted on me, particularly one who has wandering hands and a lecherous smile.'

'Pybba does have a certain reputation with women or so he proclaims.' His laugh sounded rusty.

Elene frowned. Was Hafual making a joke, rather than a cutting remark? 'All I am asking for is time, Hafual, nothing more, nothing less.'

'Do you want me and my men at the feast in case your latest scheme fails?' He gave a crooked smile which transformed his face back to the man she'd encountered before his wife's untimely death, the one who had always had a smile on his face and a kind word for her.

A bone deep weariness invaded her soul. What she wanted to do might be much harder than she first anticipated. And she needed allies, not enemies. 'Please. You might see a way to cause my father to lose his temper with Pybba, something I have missed.'

'I will not start a fight, but you have my sword, my lady.'

She tilted her head to one side and tried to dampen her rising sense of relief. 'Your being there may be enough to irritate the man. My father will immediately realise that intimidation won't work if I have an ally like you. Excellent.'

She held out her hand. He grasped it and raised it to his lips. In that heartbeat, she became aware of his height, the breadth of his shoulders and bow-shaped curve to his lower lip and forgot how to breathe.

His lips against her palm were the gentlest of touches. A warm pulse travelled up her arm. 'Your ally, my lady. Always. On reflection, I will see you home. Make sure you don't take a detour on the way.'

'Detour? Why would I do that?'

'Sometimes these things happen to people, and I am determined nothing untoward will happen to you.' He released her fingers.

She stood staring at him for a long heartbeat, watching the way the hollow of his throat moved.

'Allies, my lady.'

Elene hurriedly took a step backwards and the spell was broken. Her cheeks radiated warmth. She clenched her teeth. There were so many reasons why she shouldn't be attracted to him, starting with his late wife's death, his vow not to remarry and her determination not to be the consolation prize in any marriage.

The last thing she required was a quick alliance with a man she barely knew. She'd suffered the folly of falling head over heels for Nerian, giving him her heart, her body, her everything, and getting nothing in return. One mistake was allowed but not making the same one repeatedly.

All she wanted was time to find the appropriate man to marry, the one who would willingly cherish her and help her to protect the estate against all foes. She knew he was out there, somewhere. But Haful wasn't going to be that man. 'Ally has an excellent ring to it.'

Chapter Three

'Have Lady Elene and her dog departed? Or will you be taking them to one of her sisters?' Asida glided back in with Narfi snuggled into her shoulder shortly after Hafual returned from seeing Lady Elene safely back to her estate.

Hafual looked up from the wooden post he'd begun carving. It was the first time since Svala's death that he'd been inspired to carve anything. The curling leaves were a start, but the hall and its posts were far too plain. In the North country, gold and silver foils from important visitors would be adorning the posts of an important *jaarl*'s hall. He'd discovered the hard way that Mercia did not have the same custom.

'Lady Elene decided to return to her father and await developments. I ensured she returned safely but didn't want to waste time in case she changed her mind.'

'I had wondered where you were, but as you rarely trouble me with your comings and goings, who was I to question?'

Hafual slid a long curl of wood off the post. He would carve a horse for Narfi soon but first he needed to get these jobs done. 'I would tell you if I was going away for a few days. I would say goodbye.'

Asida set a sleeping Narfi down on his small bed. 'Lady Elene should have remained here. The runes were quite clear. I thought you understood this when I sent you to fetch her. I trust she enjoyed the porridge. Porridge will bring you to the future you desire.'

Hafual watched his son sleep. His blond hair brushed his temples. Maybe when his son woke, Hafual would get a smile. He wrinkled his nose. He'd stopped wishing for impossibilities a long time ago and Asida was seeking to distract him by mentioning porridge. 'My idea to go. And porridge will not bring me anything.'

'Have it your way, but you know I am right.' Asida led him out of the small chamber she shared with Narfi. 'Your focus means that you forget the world holds people other than yourself.'

Hafual struggled to keep hold of his temper. Asida had it wrong. He'd stopped Lady Elene from doing something rash. Her return to Baelle Heale would help her to place the threat into perspective. He'd deal with any fallout when it happened. No point in borrowing trouble, one simply had to be aware of the potential for it. 'You promised not to cast runes. Think about the danger. Think about my son.'

Asida cocked her head to one side. 'You worry overmuch, brother. My rune-casting tells me things, something you consistently fail to do.'

He crossed his arms. 'The condition of the king's gift included me and my family becoming Christian. Svala understood. Rune-casting is forbidden in this household.'

Asida stabbed her forefinger towards him. 'You, not

me. Narfi has the North running in his veins. You are denying him his birthright?'

'Narfi will farm these lands in Mercia. He isn't going to return to the North and the worn-out lands which yield little more than a crop of stones and mud and an overlord who is cruel and capricious. Those lands are in the past.' Hafual hit his hand against his head. 'Why will you not understand this?'

'I'm your sister and I'm stubborn. Runs in the family.'

'You will do as I request.'

Asida crossed her arms. 'Find someone else to teach him, if you think I'm unsuitable. Marry again. The heartbeat you do, I will stop looking after your son and filling his head with what you deem nonsense. But you won't, so allow me to bring him up as I see fit.'

Hafual struggled to control his temper. His sister's solution was always that if he rebuked her, he should find someone else. And she was right—he had no choice. He could not have Narfi with him. 'You will go too far one day, Asida.'

Asida shrugged. 'It makes no sense why Lord Wulfgar would want a man such as Pybba as his son-in-law when he could have you. You could do worse than Lady Elene. And you'd annoy Pybba.'

He frowned. 'True, Pybba has been a thorn in my side for too long but—'

'Precisely.' Asida settled in front of the loom she kept in the hall and began to weave. Although there was a hut dedicated to weaving, Asida often said that she preferred to weave in the main hall where she could keep an eye out, rather than gossiping with the other women.

The room soon filled with the clacking sound of her shuttle going across the warp threads as she created the cloth. Whenever Asida retreated to her weaving, Hafual knew she had decided against arguing with him.

'I will be going to the feast at Baelle Heale with my men, but you remain here with Narfi. You might give in to the temptation to say something we both will regret.'

'Like what?'

'Like imply some connection between Lady Elene and myself.' He cleared his throat. 'No matchmaking required, Asida.'

The loom clacked several more times. 'You said it, not me.'

'It is not going to happen.'

'Will you leave Lady Elene to be used as a counter in her father's schemes or by that horrible steward and his wife?'

'No, I hope to persuade her to join one of her sisters. It is the simplest solution. I would have sent word to them, but Lady Elene made me promise not to. Once the feast has finished, Lady Elene will see the wisdom of heeding my advice.'

Her hand stilled and her lashes swept down hiding her expression. 'You expect trouble.'

'I expect Pybba to be less than pleased to see me, but any provocation will come from him. There is a fight coming, Asida, but it will be at the time of my choosing.'

'Svala would not be happy about someone like Pybba as your neighbour. She set her roots down in this soil.' Asida's hands stilled on the loom. 'Svala would not like to see you lonely. There, I have said it.

She wanted you to be happy. She wanted Narfi to have a proper mother, not an aunt.'

'How can I be lonely when I have my duty to these lands, the king and indeed my family?' Hafual willed her to understand. He had no idea what Svala wanted at the end. Asida didn't either. She'd arrived after Svala's body had been discovered at the base of the cliff.

He hoped she'd allow the untruth. Happy belonged in the past. Content was the best he could hope for and that only happened when he was away from his memories.

Asida moved the shuttle again, faster this time, a sign that she was about to dismiss him. 'And Lady Elene? What will you do about her? Think of the advice Svala would give if she could speak, if I could summon her from her unquiet grave.'

'Stop pushing me, Asida! Stop talking about Svala and what she would have thought!' He caught the shuttle and prevented her from doing more weaving.

His sister glared back at him. 'I could, you know.'

'Beyond even your powers, Asida.' He dropped the shuttle with a loud clatter. 'More's the pity as then I would have an end to it.'

A thin wail rose from Narfi's bed. Asida went to him and gathered him up. At the sound of the Northern lullaby, the child stopped crying, stuck his thumb in his mouth and watched him with Svala's eyes. It took all his willpower not to flinch. He'd failed the mother when she begged him to follow her in that heartbeat of lucidity before she had given in to her temper and thrown Narfi towards the fire. He stopped to rescue his little boy from the fire, rather than shouting for a servant to help. He lost sight of her, only discovering her broken body at the bottom of a cliff much later that evening. Now he was failing his child. He kept completely still, watching the rushes on the floor until the child's sobs ceased.

'Someone has to tell the truth to you, Hafual, and I am the only one who can,' Asida said into the sudden silence. 'Svala will not rest in peace until you can discuss her with ease. I guarantee you that. You cannot move forward until you face your past.'

He expelled a long stream of air. 'I will protect Lady Elene the best I can. We're temporary allies against Pybba's power grab. Nothing more.'

Allies at Baelle Heale. She'd allowed Hafual to think she had them, but the truth was rather different. She had not even noticed the turnover in household servants since Ecgbert returned with his new wife until it had been too late. Ecgbert had always had a plausible excuse—a sick mother here for the assistant weaver, an unsuitable temperament there for the cook or even a love affair and marriage for the assistant pig-keeper until the servants were people who owed their positions to Ecgbert and not to her or her sisters. She doubted if any of the maids who bustled about the kitchen and worked in the new weaving hut had been here before Ansithe's marriage.

She should have paid more attention to who the servants were, but she had been away with Cynehild's wedding and then helping Ansithe with her new baby after the Great Betrayal. And before that, she had believed that Nerian would marry her eventually. She'd had her head in the clouds, oblivious to the danger.

Now all she had was the broad-shouldered Northman with his cold eyes and a half-given promise of his sword arm to assist her if she could find a way to provoke Lord Pybba into anger against her father.

'Lady Elene, mind your backside,' the steward's wife called as the assistant pig-keeper staggered in with the pig which was to be roasted for tonight.

'I was aware of the situation,' Elene said between clenched teeth.

The woman sniffed. 'Trying to be helpful to be sure, my lady. I thought you were wool-gathering again. Standing there in the centre of the room, doing nothing.'

'I was attempting to work out the number of the hogshead of ale which we will need for tonight's feast.'

'To be sure. Ecgbert has done that.'

'With the greatest respect, your husband tends to get it wrong. My sister Cynehild made mention of it the last time she visited.' Elene put her hands on the middle of her back and leaned backwards, trying to release the crick. The various servants watched her with wary and faintly pitying eyes as Ecgbert's bride began bleating on, defending him and why it was necessary not to have too much ale.

'My lady, my lady, come quick.' One of the maids who normally worked in the weaving hut rushed into the kitchen, earning a glare from the steward's wife as she did so.

'Is there a problem? Has Lord Pybba settled in?' Elene asked, her mind racing as to what the potential problem could be. The last thing she wanted was Lord Pybba or any of his men causing difficulties with the maids. The women had strict instructions to keep out of dark corners and that if any advances were unwarranted for them to scream very loudly until help arrived.

'Your father requires your presence. Lord Pybba was asking after you to be sure, but he is out on the practice yard.'

'My father knows where I am and that I'm needed here.' The last thing she was going to do was to watch two grown men practising with their swords. 'Whatever it is, it can wait.'

'Please, my lady, it is important.' The maid bobbed a quick curtsey and lowered her voice. 'It is all I know. You are to come alone and quiet like. Please, my lady. He took poorly on the practice yard after an altercation with Lord Pybba and retired to his chamber. Doesn't want anyone to know, like.'

Her father had had a fight with Lord Pybba? Her plan might work better than she had predicted. She might not require the tall Northman after all. Elene struggled to keep a straight face. She gestured towards the cook to keep stirring the sauce and followed the maid out of the kitchen.

Her father was seated on a stool in his private chamber; sweat poured from him and his face was a sort of mottled purple.

Elene knelt and gathered his cold hands in hers. Her mind raced as she tried to remember everything Father Oswald had taught her about what to do if her father took a funny turn. 'Father, what is wrong? Shall I get Father Oswald?'

Her father withdrew his hands from hers. 'That old worrywort? He'd have me in bed and resting.'

'If you know what you must do, then why not do it?'

'I overdid it today.' Her father wiped the pooling sweat from his brow. 'I wanted to show Pybba that I still had what it took to command a war band. That I could compete. That I didn't need either of my sons-in-law and their warriors to hold this land.' Her father pounded his fists together. 'Why did your sisters have to marry men from the Heathen Horde rather than men who were pledged to our King? They have caused this problem. Why would anyone doubt my readiness to raise my sword in defence of this country?'

'Did you best him?' Elene asked, refusing to panic. Had Pybba brought word of a new decree from the king, something to do with loyalty to the crown? Her brothers-in-law did not have land in Mercia as each commanded sizable war bands now settled in the Five Boroughs ceded to the Great Heathen Horde. 'Did you show Pybba that such rumours about your strength were false?'

'He ended the bout, insisting that he had no wish to overtax his gracious host.' Her father's lower jaw jutted out. 'But I knew—I'd broken him and he would have only lasted a few more breaths. He doesn't have the footwork required. You don't get to my age without learning a thing or three about warriors.'

'Do you admire him like you did in the spring?'

'Admire is the wrong word, daughter. I appreciate certain qualities. Ecgbert says Pybba's estates at Etone yield far more wool than ours do.'

'The trade in wool is growing every year, true, but his methods are not necessarily better than ours.' She cleared her throat. 'Hafual has returned. Perhaps you can ask him about increasing our trade.'

'Good man, Hafual. He often talks sense. I couldn't

figure what Pybba was on about with his notions about how a shield wall should be organised. I told him—the Hwicce would outflank us in next to no time.'

Elene schooled her features, but internally she rejoiced. Lord Pybba might have only arrived this morning but already he had managed to get under her father's skin. If he irritated her father enough, she wouldn't have to worry about the impending betrothal. 'I'm sure Hafual will agree with you. Shall we ask him at the feast?'

Her father gave a loud harrumph which she took for agreement. Maybe it was simply a case of digging her toes in, being patient and letting her father come to the correct conclusion about Pybba's unsuitability.

'I'm sure you are right about the bout you had with Pybba.' She forced a note of cheery unconcern into her voice and moved about the room, straightening cushions, rather than allowing her hands to shake. 'Lord Pybba must have been exhausted if he said that. It was you who gave him the out through conceding. You were the gracious host as always.'

'He didn't see it that way, Elene! Kept going on about the slow movement of my sword getting in his way.' Her father pulled irritably at his cuffs. 'Why do people keep making it seem that I am in my dotage. I rule these lands. I will hold these lands.'

'Father, you are the ealdorman of Baelle Heale. I dare any to say differently and live.' She made a quick curtsey. 'Now as you choose to ignore my advice about calling Father Oswald, I will return to the kitchen and the roasting of the pig.'

'Always so impatient, Elene.' A racking cough shook his frame. 'I wanted to spend time with you. Ecgbert told me earlier that his wife had heard rumours about you going on a trip to visit one of your sisters.'

A deep shiver went through her and she felt like she was teetering on the brink of a precipice. One mistake and she'd fall, taking the future of the entire estate with her. Thankfully, she hadn't done anything rash like setting out for either of her sisters. Ecgbert and his wife would have twisted that sort of action to be seeking an army to fight Pybba.

'Why would I leave? My sisters are in no danger or in need of my help. Both are content with their husbands and children.' She forced a smile. 'But I did want to speak with you—it might be best if I remain in the kitchen during the feast to ensure nothing gets burnt.'

'What nonsense. Since when have you become shy, Elene? You must be seated at my right, and in your best gown.'

'My best gown?' Elene took a step backwards. 'I had rather thought one of my other gowns for tonight. That gown should be saved for court. I'd hardly want Pybba to make sneering remarks when we encounter him at court during the Yuletide.'

Her father thumped the table. 'Do you wish to shame me?'

Elene rapidly bowed her head. Her father in this mood wanted a fight. It didn't matter with whom, but he wanted an excuse to give in to his temper. Unlike her middle sister who positively revelled in it, Elene had never actively sought to ignite that temper. She much preferred a quiet life. So she kept silent and stood rigidly to attention, praying that she wouldn't be forced to do anything rash. 'No, Father. I wish you to stop making yourself ill or I will have to speak with Father Oswald.'

Her father screwed up his eyes but continued in a calmer tone. 'Do as I request. For the family, Elene. Show Pybba that we have not adopted Northern ways. Whispers against me have started at court. Wrong of your sisters to disobey me and marry Northmen.'

Elene concentrated on a knot in the wooden table. She longed to tell him the truth—he'd been for the marriages when it suited his ambition. 'Speak with Hafual. He will know about any rumours.'

'Always with this Hafual suddenly. Any reason?'

Elene fluttered her lashes. 'He is our closest neighbour.'

Her father pursed his lips before fumbling with the iron-bound casket which sat at his side. His fingers were far more twisted with arthritis than Elene had thought.

'Do you want me to help? The lock can be tricky, particularly if your hands are stiff from the practice yard.'

'You would have me a cripple now!' He yanked the top open and the remainder of her mother's jewels spilled out over the table. Elene caught a jewel-encrusted brooch before it rolled on to the floor.

'Father!'

Her father hung his head and concentrated on picking the jewels up.

'I didn't mean to shout,' he said in a quieter voice, plucking the brooch from her outstretched palm. 'My hands ache from grasping a sword and no one helps.'

'When I try to help, you say you want to do it yourself. And you call me contrarywise. Look to yourself, Father.'

Her father gave a long sigh. 'I can't hold these lands on my own for much longer, daughter. I refuse to be the one who loses everything. My lineage stretches back into the mists of time with these lands.'

'It won't happen. You have two powerful sons-in-law. Who would want to pick a fight against them?'

'Your sisters live in another kingdom which might not have Mercia's interests at its core.' Her father toyed with the brooch. 'Selfish. You are all that I have, and you can't even hold a man. Nerian was a poor bet, daughter. A wrong 'un but there was no telling you, was there? And you've wasted the best years of your beauty. Ecgbert spoke of it only this morning.'

Elene carefully put some of the spilled jewellery back in the box and silently cursed Ecgbert and his wife. They had dripped poison into her father's ear without her realising it.

She opted for a brilliant smile and a fluttering of lashes. 'Why do I need to see my mother's jewels? Neither Cynehild nor Ansithe are here. You promised them to keep them safe until they could be distributed equally.'

'I want you to wear that one.' Her father stabbed at the gold necklace encrusted with garnets. 'Your mother wore it on her betrothal night.' He closed his eyes. 'I would have sworn she was made of stardust that night. Family legend was it ensures the man you are destined for will become besotted with you on your betrothal night.'

Elene stared at the necklace which curled like a poisonous snake. 'Who is getting betrothed tonight, Father? Why must I wear this as I've little intention of marrying soon?'

'Always with the questions, Elene.'

Elene folded her hands together and kept them firmly in her lap. 'Tonight is a feast to honour a guest of yours. Nothing more. I barely know Lord Pybba. I am planning to go to court at Christmas. There are any number of suitable men there for me to choose from.'

'Your chosen man married someone else.' Her father shrugged. 'You must find another, a Mercian, one who is loyal to the king, to show the king we are loyal subjects.'

'Cynehild has a son.'

'Far too young. A warrior is required. Events sit on a knife-edge according to Ecgbert. We could be plunged into war again. The men from the North are never satisfied.'

'You must speak with Hafual tonight. He will tell you the truth. You know how Ecgbert can twist rumours.'

'Hafual is a man who will not remarry.' He shoved the necklace towards her. 'Do you have something else to say? A pretend vocation? Another reason why you won't do your duty and marry?'

She kept her hands firmly at her sides. 'I won't pretend something which is not true.'

'Clever girl. My sister spent many unhappy years locked away in a convent until she died.' Her father lifted her chin so that she looked him straight in the eyes. 'Give the man a chance instead of rejecting him outright. For me?'

Elene unhappily fastened the necklace about her throat. The weight felt more like a chain than a pretty bauble. 'My sisters—'

'Both your sisters trusted my judgement in their first marriages.'

Elene tapped her fingers together. Her eldest sister's first marriage had eventually been a source of great happiness for her, but she also knew her middle sister had been deeply unhappy. 'And if I refuse him?'

'I disinherit you and make Pybba my heir. I must have a warrior who can hold these lands, Elene, not some will-o'-the-wisp man from Wessex, or worse, a warrior from the North who doesn't understand the meaning of this soil or what it means to be Mercian.'

'And Lord Pybba knows?'

'He has sworn to slay any who so much as wears a brooch of the late King. He considers them to be cowards who were incapable of holding West Mercia.'

'You mean like my late brothers-in-law?'

'Both those ealdormen are dead, child. I must keep my eyes to the future. I might not live much longer, you know. I would see matters settled.'

Elene stared at her father. His lips were nearly bloodless and his eyes sunk back into their sockets. At some point, without her noticing it, he'd become old and with age cruelty had come. If she had listened to Hafual, she might be tucked up in Ansithe's hall or halfway to Cynehild's but Pybba would have power here. 'You wouldn't dare.'

Her father's lips turned upwards in a humourless smile. 'You have no idea about what I will dare or not. Show me you are a dutiful daughter. And you never know, family legend can be true. They were with your mother and me.'

She kissed his withered cheek. His skin was like the old vellum which Father Oswald's predecessor had scratched his remedies for chilblains on. 'I miss my mother as well, Father. I will wear the necklace in her honour and for no other reason.'

'No trouble. No gambling, no arm wrestling, no singing loudly,' Hafual reminded his band of hand-picked warriors as they filed into Wulfgar's banqueting hall. 'Nothing to give Pybba an excuse to attack us.'

'But you know what he is like,' one of his men complained. 'How they taunted us this past summer. It is nigh on impossible, Lord Hafual, to hold our tongues and retain self-respect.'

'We are here to assist Lady Elene if she needs it and nothing more. You are pledged to me, and I'm pledged to the Mercian king and will keep the peace.'

The men grumbled good-naturedly, but he knew they would obey him. They were his last line of defence if Pybba attempted to force Lady Elene into an unwanted alliance. He would get her to her sisters, kicking and screaming over his shoulder if necessary.

He would not be taking up Asida's suggestion of making a marriage offer for her. Sometimes Asida had to accept that she'd read the runes incorrectly.

Marrying Lady Elene would be a mistake. However, a little voice in the back of his mind which had grown more insistent kept asking what was wrong with the idea. He ignored it and focused on choosing the best possible place to ensure he could keep his promise.

A spot on the lower tables which afforded him a good view of the high table where Wulfgar, Pybba and Lady Elene would sit appeared to offer the most advantage. He motioned to his men to follow him.

'You came.' Lady Elene materialised by his side, carrying several horns of ale.

Her hair formed an intricately braided crown, and she wore a deep blue gown which brought out the blueness in her eyes. The golden belt she wore about her waist emphasised its smallness in relation to her bosom. Hafual forced his gaze upwards away from the generous mounds and ignored the scent of crushed rosemary and lavender which seemed to surround her. Asida's earlier teasing about the best solution to the Pybba conundrum was to become betrothed to Lady Elene was doing things to his brain, making him notice things which were best left unnoticed.

'I keep my word. Always.'

Her neat white teeth worried her bottom lip, turning it a deep red like the garnets she wore around her neck, the sort of red which begged to be tasted. Hafual cleared his throat and straightened his back. He'd always known Lady Elene was the beauty of the family.

'My offer remains, my lady,' he said, keeping his voice low. 'Your sisters will welcome you with open arms. Say the word and I will get you out of this place.'

Her lashes swept down over her eyes. 'Are you asking me to be a coward?'

'How could I when we both know about your bravery?'

She made a mocking curtsey. 'I think you try to flatter me, sir.'

'Is that wrong of me?'

'Leaving would be a grave mistake,' she said, lowering her voice to gentle purr. 'My sisters would never forgive my failure if my leaving meant Baelle Heale

passed out of the family because I selfishly refused
to marry.'

'Your discussion with your father failed to go as
you planned. I did warn you, my lady. It would not be
as simple as having him lose his temper.' He gave in
to temptation and touched her elbow. 'The plot will be
well advanced.'

'Early days.' Rather than moving away, she glanced
towards the high table where Lord Wulfgar was seated,
holding forth on some subject. 'Rumours at court have
questioned his loyalty to the king and it has been suggested that one way to dispel the rumours would be
for his youngest daughter to marry a Mercian warrior.'

'I will pay my respects and reassure him that no
such rumours exist. King Ceolwulf spoke highly of
him when I last saw him.'

'Yes, that might assist. Thank you, Lord Hafual.'
She curtseyed low and Hafual caught a glimpse of her
full breasts with the garnets nestled between. A rip-
ple of awareness of her as a desirable woman coursed
through him. He'd never considered Elene as anything
more than a friend. At first, he'd been involved with
Svala and felt he owed her loyalty to pay any notice
to other women. Then he'd had too much respect for
Nerian and finally it had become a habit. But now that
he'd noticed, he knew his body would keep on noticing her charms.

'I'm certain it will.' Without waiting for her answer,
he started towards the high table.

'My lady? You entertain a Northman in this hall?
After what the king has been saying…' The distinct
nasal whine of Pybba made him halt. He motioned to
his men to remain perfectly still.

'Lord Hafual is our neighbour and serves our King well.' Lady Elene motioned to her ladies to bring forth more horns of ale for Pybba's motley crew of hangers-on.

'Pybba and I did the king's bidding this summer,' Hafual said in a mild tone and dared Pybba to say something different.

Pybba took a horn of ale with a curl of his lip. 'I had not appreciated you were Wulfgar's friend as well as his neighbour.'

'Friendly relations between neighbours make the area more peaceful.'

Pybba made a noncommittal noise and tried to put an arm about Lady Elene's waist which she deftly avoided by twisting away to fill more horns with ale. Without pausing Pybba squeezed one maid's waist before patting another one's bottom. Both women called out in surprise. Hafual's hand inched towards his sword.

Lady Elene cleared her throat and directed the women to other tasks. 'Lord Pybba, I expect you to remember that you are a guest in this hall.'

Pybba gave an unrepentant grin. 'When I see delights like that...'

'Guests should not abuse hospitality.' The words sprang from Hafual's throat before he had a chance to check them.

'Must I have a lecture from you every time we meet?' Pybba growled.

'Is it my fault that you keep making simple errors like you did this summer? Water does not run uphill and the Hwicce seldom hide in haystacks.'

Pybba turned a sort of mottled purple. 'There was no proof that any of it was my fault. If we were not guests in this hall, I would challenge you to combat for that insult.'

'Pity.' Hafual shrugged. 'But you know where to find me.'

'One of these days, perhaps, I will.'

'I would have harmony in this hall, the better to hear the skald who has promised quite the exciting tale,' Lady Elene said, stepping between them.

Pybba made an elaborate bow. 'I do apologise, my lady. Your hospitality is legendary.'

'Apology noted,' Lady Elene said.

'I apologise as well, my lady,' Hafual said. 'I do look forward to hearing this tale of your skald's. The entertainment is always such a high standard at your father's table.'

Pybba flushed and muttered about Northmen needing to learn their proper place when he jostled Hafual's shoulder on the way to the high table. Hafual forced his hands to relax and kept a smile on his face. His men followed his lead and did not respond to the provocation.

'Thank you, Hafual, for being here,' Lady Elene murmured as she went passed. 'But there is no need for you to fight.'

'It is what I am here for—your protection.'

Elene pursed her lips like she wanted to say more but thought better of it. 'Let us hope I remain protected in my father's hall.'

'And the betrothal? Has your fear of that ceased?'

'I have to hope my father's word remains true.' She pressed a hand against her bosom. 'If not...'

Hafual schooled his features, but he silently vowed the warrior would not get the better of him or be allowed to harm Lady Elene in any way. Whichever game Pybba was playing, he was going to lose and lose badly. He would not allow his enemy to become his neighbour and oust him from his lands. He was not going to become his father and spend the remainder of his life lamenting lost chances of disabling an enemy before the enemy became too strong. He would strike when the first opportunity presented itself.

He caught her hand and raised it to his lips. Her palm tasted of honey. He hastily stepped back and regained control of his body. Whatever Lady Elene was to be, she would always be forbidden to him. He knew about his past. She didn't. 'Allies keep the faith, my lady.'

Chapter Four

'You picked at your food, daughter.' Elene's father made an extravagant gesture with his horn of mead, sloshing some of it on the wooden table.

Elene winced. Her father's consumption of the mead was far greater than at most feasts as he seemed to be having an unspoken competition with Pybba, matching him horn for horn with the jokes and quips growing ever louder.

'Are you going to say something, daughter, or are you going to sit there with that superior little smile on your face?'

'Like my mother used to, Father?'

'Perhaps.' Her father broke into a hearty laugh. 'Yes, you remind me more and more of your mother. Headstrong and not easy to tame.'

'But you loved her.'

'Aye, daughter, that I did. Now eat, drink and be merry, else our guest considers you a scold.'

Elene opted for a quick smile, rather than confessing the truth—even with Hafual in the hall and pledged to her protection, whatever that meant, she worried that before the night ended, she would be married to the wrong man.

Earlier, she had visions of Hafual throwing her over his shoulder, carrying her out of the hall and riding as if all the furies from Hell were behind them to one of her sisters. And keeping Baelle Heale would be a distant dream because her father in a fit of pique would gift the estate either to Pybba or even Ecgbert which might have been Ecgbert's scheme all along.

Elene pinched the bridge of her nose and tried to concentrate on her trencher. Her worries were foolish nonsense. Her father would give her a little time to make up her mind. She would be able to find the appropriate excuse. Her brain had never failed her before.

'Are you sickening, Lady Elene?' Ecgbert's wife asked with an all too solicitous grin. 'You've barely touched your food. Your father always says what a hearty trencherwoman you are. Not that you can tell it from your waist.'

The woman's laugh grated on Elene's skin. The steward's wife was like that with her false compliments and barbs. No doubt she thought herself very clever, but after enduring her family's teasing when she was growing up, such things bounced off her. Elene opted for her usual unconcerned strategy, or as she thought of it, pretending that she hadn't noticed the sting in the remark.

'Too busy worrying about the entertainment for after the feast.' She speared a piece of meat with her eating knife. 'Cynehild is bound to ask everyone what I did wrong when I next see her. Quite the stickler is my sister. Always wanting control even from a great distance.'

The woman exchanged a significant glance with her husband. 'Do you plan on seeing your sister soon?'

'Both my sisters are ever welcome in this hall.' Elene nodded towards her father. 'My father would like them to visit more often than they do. He was mentioning this earlier. He does value the advice my brothers-in-law give him about keeping sheep. The yield with the sheep's wool has increased considerably in recent years. We are looking for new markets.'

Her father made a non-committal grunt and drained his goblet before gesturing towards one of the maid-servants for more mead.

Lord Pybba took advantage of the distraction, reaching his hand under table and brushing her thigh.

Elene stabbed down with her eating knife, connecting with flesh. Pybba scowled and rubbed his hand. Elene smiled back and calmly cut up some of the meat in her trencher.

'You should inform your daughter that she needs to relax,' Lord Pybba said, sloshing some of her father's best mead over the table. 'She is behaving like a scared rabbit. All jumpy. Get it. Rabbit. Jumpy. Get it. My wit surpasses all.'

His coarse laugh rang out and his men joined in, but everyone else sat in stony silence. Elene tightened her grip on the knife, ready to strike if Pybba's hands wandered again. Next time, blood would spill, and it would belong to someone other than her.

Her father frowned. 'My daughter is normally very steady. No one Father Oswald would rather have at his side when one of the men are injured. She helped with a trepanning. One of the farmers' lads fell off the ladder, bashed his skull. Right as rain now. My daughter ensured that.'

'The minstrels appear ready to begin,' she said in a

clear voice before Lord Pybba could make a sour comment about how ladies were not supposed to do such things. 'It would be wrong to delay them, Father. Let us go on to the more pleasurable part of the evening—the songs and the tales. Perhaps Lord Hafual will have one of his men recite *Beowulf*. I seem to recall one does Grendel's mother very well.'

Hafual gave a nod from where he sat near the entrance.

Her father waved his goblet about, sloshing more mead. 'Quite right. Music. Then the part of *Beowulf* with Grendel's mother.'

Elene motioned for the skald to begin. Inwardly she relaxed. Two songs, a stanza or three of *Beowulf* and she'd be able to depart un-betrothed. Pybba with his cutting across her father's words, and argumentative stance, made it easier than she'd considered. All she had to do was to wait and her father would end up in a fight with Pybba. Patience. Then she could thank Hafual kindly for the offer to ferry her to her sisters', but it would be unnecessary.

'Enough with the music, Wulfgar. And I loathe *Beowulf*. To the business at hand.' Pybba banged his hand against the table after the first song. 'We need to celebrate our coming together…in mutual friendship and respect in another fashion, Wulfgar, like we discussed earlier.'

Elene's father tapped his goblet and the entire hall, including the minstrel's lyre, became silent. He rose unsteadily to his feet. 'We are gathered here tonight because I have an important announcement.'

Elene toyed with the idea of jumping up and rushing out of the hall, but that would make matters worse.

She was aware Hafual watched her like a hawk, waiting for a sign that she wanted to be rescued.

Elene took another sip of the sour wine and contemplated throwing it in Pybba's jowly face.

'Get on with it, man,' Pybba said.

'I have the honour of announcing my youngest daughter's betrothal to—'

Elene sat, stunned. Until he said the words, she had doubted that he'd go through with the threat tonight. She had anticipated that she would have several days to win her father around and tonight was merely a precursor to her having the final say.

Hafual rose to his feet. In the flickering firelight, his shoulders appeared broader than ever. She quickly shook her head, but his face merely became more severe.

'I beg your indulgence, Lord Wulfgar, allow me to speak before you say anything rash.'

'Speak? Why should this…this Northman speak about anything? His rudeness is astonishing.' Pybba's nasal whine grated on her jangled nerves. 'Showing up where he is not wanted and unable to take a civilised hint to leave. What is your table coming to that you permit Northmen to dine at it like they are civilised?'

'I think we should hear Lord Hafual speak. Like you, Lord Pybba, he is a guest here, but unlike you, I doubt he has drunk as much mead or ale.' Elene pointedly gazed at the splatters of ale, mead and blobs of grease which now adorned the man's tunic.

How could anyone think she'd ever accept such a man? She silently prayed that Hafual had found an excellent reason why her father should delay.

'Are you accusing Lord Pybba of something, my

lady?' the steward asked. 'He merely mentions the truth which all true Mercians know, or has this become unspeakable at this table?'

'Lord Hafual has pledged his service to our King and therefore is now a Mercian,' Elene said, trying to control her temper. Ecgbert had obviously forgotten that he owed his life to a Northman. 'Lord Pybba and Lord Hafual served together this summer. Long past time you stopped speaking of him as a Northman and started speaking of him as a Mercian lord.'

'My daughter has a point—Lord Hafual is pledged to King Ceolwulf,' her father said, pounding the table with his fist. 'I will hear you out, Hafual, as we are neighbours and bound in friendship and loyalty to the king. It is the right and proper thing to do.'

Elene released the breath she'd been holding. Her father retained some semblance of reason.

Hafual came forward with a firm step and a determined glint in his eye. 'Thank you for hearing me and my petition, Lord Wulfgar. Hopefully this matter can be cleared up quickly and we can all continue to enjoy the feast. *Beowulf* is a poem I know and love. But once I speak, I trust you will understand the urgency of my request.'

Elene slowly relaxed her grip on the eating knife, undecided whether she should run to his side or duck under the table and attempt to make an escape that way. Neither option struck her as particularly dignified, so she remained seated and silently prayed for a miracle.

'Why the urgency?' her father asked. 'Why does my daughter's marital status concern you?'

Hafual held out both hands. 'Lady Elene and I have a deep and abiding understanding.'

The entire hall fell silent at the shock announcement. Her father sank back in his chair. The colour drained from Ecgbert's face. Ecgbert's wife dropped her spoon which broke the spell.

'You and my daughter? What understanding, Hafual? How long has this relationship been going on under my nose?'

Hafual paused and looked directly at her. His face was studiously blank, but the warmth from his deep blue eyes appeared to penetrate her soul. Elene swallowed hard. He knew what her father had planned and was attempting to save her. He understood that running away now was going to be the worst thing. He was asking her to lie in a way that she'd never done before—he was asking her to pretend that they had a binding secret betrothal.

She lifted her eyes to the ceiling and blinked hard, regained control of her emotions. A secret betrothal which they later broke? It could work but it also could end in disaster. She felt like she was a bird teetering on a branch, getting ready to fly for the first time.

When she regained control of her racing heartbeat, she nodded and held out her hands towards him in a mute plea for help and understanding that she placed her future in his hands. He imperceptibly nodded before turning towards her father and Lord Pybba.

'We made our pledge…in the green wood after I returned from my summer of warring in the king's name. I have come here today to speak to you about this very subject.' He cleared his throat. 'Your daughter is not in a position to offer her pledge to anyone else.'

'You?' Her father sat down with a thump. 'My daughter gave you her pledge to marry.'

'Do you doubt my word?'

Elene risked half a breath. Hafual was treading a fine line trying to see off Pybba without actually making a firm commitment.

Her father tugged at his tunic. 'I had no idea this was in the offing. When you returned. A few days ago. That explains about several things earlier. I had thought Elene was merely being evasive about where she'd been.'

'He is seeking to pull the wool over your eyes, Wulfgar. There is no marriage agreement between the pair,' Pybba called. 'Ask the precise words. With Northmen, one must always be certain you are asking the right question.'

'Is your daughter choosing me so hard to believe, Wulfgar?' Hafual's features became set in stone, devoid of any warmth. 'Perhaps Lord Pybba would care to fight for the privilege, but I suspect you will allow your daughter the pleasure of following her own inclination.'

'She has little idea what is good for her,' Ecgbert said.

Her father placed his hands on the table and rose. 'My daughters have always known what is best for them, Ecgbert. You often remark on their strong wills. They take after their mother.'

'My late mother would agree with me—her daughters must have a say in their marriage.' Elene clasped her hands to the necklace. 'It is why I wore her necklace tonight, because I knew Hafual was coming but I… I didn't want to spoil the surprise.'

Hafual tilted his head and gave her a hooded look. She smiled back at him. A few more subtle nudges and

Pybba would lose his temper and storm away. Ecgbert's machinations would be exposed. Then in a calm and collected fashion they could work out what needed to be done. The pledge was simply a way of buying time.

'I believe you gave your oath that your daughter's wishes were to be respected if they involved anyone who had assisted in obtaining your freedom,' Hafual continued as if she had remained silent. 'Are you an oath-breaker, Wulfgar?'

'That oath pertained to…' Her father's voice trailed off. He swayed before standing straighter and attempting to regain his dignity. 'I stay true to my oaths.'

'Good. Your daughter will be glad to hear that. Your daughter is very precious to us both.'

Elene studiously studied the trencher with its remains of her meal and tried not to laugh. Hafual knew precisely how to play her father.

Pybba thumped the table, making the dishes jump. 'Your daughter has been with this…this heathen?'

'What are you accusing my lovely and innocent daughter of?'

Elene concentrated harder on the table, not looking up at anyone. Her stomach tightened and she began to hope that there was an actual solution to her problem which didn't involve running away, entering the church or abandoning her people.

There was another path she could take. All she had to do was follow Hafual's lead and allow certain assumptions to be made, then Pybba's own prejudice would do the rest. Goodbye to unwanted entanglement, hello to freedom and opportunity. They could decide they didn't suit after getting to know each other properly, and she could go to court and discover someone more suitable.

Liar, a little voice in her mind said. Until tonight, she'd failed to notice or allow herself to consider the breadth of his shoulders, the hollow place at the base of his throat, the torchlight glinting off his dark blond hair or how his eyes crinkled. There was something solid and forthright in the way he moved which she'd failed to appreciate before. He was a man to stand beside his woman in times of trouble. She silenced that voice. Hafual had vowed to remain loyal to his dead wife.

'Lady Elene should speak and give her version,' Lord Pybba said with a smug expression on his face. 'I know from bitter experience the sorts of tales you spin, Hafual. You say one thing and mean another, all the while protesting that you are simply a blunt warrior who is unfamiliar with our language.'

'Webs and traps now, Pybba? Sounds like you come perilously close to calling me a liar.'

'I merely wish Lord Wulfgar to be aware of the sort of man you are.'

'Daughter?' her father asked. 'Will you confirm what Hafual is saying?'

Summoning as much dignity as she could muster, Elene stood, went over to Hafual. Rising on to her tiptoes, she brushed his cheek with her lips. He half turned and their mouths met for the briefest of heartbeats.

She took a small step backwards and allowed the air to rush between them. Her heart raced as if she had run up a long hill. She dug her fingernails into the palms of her hands and bid the rush of attraction to be gone. She needed to confirm the rules of their pretend engagement, but to do that she needed to speak with him privately.

'We were in the wood together. Alone.' The words

came out as a whisper. Elene swallowed hard and felt Hafual's warm hand in the middle of her back. She increased the sound of her voice until it rang off the walls. 'Words of a specific nature were spoken. With your sudden arrival and the preparations for the feast, Lord Pybba, I missed the chance to speak privately with my father. Certain matters are best spoken about within the family before being shared with the wider world.'

Hafual moved his hand to encircle her waist and pulled her close. The subtle scent of wildflowers, woodsmoke and something utterly masculine engulfed her. She was aware of how his broad chest rose and fell, inviting her to lean her head against it.

Pybba's mouth dropped open and he rose quickly from the table, nearly falling backwards in his haste as if he was about to become soiled. 'You have an intimate agreement with this man? An agreement your father knew nothing about? That your father's steward knew nothing about?'

Ecgbert and his wife exchanged panicked glances. From that look, Elene knew her earlier hunch had been right—they were seeking to undermine her and her sisters for their personal gain. She wondered what had been offered or hinted at—lands, jewels or simply an appeal against all Northmen. Ecgbert had always been bigoted against them, even if he modulated his tone around her sisters' husbands. And with an eye towards the main chance, Ecgbert now felt he had miscalculated. She suspected that he would quickly try to pretend it was entirely his wife's influence. The one thing which was consistent about Ecgbert was that he tried to save his own skin first.

'Our new arrangement suits us both. We are such

good neighbours,' she said, turning more towards her father and away from the appeal of Hafual's broad chest.

'Elene has captured the situation perfectly.' Hafual's lips brushed the top of her head, causing a curl of heat to start deep within her.

She lifted her eyes to his and tumbled into the deep pools. When had they become so deep blue and had such depth? 'Glad you approve…dear.'

He brushed his lips against hers again. Longer this time. And the curl of heat swooped and circled about her insides, making her knees weak. She splayed her hands against his chest to keep from falling.

'Why?' she whispered.

'To get the point across,' he murmured against her ear.

The hall resounded to people stamping their feet in approval and cheering. A surge of triumph went through her. No one had guessed that the performance wasn't real.

She stepped away from Hafual's encircling arm and held her hand out to her father. 'You see how it is. An intimate understanding. Or does Lord Pybba disagree?'

Pybba visibly shrank away from her and regarded her as if she was a clod of mud he'd removed from his boot. 'What you do is of no concern to me, but your father, all right-thinking people, must be appalled.'

Elene struggled to keep her face straight. If she appeared triumphant, she could lose everything.

'Father, say something,' she said, injecting what she hoped was the right amount of supplication and pleading into her voice, as if this scheme truly mattered to her. 'Tell me that you are proud of me.'

'Are you saying what I think you are saying, Daughter? You have accepted this Mercian lord without consulting me?'

'Is there something wrong with Lord Hafual, Father?' she asked in her lightest voice. Whatever happened, she had to keep to the truth as much as possible and not make too many exaggerations. It made telling the slight untruths easier, something she'd discovered when she was with Nerian. 'I thought you admired him, particularly as he's renounced his heathen ways and pledged his service to our King. His sword arm is beyond compare. And while I have never considered myself maternal, his young son brings a smile to my face on dark days.' She went over to him and grasped his gnarled hands. 'Please, Father, do not deny me this.'

Her father tightened his fingers about hers and then let go. 'You and Hafual? Came to your own arrangement? About your future? Without consulting me? Ansithe and Cynehild at least waited until their second marriages before ignoring my wishes.'

'I take after my mother.'

Her father's face crumpled. 'I've led a quieter life since your mother's death.'

'King Ceolwulf accepted me as a liegeman when he gifted me my lands,' Hafual said. 'Your daughter and me? The arrangement suits us both. I discovered she was free, her heart no longer pledged to another. I acted. Are you objecting to where I was born?'

Her father visibly paled. 'Unexpected. I mean nothing by it. I simply never considered the possibility.'

Pybba's expression grew more horrified by the breath. 'You are considering it now, Wulfgar? You can't be. He is a Northman.'

'Lord Wulfgar does more than consider my proposal. He sees the merits of a son-in-law who is close to the king,' Hafual said in an ice-cold tone.

'The lies drip from your mouth,' Pybba declared.

'Is that a challenge, Pybba? Name the time and place.'

'You know full well King Ceolwulf has listened to his wife. Any duel between members of his inner circle is forbidden until he rescinds the order.'

Hafual's hand went to his sword. 'You can't keep hiding behind the queen's skirts for ever.'

'Lord Hafual is a guest under this roof as are you, Lord Pybba.' Elene stomped her foot hard on the rushes and gained a few heartbeats of silence. The king would never forgive her father if the men broke their oaths. Starting a feud with Pybba's kin would send Baelle Heale and Mercia spiralling back towards the civil unrest she'd experienced as a child. 'Hospitality is all. We will have no challenges or fights at this feast. We have all broken bread together.'

'Yes, we have indeed, daughter.' Her father appeared to understand the danger. 'I will need time to consider.'

Silently she willed Pybba to take that final step off the cliff he teetered on, rendering his own suit irredeemable without her having to do anything more. And without there being any bloodshed. 'What is there to consider?'

'Honour our agreement, Wulfgar,' Pybba thundered. 'Force your daughter or face the consequences.'

'Pity, but my lady has spoken, Pybba,' Hafual said with a curl in his lip. 'No one will be forced today.'

'Did you invite me here to humiliate me?' Pybba's eyes narrowed. 'Or was it something much more sinister? Something cooked up between you and your steward? Was I the bait to smoke out your real target? They said you were a tricky customer at court and your youngest daughter flighty. I now understand why, Wulfgar.'

'You appear to be excelling at the humiliation without any assistance,' Haful said. 'Or is it the mead speaking? I will accede to my Elene's wishes. No fight tonight but say the word, Pybba, and I will happily meet you on the field of honour. Name the time, the place and the weapons.'

Pybba turned beet red and muttered again about the queen's command.

Elene marvelled at how Hafual commanded the room with a curl of his lip. Pybba feared him. Hafual was right—Pybba did hide behind the queen's skirts and that made him dangerous.

'Father,' she said in a low voice. 'We need to change the mood from anger to joy. I've done as you requested.'

'Daughter, you are the voice of reason.' Her father clapped his hands. 'More mead and more songs. We must rejoice for my youngest daughter has finally made her choice.'

'The right choice,' Hafual said with a grim smile.

'Wulfgar, are you going to allow this man to insult me?' Pybba raised his hands up to the ceiling. His chins trembled. 'I, who am a guest under this roof? Someone who had every expectation of marrying your daughter? You led me astray.'

'Are you accusing my father of underhanded tricks, Lord Pybba? Is that an abuse of hospitality?' She kept her chin up and tried to keep her voice steady, rather than allowing it to race like it did when she was excited. 'Father, no one has consulted me on views of a betrothal to this man. Ever. I would not take him, even if I did not have an understanding with Hafual—his rudeness towards you has been astonishing.'

She looked forward to explaining the final coup de grace to her sisters. Whatever happened with Hafual, and however they ended it, she would not be marrying Pybba.

Her father's hand trembled. 'Do you think he is being rude to me?'

'I heard his words, Father,' Elene said in an undertone. 'Judge his actions. Is this the sort of man you require as a son-in-law and guardian of Baelle Heale?'

Pybba slammed his hand down on the table. 'Three daughters. All married to perfidious Northmen. You don't deserve to be called an ealdorman of Mercia.'

'You insult Baelle Heale hospitality and my father! You are the one who is unworthy!' Elene shouted. The hall erupted with feet stamping and a chorus of approval for her.

Pybba made a rude gesture and strode out of the hall swiftly followed by his men and Ecgbert, who appeared ashen-faced at the sudden turn of events.

Elene held her face still and tried to ignore the small curl of panic. What was it that Ansithe and Cynehild used to say about her schemes—she always ended up making things worse? She glanced at Hafual's remote face and hoped that they could solve the tangle of the pretend betrothal without too much difficulty.

Chapter Five

Hafual waited until Pybba and the steward had exited the hall before he released his breath and willed the ache in his right shoulder to go. It was easier to vanquish Pybba than he had considered at the start of the evening and his only regret was that Pybba had not agreed to single-handed combat. That fight was coming, he silently vowed, and it would be on his terms.

He glanced at Elene's mutinous face. Now he had to deal with the fallout from their announcement and pretend understanding. Implying that he and Lady Elene had a marital agreement was different from marrying the woman. However, he'd marry her if he was left with no other choice as his sense of duty and honour would demand it, even though he knew he was not the sort of person to make any woman a good husband.

He'd proved that with Svala. He'd been the one to force her to come to Mercia when the autumn storms had started, causing their baby to die on the voyage. He'd been the one to say that they must try again, seducing her that night, and had watched helpless as she sunk into lethargy and depression after she fell pregnant. Rather than staying with her, he'd found solace in his work for the king. And it had culminated in their last terrible fight when he made the wrong choice.

'My lady,' he said in an undertone. 'I believe the time has come for my men and I to take our leave. There's little more for me to do here tonight. You are safe. You will not marry Pybba. I swear this on my life.'

'I hope Ecgbert fails in his mission to change Pybba's mind. Actually, he should go with Pybba and never return. The man has been a disaster for Baelle Heale, but my father thinks highly of him,' Elene murmured, reaching over to squeeze his hand. Her bountiful charms once again captured his attention, reminding him Lady Elene was all woman, the sort who deserved a proper husband rather a hulking wreck like himself.

A pulse of warmth went up his arm, making him remember what it was like to be alive instead of half dead and burdened with guilt until his throat nearly choked from it. He rapidly lifted his eyes to where her father sat with a speculative look on his face.

The sly old fox was up to something. A faint prickle of unease slid down his spine. The bride price and his morning gift to the bride needed to be properly negotiated. Some of his work for the king had been spent overseeing various marriage contracts of heiresses.

'We both do,' he said out of the side of his mouth. 'The neighbourhood would be a more peaceful place without Ecgbert. The man lives for conflict and lining his pockets, I swear it.'

'You and me both, but my father listens to his blandishments and flattery. He won't have him put aside. Moir and Ansithe have tried. Cynehild says that Ecgbert's heart has Baelle Heale carved on it, but she always sees the best in people.'

'And you? You are the one who has your father's ear.'

She toyed with her necklace and a distant look came into her eyes. 'Ecgbert saved my life once. He braved the bandits and raised the alarm which allowed Ansithe, Moir and the remainder of the *felag* to rescue us.'

'Don't allow him to throw it away, then,' he said, giving in to temptation and touching her arm.

The pensive look vanished. 'One less suitor. Thank you. You were as good as your word in being my ally.' She put her hands together. 'I was wrong earlier to think I didn't need rescuing, but it is over.'

'Is this rescuing? Much easier than I had considered but then Pybba was always a blowhard coward.' Hafual smiled down at her and vowed to keep her in ignorance of the peril she faced. Pybba was a snake and more dangerous when cornered.

He'd never known the man to give up easily if he wanted something, but this time he had. What game was being played? What had Pybba wanted if he didn't want Elene? A pain started behind Hafual's eyes. He was missing something vital, something that Pybba was doing in this game of *tafl* they were playing. It would come to him, but for now, he was victorious.

Her laugh had a certain amount of false bravado to it. 'Will you go hot on Pybba's heels to ensure he doesn't make any mischief at court?'

He looked around at his men, who remained seated. His gut instinct told him mischief could still be done tonight, but he refused to worry Lady Elene further. 'We stay until after the recitation of *Beowulf*.'

'Thank you.' Her look of relief made something he'd considered long dead turn over inside him. It surprised him that the empty place inside which he'd carried about for so long—after Svala's confession about how she'd tossed their baby screaming into the sea because she could not stand the noise any longer and was convinced that the baby was calling to the demons of the storm—had lessened. He was alive, rather than merely existing after all.

'You are welcome.' Giving in to impulse, he brushed his lips against her smooth cheek. 'Go. Get the feast restarted.'

'Elene, why are you whispering like that? What else are you plotting?' Lord Wulfgar called out from the high table. Hafual noticed the steward's wife had returned to the hall and stood close to the elderly ealdorman with a smug smile on her face. Ecgbert joined her and pointed towards Lady Elene. Hafual wondered how much gold Pybba had promised the pair.

'We celebrated too soon,' he murmured, absently patting Elene's hand. 'The worst may be yet to come. Ecgbert and his good lady have more than one trick up their sleeve. Shall I sit at the high table?'

'Ecgbert is loyal to my father.'

'You are being naive, my lady. Pybba has bribed him with what I've little idea, but the man has sold his soul.'

Elene forced her head up and moved away from the comfort of Hafual's bulk. Her father's face had gone a mottled colour and his jaw worked up and down, but no words emerged, just inarticulate squeaks.

Elene's heart sank. She struggled to remember the last time she had seen her father that angry. Possibly when she had broken his favourite sword by stamping on it when she tried to jump over it. 'Allow me to handle this. More mead will restore his temper.'

'We go together and discuss things privately.'

Elene put her hand on her hip. Hafual was being like every other warrior she knew—overbearing. 'You doubt my ability. Remember, I pushed Pybba into his temper tantrum.'

'What I believe makes no difference. I was concerned about your safety. Among other things, your quick thinking and skills with herbs saved my comrades back when we were fighting the outlaws.'

Safe. What a lovely word that was. She certainly felt far safer now than she had before. His half-smile made her insides flutter. 'And you keep your promises.'

'I make every attempt to.' He leant closer so that his breath touched her ear, increasing the fluttering. 'I thank you for the kiss, my lady.'

Elene fixed her best smile to her face, ignoring the weakness in her knees. She clapped her hands and motioned to the serving maids to begin clearing up and for the minstrel to start reciting *Beowulf.* The sooner this feast finished, the better for everyone. She gestured towards where the bard sat, plucking his lyre. 'You always enjoy *Beowulf*, Father. Perhaps where the monster's mother comes to avenge his death, now that Lord Pybba is not here to object.'

Her father's mouth opened and shut several times. He jabbed at the air with his finger and a growl escaped his throat. 'You will be getting married. I will not have any more excuses or indeed recitation of *Beowulf.* Hafual made an offer. You accepted. You will not dishonour the family by repudiating it like you did with that Nerian fellow.'

Elene stood up straighter. Her father had consumed far too much. Nerian had jilted her. She had been waiting for him to formally approach her father at long last when word came, he'd married that heiress. The rational part of her brain knew she could not hold Hafual to anything more than a betrothal, which would fail during the negotiations for the bride price. He had famously said that he was through with marriage at his wife's funeral. 'We have an arrangement, yes. Hafual can explain its precise nature. We both accept there must be negotiations about the bride price.'

'Do you know the nature of the negotiations?'

Her stomach knotted. Time to redirect her father's attention and remind him of his irritation with Pybba. 'But I much prefer it to anything you might have arranged with Lord Pybba. That man made my skin crawl. His disrespect of your hospitality astonished me.'

'Was this scheme another of my daughter's fancies, Hafual?' Her father rapped his goblet on the table. 'You have known her long enough to spot them. She gets everything in a tangle and expects someone else to sort it out. Has she entangled you in one of her more fanciful schemes or are you willing to marry her in truth?'

Hafual stepped forward. His blond hair shimmered in the torchlight and his strong jaw jutted forward. 'I am no liar, Lord Wulfgar.'

Elene hurriedly linked her arm about his. He pulled her towards him, making her body collide with the hard planes of his chest. She fluttered her lashes. 'Why should you refuse our neighbour's reasonable request? He is everything that you could wish for in a son-in-law. Is it my fault that you went behind my back and tried to make an alliance with a man like Pybba?'

'If Your Lordship pleases,' Ecgbert's wife said with a low curtsey. 'You will see what the trouble will be if you consult a priest. The king has become more religious of late, and Lord Hafual has a certain reputation for ignoring the delicacies of mass.'

Elene gritted her teeth. The woman was a complete bigot and deluded. 'Call Father Oswald. Wake him from his slumber. See if he prepared him properly for baptism.'

Her father bellowed for Father Oswald, who came at a shuffling run behind the new assistant pig-keeper. He was busy doing up his robe and looked as if he had been woken from a sound sleep. 'Are you prepared to marry them?'

Father Oswald blinked like a startled owl. 'Who?'

'Elene and Lord Hafual? Will you marry them? Tonight? Is there an impediment to the marriage?'

The priest widened his eyes. 'Lord Hafual was baptised several years ago. He remains a devote Christian.'

'No impediment, then. Good. Then you will marry them.'

'You mean right now? I thought perhaps we could wait…until…' Father Oswald turned towards Elene with a pleading expression on his face.

'Until Brother Palni returns from my sisters',' Elene said, her mind racing to find a reason why a marriage should be delayed. 'He has been instructing Hafual in our religion, to ensure if his conversion was more than mumbled words. But you know how Brother Palni is, always wanting to ensure everyone understands the importance of the opportunity Christianity affords. He would want to be here. And my sisters as well.'

Father Oswald bowed low. 'Precisely. Brother Palni is this man's confessor.'

Her father's countenance darkened. 'My daughter is capricious like the wind. I require her to be married as soon as possible.'

Elene disentangled herself from Hafual. The cool air rushed between them. She could not beg him to marry her. She had her pride. 'If I want my sisters to attend? A wedding should be for family.'

And the time it took for her sisters to arrive would give her time to figure out a decent solution to the conundrum about what sort of marriage she and Hafual would make, if indeed there was to be a marriage.

'I warned you earlier, Elene. You must find a suitable man to marry tonight.' He began to cough, and his skin had that parchment quality to it.

'Hafual is suitable. Why the haste?'

Her father's smile became mirthless. 'I shall send a rider to catch Pybba. I will inform him that I have no daughter and that I wish him to become my heir.'

'You can't do that. My sisters—'

'Your sisters have their own estates with their husbands who have pledged their loyalty to a different king.' Her father shrugged. 'To keep our lands, you must marry someone who is loyal to our King and has his ear. Elene, you are not a child who requires an explanation about my health.'

Elene clenched her fists and would have walked away if Hafual had not been keeping her pinned to his side.

'Easy,' he breathed against her hair. 'Remember, Pybba has bribed Ecgbert. He wants the estate.'

Her father pounded the table. 'You have turned too

many other good men down for silly reasons. Simply because you were besotted with that Wessex warrior. Then you had the temerity to send him away!'

'I didn't. I swear it. I thought he was going to return.'

'Every chance you waste. You should have ensured it through your feminine charms.'

Elene examined the rushes, rather than looking at the shocked faces of the servants and her father's men-at-arms. Her father normally kept his harsh words for their private conversations, instead of humiliating her like this in front of the guests.

'Elene, why are you silent?'

'Your mind has been twisted and you've had too much mead, Father,' Elene began, giving her father a hard stare, the sort her eldest sister used when their father spoke out of turn. 'We will speak in the morning when you are rested, and all can be properly explained and sorted.'

'Elene,' Hafual said in a low voice, putting his hand in the middle of her back. There was something safe and solid about his hand. He put his finger to her lips. 'Let me speak. I know my own mind. I have had very little to drink. We do not need to wait for anything. Can you do that for me?'

She nodded and hoped that he had seen a way to bring her father around to the situation where they might be betrothed until such a time that a solution could be worked out.

He turned towards her father and held out his hands. 'Wulfgar, there is little need to send for Pybba or to wait for Palni. I will marry your daughter tonight if Father Oswald is willing and you insist but only if you insist. You must accept the price I ask for her.'

The sudden silence in the room was deafening. Elene stared at him in astonishment. Hafual, the man who had sworn never to remarry, was offering to marry her. Tonight. And it appeared that the pink-cheeked and very much awake Father Oswald would agree. He bustled forward and indicated that he would give his blessing if Lord Wulfgar deemed it necessary.

The steward's wife gave a small cry and hid her face in her hands. Ecgbert's throat worked up and down, but no sound emerged. He started gesturing wildly with his arms.

'Is there some problem, man?' her father asked. 'Your wife assured me that forcing the marriage was the way to tell if my daughter lied.'

'They are up to something, Lord Wulfgar,' Ecgbert gasped out. 'I know it. Your daughter and Lord Hafual? Impossible. I know Hafual's history, how he vowed that he'd never marry again after his wife's accident, and how Lady Elene has always said that she would never be second best.'

'It is not Lady Elene or me who is up to something,' Hafual thundered. 'What has Pybba promised you? What has he paid you personally?'

The steward shrank back, bleating about the unfairness of it all and how he'd only wanted what was best for Baelle Heale, and it had been a business deal over wool, that was all.

'Do you insist on me marrying your daughter tonight, Lord Wulfgar?'

Her father blinked rapidly. 'You wish to marry today, Hafual. Without negotiating a bride price. Why?'

The planes of Hafual's face became harder and more remote. 'As you said, your daughter can be capricious.

And I now know her dowry is to be Baelle Heale. Why would I turn down the chance to increase my holdings and to keep my sworn enemy from my doorstep?'

'You are not one to miss an opportunity, that's for certain!' the steward's wife called out. 'You have been played, my lady. Mark my words, you will regret this. Sooner than you might think. Best to call for Lord Pybba now before you are wed to this barbarian. He is scheming behind your back already.'

'I think you will discover that I am negotiating in full view of Lady Elene. Why should I hide my reasons for desiring the same treatment as Lord Pybba from my bride?'

Elene glanced up at Hafual, but his face was inscrutable. And she longed to ask him why he'd done this and what their marriage would be like. Questions buzzed in her brain like a swarm of her sister's bees. Was he only marrying her to get the estate? Why were he and Pybba sworn enemies? Did he care about her as a person, or would she be a counter to advance his political career?

'What say you, daughter?' her father asked. 'Will you marry this man? Or will you do as I bid?'

Elene held out her hand. Hafual's strong fingers instantly curled about it, steadying her. She lengthened her neck and stood as proudly as any woman in her family had ever done. 'As Father Oswald is willing, it would be my pleasure to wed Hafual tonight and begin my life as a married woman. Now if you will excuse me, I must find the circlet which belonged to my mother. I like to think that she would want me to wear it for the ceremony.'

* * *

'I need to get that eagle brooch which belonged to Ansithe. I want to wear something from each of my sisters as well as my mother's circlet.' Elene gave a nod to the maids who were guarding her. 'There is no need to come with me. I know precisely where Ansithe left it.'

Without waiting for an answer, Elene slipped out of her chamber. She whispered a silent prayer that she'd be able to discover Hafual alone and they could have a sensible conversation. Things needed to be settled between them before they married. She knew she should confess about Nerian taking her virginity, and how disappointing the act had been. It would also mean confessing how he'd altered towards her and her suspicions that it had been her failure rather than his that the experience had been so lacking. She pressed a hand to her head. It would be better to come up with a reason why the wedding night should be postponed.

'Lady Elene.' Silver starlight outlined Hafual's form, making her aware of his height, the breadth of his chest and the narrowness of his hips. She had never considered him beyond a friendly face before, and now she couldn't stop noticing him as a man. She straightened her shoulders and tried not to think about her failures as a woman. If she had been better in bed, she could have held Nerian. Nerian had panted for her until he'd had her.

'My lady, is everything well?'

'We need to agree terms,' she said, far more forcefully than she intended.

'Terms? Your father and I have agreed the dowry, the bride price and the morning gift.'

'Set limits to our marriage. What we each expect. Little need to pretend, Lord Hafual, our marriage is one of convenience rather than of desire.'

'Most marriages between Mercian noble families are matters of property rather than of the heart.' He inclined his head. 'My time at court has given me the opportunity to study this closely.'

Elene pleated her gown between her fingers. 'We need to see if we are compatible before…before we do anything rash.'

'Does your heart remain in Wessex, my lady?' The words were no more than a whisper.

'What do you know about that?'

'The court was alive with rumours when he married. And you failed to appear at any of the feasts this last spring.'

She swallowed hard. 'I've no intention of asking you about your late wife. Please offer me the same consideration about Nerian.'

He stood silent in the starlight. She forced her mouth to remain shut, rather than rushing several meaningless sentences about the weather.

'Do you wish for the marriage to be in name only?' he asked finally when the silence had become unbearable.

'It seems the best way to proceed…until we know we suit.' Someday she would find a way to confess about Nerian and how painful coupling with him had been. 'I've thought about the marriage bed and how to handle the sheets in case my father decides to inspect them in the morning.'

'Indeed.'

'Best to be prepared.' She put her hand on his arm. 'Everyone knows about your devotion to your wife.'

He removed her fingers from his arm. 'Svala is dead.'

Elene swallowed hard. She had made a mess of it. 'Why do you want to marry me?'

'You have to admit Baelle Heale is a considerable prize. Having it will ensure I can protect my lands more easily.'

'You are only doing this for the land?'

'What other reason could there be?'

Elene held out her hand. 'Then you agree to the sort of marriage I propose.'

'For now.'

She heard the steward calling her name, wondering where she had disappeared to.

'Go now, my lady. All will be well. I promise.'

She picked up her skirts and hurried away. It bothered her that she did believe him.

'Here I find you, brother dear, wandering aimlessly in a church like some lost soul.'

Hafual groaned inwardly when Asida's voice resounded throughout the near-empty church where he'd gone after his unsatisfactory interview with Lady Elene. The woman still harboured feelings for Nerian. The agreement for a marriage in name only would give them both time. He'd never forced a woman, and any woman he had lain with he wanted her to be thinking of him, not some other man, when she was in his arms.

Marrying Lady Elene was the right thing to do for Narfi's future, the land and to prevent Pybba gaining a foothold so near to his family. That Lady Elene's hair had gleamed in the torchlight, or her mouth was the colour of a summer sunrise, had no bearing on his decision. That part of his life had died when Svala drew her last breath. When he'd discovered her body, the ice entered his soul. He knew all the things Svala had said in their last quarrel about him were true. He had tempted her away from his distant cousin to spite the man; he should have returned North and travelled with her and the baby instead of simply sending word and expecting her to travel on the storm-tossed sea; he'd stayed away doing the king's bidding when he could have returned; and he wasn't the husband she required. If he had been a better man, she'd never have flung herself off that cliff.

'Hafual, aren't you pleased to see me?'

'Asida. Sister.' Hafual adopted his coldest tone and gave her a stare which would have one of his warriors quaking in his boots. 'You were under orders to remain with my son. Away from this place.'

'Narfi is safely asleep with the servants. I gave him a kiss before I left. He will have the sweetest of dreams tonight instead of the restless ones he has been having. He is to have a proper mother at long last.'

'Wonderful that you know my son's dreams now.'

'You are being grumpy, Hafual. You should be pleased to see me. The entire hall buzzes with what you have vowed to do. Best done wearing this coat instead of the tatty one you are wearing.'

'I like my cloak.'

'Your bride has taken the time to change.'

'How do you know that?'

'I have ears, brother dear, and I listened before I came to find you. Stop being difficult.' Asida glided up to him, carrying his best kaftan coat, the one he'd purchased in Ludenwic with the heavy gold and silver embroidery on the facing and cuffs. A coat fit for the sort of lord he was destined to be, or so Svala had proclaimed when she saw it. She had told him to wait and wear it at the Christmas feast at court and to put all the Mercian lords to shame. In the event, she'd been too sick from the pregnancy, and they had not gone.

Returning from her funeral, he had carefully packed it away in his smallest iron-bound trunk, intending never to look at it and his foolish dreams again.

'You went through my things?' he asked, eyeing the coat warily.

'Your hiding places are so obvious.'

'My hiding places are not— Give it here, as you appear determined.'

Asida shoved the coat towards him. The coat was heavier than he recalled, laden down with a king's ransom of gold and silver.

She gave an ironic curtsey. 'Before you ask, I had little idea that you would be getting married tonight.'

'Your *fylgjur* didn't tell you that? How remiss of it.'

Asida smiled, looking precisely like one of the house cats who had discovered a bowl of unattended cream. 'Absolutely silent on that particular point. Now put the coat on and stop being awkward. You don't want to shame the family.'

'I've done that enough already, according to you.'

'According to our half-brother if you want to be strictly truthful, but you know I rarely listen to him.'

He put the coat on over his thick wool tunic. It was slightly tight on his forearms but otherwise it fit like it had when he was in Constantinople back when he thought the world had possibilities. If he remembered correctly, the colour brought out the blue in his eyes. 'You are interfering again.'

She gave him a playful punch on his arm. 'Admit it. You want me here. You need me here before you do something which makes life more difficult for everyone. And you will want to look your best for your bride. Elene is the sort of woman I want as a sister.'

Hafual concentrated on doing up the silver clasps at the front. 'I am perfectly capable of looking after my interests. The estate will go nicely with my holdings.'

A tiny smile hovered on her lips. She dusted the coat down and straightened the collar as if he was little older than Narfi instead of her older half-brother. Hafual gritted his teeth, but with Asida in this sort of managing mood, he knew better than to risk a scene.

'It is good that someone in the family will be here to support you.' She took a step backwards and nodded. 'You may have need of me before this evening is finished, Hafual. I consent to being used as a counter if it comes to it.'

Hafual clenched his teeth. Asida was so certain about her own importance in this thing. 'Mercia is not like the North. They do not require hostages from the bridegroom. But your *fylgjur* might not understand that, seeing as you refuse to learn anything about the country in which we now live.'

She rolled her eyes. 'You are the one to mention such a possibility as hostages, not I. I am here because I'm your family and I thought you might need assistance in some sort of unknown capacity.'

'As the coat-carrier.'

She laughed. 'You made a joke. First time since...'

'You are my sister. Try not to make it more difficult.'

'From everything you said over the past year or so, Lord Pybba is a permanent thorn in your side and potentially a formidable foe. I suspect he might have had help from certain quarters…'

'You are to do nothing about that. Leave them to me.'

She fluttered her lashes. 'What sort of sister would I be if I failed to help? I like Elene. I look forward to you expanding the family.'

Hafual hated the sudden lump which came into his throat. Asida knew what could happen at weddings in the North and wanted to help. 'Leave me to expand my family in my own good time.'

His half-sister straightened the folds of her gown. 'Curiosity made me do it if you must know. After your marriage, you will have a new wife who will rule the hall and look after your son. My life starts afresh. I have laid my plans.'

'Curiosity killed a cat, you know. I like you alive.'

She made an annoyed noise. 'You never had a sense of adventure.'

'Self-preservation.' He nodded towards the priest, who stood with Lady Elene and her father. Elene wore a circlet on her head and carried a makeshift bunch of flowers. The deep crimson gown more than hinted at her generous curves. She stood with her head proudly erect, every inch the lady. Hafual drunk in her looks and belatedly realised he was staring, much to Asida's silent amusement.

'No interest in your lady, brother? I suspect you will expand your family very quickly. A part of your anatomy agrees with me.'

'Asida!'

'I'm from the North and am not a prudish nun. But I won't embarrass you, brother dear.'

Father Oswald stifled a yawn and signalled towards him. Elene's smile trembled on her lips as if she expected life to disappoint her. A surge of unfamiliar protectiveness surged through him. He silently vowed that he'd ensure the marriage worked within the parameters they agreed. This time, he would be a better husband.

Hafual put a hand on Asida's shoulder. 'The next part of my life waits for me.'

'We really need to do something about your sense of fun, brother. You look like you are about to face a hundred berserkers instead of a comely bride.'

Chapter Six

The actual wedding ceremony passed in a blur for Elene. It was more like a series of still images—the torchlit church, Father Oswald intoning in his deep voice while Hafual stood at her side with his eyes focused on the priest, the passing of the gold wedding ring on the blade of the sword, an old Mercian custom which meant that the groom pledged his sacred honour to his bride. The intricate ring held subtle warmth from Hafual's finger when she slipped it on.

Hafual had changed into a deep blue leather coat with gold and silver embroidered trimmings, a coat far finer than she had seen before. A reminder that she knew very little about his prospects.

Asida stood directly behind Hafual, with a bright smile on her face. Elene wondered why the woman had brought the coat so late in the day. Had this marriage scheme been planned in far greater detail than she realised?

She'd had to make a choice between Pybba, who would be no good at all for the estate, and Hafual, whose estate prospered. Elene placed a hand on her stomach. When he turned towards her, she sought the warm spark in his eyes she'd glimpsed earlier, but all she glimpsed was a steely cold hardness.

'You may kiss the bride,' Father Oswald intoned, breaking through her thoughts, and reminding her of what needed to be done.

Elene obediently lifted her mouth, expecting the lightest brush of his lips, a token gesture no more than that. Silently she prayed it would be enough to satisfy her father and that he would not demand any other sort of demonstration of Hafual's commitment to the marriage. The last thing she required was someone inspecting the sheets or waiting outside the bridal chamber until the task was complete.

'We need to make this meaningful,' Hafual murmured, cupping her face.

Her eyes traced the faint silver scarring on his cheeks, a relic from some bygone battle. She gave in to the temptation to touch it, silky smooth against the pads of her fingers. Everything appeared to hang on that heartbeat.

'We should do that.' Her voice was far too breathless for her liking. She wet her parched lips. 'I mean, yes.'

Hafual lowered his mouth. A feather-light touch but one which promised something more as his lips moved over hers. An unexpected pulse of heat went through her. As her mouth slightly parted, she tasted him— honey, and something indefinably him. He lifted his lips and raised a quizzical brow and then repeated the performance to the cheers of the people in the church.

Then it was over. He moved away from her, stopped. She realised she had grabbed hold of Hafual's coat. She forced her fingers to let go and took a step backwards. The kisses she'd shared with Nerian seemed to be pale and puny in comparison, belonging to girlish dreams, and yet she instinctively knew it had been the lightest of touches, something which meant nothing to him, a signal to any of Pybba's spies that they were married and she now belonged to him.

She turned towards where her father stood with a self-satisfied grin on his face.

'There, it is done, Father,' she said, a little too loudly as not to show how off balance the kiss had made her. She refused to repeat the mistakes she'd made years ago—believing an accidental brush of shoulders, a touch of hands and a stolen kiss or three meant something deep and profound, instead being a deliberate seduction because all the man in question required was a warm body in the night.

This time, she was not going to ask for more than Hafual was prepared to give. This time, she was not going to wear her heart on her sleeve. But this time, she wasn't going to be seduced until she knew Hafual cared for her as a person, not simply a means to an end. She was going to keep her heart safe.

'What is done, daughter?' her father called and more ribald shouting about the power of that kiss rang out.

Father Oswald frowned. 'This is a place of worship, not a hall after the stories have been told.'

'Must you kill joy, Father Oswald?' Hafual's sister called back. 'We are celebrating a wedding.'

'We should go to the hall,' Hafual said in an undertone. 'My sister can be forceful with her opinions at the best of times.

Elene nodded to show she understood. 'We will go to the hall.'

'Yes, to drink toasts!' Hafual clasped her hand and raised it above their heads. 'Who will drink to our good health and happiness?'

* * *

'I like your sister, Hafual.' Elene's father leant towards Hafual after more mead was poured and the first of the toasts had been offered in the hall. During the feast with Pybba, the noise had been subdued as if everyone was expecting the worst, but now the sound reverberated off the walls. People appeared to be genuinely pleased with the situation, but despite the urging, Hafual had not kissed her again. And it bothered her that a vague sense of disappointment had settled in her belly.

'I can hear the objection in your voice. Don't be shy, Wulfgar. We are related now,' Asida said from where she sat, her face flushed pink from the mead.

'But she should find a husband. Someone who can control her tongue.' Her father banged his fist on the table and glanced about as if he had said something witty.

'Let my marriage be an end to all your scheming,' Elene said before Asida could reply and make the situation worse. Her father had drunk more mead than was good for him. 'You've done your duty, Father. All your daughters are married. Baelle Heale will be safe for years to come.'

Her father extended his arms. His eyes glistened with tears, but whether they were real or mead-induced, she didn't want to say. 'All I have wanted. My youngest has married a warrior who can defend this land if called upon. Someone who is loyal to our King.'

Elene stood very still but longed to hit something quite hard. Her father was being difficult and damning with faint praise. 'My brothers-in-law are good men and would defend these lands.'

'Without being pledged to our King, they are no

use to me. Even my grandson is being brought up in Dane-law country, not in Mercia.' Her father pinched the bridge of his nose. 'There you go. Getting me in a muddle, Elene. I only want what is best for you. You are far too stubborn for your own good as Ecgbert confided. But you are married now. All is well even if the wedding was rather abrupt.'

Elene pressed her lips together and held back a swift comment asking whose fault that was. Hafual, she noticed, carefully avoided her eye. 'Father, this is not the time or place.'

'Should we have another toast to the happy couple?' Asida called out. 'Or has the mead run out?'

'The mead will never run out, dear lady,' her father said and called for more mead. 'The chamber must be prepared for the happy couple. It must be a proper send-off.'

Elene winced. The traditions of a Mercian wedding night were well known to her. Every bone in her body ached. The last thing she wanted was Hafual being forced into the sort of display required.

Hafual put a firm hand on her shoulder, after yet another toast was drunk to the bride and groom. 'My bride and I will bid you goodnight and leave you to drink the fine mead.'

'Of course, the marriage will need to be consummated,' Ecgbert's wife said in her nasal tone. 'I made sure the sheets in your bedchamber are clean, Wulfgar. Nothing but the best for the daughter of the hall. These things should be done, according to Mercian custom.'

'Mercian customs are barbaric,' Asida said to no one in particular. 'I always feel sorry for the poor bride in these situations, but then what do I know being an unmarried woman from far away?'

'Precisely.' Ecgbert's wife sniffed loudly. 'Our traditions are our traditions. Nothing foreign.'

Hafual's eyes burned blue fire. 'Asida, sister, do not antagonise our hosts. Their traditions are now our traditions. We are Mercians.'

Asida hung her head. 'I apologise, Lord Wulfgar. But there must be a better way. Dignity for your daughter and you being able to sleep in your own bed.'

'Asida!' Hafual's voice held a warning note. 'We discussed this earlier. Mercian customs hold sway.'

Elene froze. Hafual had discussed the terms with Asida.

Asida curtseyed low and Elene noticed the way her father in his drunken state ogled the woman's breasts. 'I merely wanted to suggest following Northern customs. A suggestion, no more than that. More dignity for the woman. I apologise if that is wrong. But it comes from my heart.'

Her father wiped his mouth with the back of his hand. 'You planned on doing something different than the usual send-off, Hafual?'

'Where I come from, normally the groom captures the bride and takes her away from her family. They spend the night. Alone.' He gestured towards his sister. 'Asida volunteered to remain here until we return.'

'For as long as it is necessary, brother,' Asida called back with a wave and a brilliant smile. 'Lord Wulfgar and I shall become excellent friends. We share an interest in mead and I think perhaps *tafl*. I've longed for someone to teach me the intricacies of the Mercian game.'

Her father waved his goblet. 'Such a charming creature.'

Ecgbert and his wife appeared to have swallowed exceptionally sour plums.

'All settled. I shall take up the position of hostage as you suggested, brother.'

Elene's knees went weak. Hafual was offering Asida as a hostage? The knowledge hit her. He'd planned this. Why else would Asida have appeared in the way she did?

'I hardly think that is necessary. Do you, Father? Asida needs to return to your hall so she can look after your son, Hafual.' She hoped he'd take the hint and suggest that Asida return to the hall with them. 'We are friends here. Family now.'

Hafual's face offered little comfort. 'Up to your father.'

Her father tugged at his tunic. 'I've no objection to Asida remaining here. I look forward to the change in company. Your son as well, Hafual. He will come to no harm in this hall. We are family now after all, as my daughter said. You and your bride should have some time alone.'

Asida linked her arm with his. 'There, Hafual. It is all decided. You may take your bride away for a proper honeymoon instead of finding an excuse to leave immediately. Such as King Ceolwulf requires you and your advice on the price of wool.'

Hafual lowered his brow, and his face became carved from granite. And Elene knew with a thumping heart that he had intended to abandon her. She should be happy about that. It was the sort of arrangement which suited them both—a distant marriage. But the world also became a little less bright. She once again was going to be the person who was overlooked and under-regarded like she had been when she was growing up.

'Would I do such a thing? Leave my bride alone?'

His sister fluttered her lashes. 'As you are my brother, I make it a point never to be surprised. But I have no plans to play the gooseberry between a bride and her eager groom. I have brought some embroidery that I have intended to work on for ages.'

Hafual closed his strong hand about hers. Elene knew she could not pull away even if she wanted to. 'My bride commands my utmost attention, Asida.'

'Yet you have ignored all the calls to kiss her.' She held out her hands, obviously playing the crowd and enjoying taunting her brother. 'Hasn't he?'

The crowd immediately began stamping their feet and calling for another kiss. A muscle jumped in Hafual's jaw, and he made a rumbling sound in the back of his throat.

Even though she knew what Mercian wedding feasts could be like with their ribald jokes and rowdy behaviour, Elene wanted the floor to open up and swallow her.

'Please,' she whispered and silently prayed he wouldn't publicly reject her.

A dark light appeared in Hafual's eyes, and his mouth descended onto hers. Fierce and hungry. Demanding, with something else besides, something which called her deep within, awakening a curl of fire that threatened to consume her. Then he let her go. The crowd went mad with approval.

'Will that suffice for my intentions?' he asked in a low voice.

Elene gave an uncertain nod as her fingers explored her now tender mouth.

'It is your bride you will have to satisfy, not me. Unless things are different in Mercia,' Asida called back as if Hafual was speaking to her instead and acted like a sudden splash of cold water, bringing Elene back from that cloud where she'd been rapidly spinning dreams.

Impulsive. Apt to act first and require rescuing. Her sisters' taunts about how she never noticed things until too late washed over her. This time she was not going to allow desire to cloud her judgement like it had with Nerian and his soft kisses, and implied promises. Hafual had agreed to her suggestion of a marriage in name. She would hold him to it.

'Do I carry you over my shoulder or do you wish to walk to the horses?' Hafual gave an apologetic half-smile. The dark fire had gone from his eyes, and he was back to the unapproachable person from the other day. 'I pulled my shoulder a few months back.'

Elene tightened her fingers about his briefly. 'I will walk.'

'Over the shoulder would be more appropriate,' Asida called out, much to her father's amusement.

'Attention to propriety is something our family rarely adheres to.'

'You have me there, brother.' Asida made a shooing motion with her hands. 'I will see you both soon. Enjoy your wedding night.'

Elene ignored the curious stares as she exited the hall, matching her step with Hafual's.

Hafual attempted to control his anger at the situation and how Asida had outmanoeuvred him. The kisses he'd shared with Elene unnerved him with their latent passion. He'd been within a hair's breadth of giving in to the dark passion which swept over him at the hall. He'd tried to tell himself that it had simply been that long since he kissed any woman like that, and his body just needed the release, except a small voice called him a liar. He had wanted to kiss Lady Elene and explore her mouth. He had known many men desired her. Several members of his old *felag* used to worship the ground she walked on, but he'd held himself aloof from their ribald behaviour. She had only had eyes for Nerian and he had longed for the woman he'd left back in the North. But now he noticed the way her breasts had touched his chest, the faint floral scent of her hair and the curve of her bottom lip.

Not trusting himself to speak, Hafual untied the reins of his horse, Bretwalda, a large black stallion, while Lady Elene watched him with her arms wrapped around her waist. He willed her to say something which showed she understood that he had no choice.

He could have killed Asida for her suggestion about following Northern ways and her unasked-for interference in his marriage. The road to Wulfhere's Clearing could be dangerous at night and particularly tonight.

If he had been Pybba, it was where he'd wait and strike. However, there was little point in worrying Lady Elene about it. The last thing he wanted was to have his bride frightened unnecessarily, but he'd had the wedding night all under control until Asida opened her big mouth and volunteered to be a hostage. The saints preserve him from family.

'Where are we going?' Lady Elene asked, finally breaking the silence. 'To court to see King Ceolwulf?'

'To my hall. I've neglected it for far too long. My sister was right about that.' He tried for a smile but was aware it was more like a grimace. 'But you mustn't tell her. Her head is far too big already.'

'Sisters can be like that.'

Hafual sobered. Lady Elene would be easy to like and then he might be tempted to confide in her, and he knew the danger that lay in that. He knew how Svala had reacted when he'd tried with her. 'Any wedding trip will have to wait, my lady.'

'Your son must remain with us,' Lady Elene said, her eyes big in the moonlight and her generous mouth shadowy, almost begging to be tasted again. Hafual forced his attention back to his horse. 'No need to send him here to be with Asida in the morning either. I welcome the chance to show him that I intend to be his new mother.'

His hands trembled in his adjustment of the saddle, glad that the darkness hid his features. More than he hoped for. Elene had a good heart.

'That is very noble of you. My sister has been complaining that she is his aunt, not his mother.'

'Not noble, I can assure you, but practical. I intend to run my own hall. What better way to do so than to start with my stepson? I intend to be his new mother, not like the woman I had as a stepmother, who was more interested in court intrigue than the three daughters she'd inherited.' Elene stopped, aware her words had run on too long and too fast. She had perhaps revealed too much about her fears of being inadequate. Nobody wanted to know about them. Ever.

'Shall we saddle one of my father's horses for me?' she asked to change the subject away from her fears about failing.

'You will ride on my horse.' Hafual's words allowed for no dissent.

Riding with him, with his hands on her waist, her body jostling into his hard muscles... Elene screwed up her eyes and bade the image and the curl of heat to be gone. His earlier kiss had been for a specific reason. She refused to turn into a panting female like she'd been for Nerian. Looking back with the benefit of hindsight, she could see Nerian really pulled away from her after they had been intimate, how she'd clung and how he'd pushed her away. It reminded her of how Ansithe and Cynehild had only grudgingly allowed her to play in their games as a child and how she'd never enjoyed the games very much.

'I am perfectly capable of handling a horse. You've seen me ride before.'

'Nevertheless, I will feel safer if you are on this horse.' He gestured to the horse. 'Do you require a hand up?'

'More in keeping with your tradition of abducting the bride?'

'More like no one accidentally getting lost in the dark or confusion.'

A prickle went down her spine. Accidentally getting lost or having the horse led away. 'You think Pybba is out there? That he will seek to cut us off and prevent us from reaching your hall?'

Hafual finished tightening the saddle and turned back to her. 'He left. Horses pounding in the dirt, headed for Watling Street and ultimate destination unknown.'

'You are stating the obvious.'

'Would you like it better if I lied? Should I say that I want to feel your body against mine and have the faint floral scent from your hair in my nostrils? Would that appeal to your romantic sensibilities, my lady?'

'Romantic sensibilities? Now I wonder who has drunk too much mead. I stopped having those years ago. Truth, not indigestible sweetmeats.' She started to get on the horse, but her gown was too tight about her hips and prevented her. A snort of frustration escaped her throat.

He put his hands on either side of her waist and lifted her on. The horse pawed the earth. 'We go together in case of attack. My sister has left my hall unguarded. I've no wish to fight to get it back should that be Pybba's destination. I would not put it past him.'

Elene stared at the horse's twitching ears. She had reached the wrong conclusion again. He was worried about his lands, rather than seeking to protect her or, even more fancifully, seeking to get closer to her. 'I see.'

'I am pleased you do.'

'Can my dog come with us? She will fret otherwise.' Elene's heart pounded. 'She can keep up. And she isn't a bother. She gets on with any animal.'

He tilted his head to one side. 'Why would I wish to deprive you of your dog? Do you consider me little better than Pybba?'

Elene winced. Her words had been less than tactful. 'My sisters always say that I spend much time with my foot in my mouth.'

'I'm not your sisters. Not the least like them.'

Elene was glad of the darkness as her cheeks suddenly burned at his gravelly tone. It made her think of the kiss and his hands on her back and how her body had pressed up against his. All things she did not want to explore.

To distract her thoughts, she whistled for Bugge again, this time far louder, one of her piercing sounds which always made her father complain that his ears hurt afterwards.

After hearing Elene's second whistle, Bugge appeared. She immediately went to Hafual and wagged her tail furiously. And the mood altered.

'It would seem your dog approves that you are going with me. Interesting.'

'I suspect she wants the dried meat you stored in your pouch.'

Hafual adopted a look of injured innocence. 'How do you know I have that? It could be that dogs naturally like me.'

'Twice she has nosed the pouch which is hanging off your belt.'

Hafual laughed and gave Bugge a piece of dried meat. 'I admit it. I did think it might come in handy in case of unforeseen circumstances.'

'Are you going to ride with me?'

The instant the words were out of her mouth, Elene winced. She sounded like she was inviting him to hold her.

He shook his head. 'Walking with my men will suit me fine. We will go at your dog's pace.'

'Bugge's pace will be lovely.' Silently Elene vowed that she was not going to make any more mistakes. She refused to trust anything. This time she wasn't going to wear her heart on her sleeve. This time she would be wary.

Chapter Seven

Elene disliked the all-pervading darkness combined with silence which enveloped her and the rest of the group as they made their way through the woods to Hafual's hall. A distinct wet earthiness invaded her nostrils. Everything reminded her far too much of the time the outlaws had attacked her group on the way back to Baelle Heale with Nerian. The outlaws had received information and had been lying in wait for them on their return journey from the summer court. At the time, no one had realised that it was an attempt to ensure Moir and his *felag* perished. There had even been the same steady drip from the low-lying mist.

'Are you sure we are going the right way?'

'I do know the way to my hall,' came the answer. Hafual paused. Elene thought she could see his body shaking with silent disapproval. 'For the fifth time.'

Elene tucked an errant strand of hair about her ear. Had she really asked five times already? It was on the tip of her tongue to confess about her fears, but she swallowed hard instead. 'Trying to make conversation.'

'Sometimes silence is preferable.'

Elene sat up straighter on the horse and peered into the darkness. The horse seemed to recognise her nerves and get tossing his head about and gently pawing the ground. 'This is not one of those times.'

'Nervous, my lady?'

'No,' Elene lied. 'Why would I be? It has been a long day and I am anxious to get to bed.'

'Always good when a bride wishes to go to bed.'

Her cheeks burnt and Elene was suddenly glad of the darkness. 'That is not what I meant.'

'I stand corrected. Now, my lady, eyes on the road and breathe slowly. Bretwalda can sense your feelings, even if you want to deny them.'

'You named your horse for the High King?'

'See how he holds his head high and paws the ground? He knows that he is the master of all he surveys or at least I let him think so. I thought it a good name for a horse, particularly one I might ride into battle. I liked the idea of saving the country.'

The silence descended again but a crack of a twig further ahead resounded. Elene jumped and gave a muffled scream. Bugge stopped and growled in the back of her throat.

Hafual halted and motioned to his men. Elene stuffed her hand into her mouth and longed to ask for reassurance.

A white barn owl glided across the road. Elene remembered how to breathe.

'An owl is a good omen, my lady.'

Elene let out a breath. 'Nerves. That is all. They attacked at night and the first sound was the breaking of a twig. I had suggested we go on, you see, and I was in charge. It was my fault.'

'That attack wasn't your fault. You were tracked. That much was established.'

Elene's neck muscles relaxed slightly. He had not laughed at her. 'I suppose you are right.'

'You are safe with me. My strong arm is a match for any owl, my lady.'

'It is why we are allies. United against bumps in the dark.'

Hafual breathed easier when the outlines of his hall came into view, and they entered the darkened yard with Elene's dog easily keeping up with them. There had been a breath when a barn owl glided over the path; the dog stiffened and Hafual had been certain Pybba and his men were waiting for them around the bend. But silence had greeted them, and he'd been able to relax his grip on his sword without alerting Lady Elene to the possible danger. She appeared nervous enough before that, worrying about the long ago attack as if she had had anything to do with that.

If he had his way, she would never discover the true threat Pybba posed. It was the way his father taught him to be—shouldering the burden to keep others safe rather than telling her the absolute truth.

'Here we are,' he said, forcing a heartiness into his voice. 'Safe and sound.'

She lifted her chin. 'I didn't expect it any other way. Pybba is a coward of the highest order. He will have left the neighbourhood. That's what you said before we started out. Why should I doubt you now?'

His neck muscles relaxed. She had not seen the possible danger of Pybba attacking him at court. Good. Her nervousness about travelling gave him a good reason to leave her at Wulfhere's Clearing and go to meet Ceolwulf alone. The idea which had seemed so appealing only a little while ago was less now that the taste of her lips lingered on his. He wanted to explore the attraction and to see if she felt it as well.

The dog gave a sharp bark and raced ahead to the door, breaking into his thoughts.

'Bugge, come back and be silent. You will wake people.' Lady Elene clapped her hands, but the dog ignored her in favour of scratching at the door. 'Bugge is not usually this forward.'

'She knows it is her new home where none will hurt her.'

Lady Elene put her hand over her mouth. 'I hadn't thought about it in that way. I suspect it will be different than either of us planned earlier.'

Hafual gritted his teeth. Did Lady Elene intend to make their marriage last or was she more intent on avoiding marriage altogether? He could take her to one of her sisters but then she'd have to explain about what happened. He was not going to be blamed for the marriage.

Before he could pursue the thought, the servants came out with sleepy eyes and torches. Hafual explained he'd brought Lady Elene back as his new lady and waved them back into the hall. Several muffled cheers rang out before the servants followed his orders and returned to the relative safety of their quarters.

Hafual motioned to his men to stay on guard. They nodded, understanding the signal. A necessary precaution but Hafual doubted that Pybba would attack him outright and risk Ceolwulf's displeasure.

'My sisters will be astonished to hear I'm married.'

Elene's voice sounded strained from where she sat on the horse, making no effort to alight.

'They will understand the necessity.'

'Provided it is explained correctly. Ansithe has trouble controlling her temper.' She smiled down at him. 'She is far grouchier than I am, and she likes to be consulted on everything. Cynehild will probably murmur that we did the right thing.'

'Thank you for going along with the scheme. I was the best groom I could think of at short notice,' he said, lifting Elene down. He was careful to keep her away from his body, but he was intensely aware of the way her dress moulded against her curves and how the moonlight highlighted the sweep of her neck. He wanted to reach out and move that tendril of hair which nestled against her neck. He forced his hands down to his sides.

'Short notice?' Her lips tilted upwards. 'You mean you did not plan for Asida to appear with your coat?'

'Asida took it upon herself.' The words sounded feeble to his ears. 'Asida is a good guesser about such things. She anticipated I might need it.'

'Have you done this before? An impromptu marriage?'

'Is that what this is?'

'As good a name as any.' Her face was tilted upwards in the moonlight with her lips softly parted, almost begging to be tasted. Earlier they had tasted of honey and everything good.

He rapidly stepped away from her. 'We need to go in, out of the night air. It can cause problems.'

Elene dipped her head and smoothed her skirt down with an unconcerned flick of her hand. He tilted his head to one side, wondering if she had felt the same flare of heat that he had.

'Is your shoulder bothering you?' she asked.

Hafual rolled his arm, grateful for the change of subject. His shoulder had never healed properly from this summer's dislocation. He'd saved his men but hurt his shoulder. He knew which was more important. 'It is getting better.'

'I can make ointment for it. I've made some refinements to Father Oswald's recipe. I believe it is much improved. You see I'm determined to be a practical, not decorative, wife.'

She started towards the hall, but Hafual reached down and scooped her up.

She pushed her hand against his chest. 'What are you doing?'

'Carrying you across the threshold. I've no wish for anyone to say I courted bad luck with this hasty marriage.'

Her struggling stopped and he was conscious of how her breasts brushed his chest and how right she felt in his arms. He carried her like he'd carry a vessel of precious glass. Someone had laid a broom across the doorway.

He set her down abruptly to the applause of the servants. Hafual glared at them, and they melted away.

'There, it is done.' Elene's voice was pitched far higher.

'No harm to my shoulder either. You're far lighter than you look.'

'What? Do you think I am too large?'

'Your figure is perfect, and you know it. You are only seeking compliments.'

She put her hand on her hip. 'Proving your shoulder was fine, was that what this demonstration was about?'

Haful shrugged. 'I've little idea if Pybba has spies in my household. One day we will meet in combat, and I will best him.'

Elene nodded towards the high table. 'Were you expecting company?'

He looked towards the table and groaned. Asida had left two goblets and a flagon of ale out on the table and what appeared to be sweetmeats, the sort of thing one might use for a seduction.

One of the servants curtseyed and asked if she should take the tray into his chamber as Asida instructed before she departed.

Haful gritted his teeth and refused abruptly. Elene gave him another sideways look. Haful didn't care. His sister had taken far too many liberties. He dreaded to think what she had left for them in his chamber.

'Are you fine with the marriage?' he asked to cover the silence of the maid's departure from the hall.

'Did I have much choice?' Elene smoothed her skirts. 'My father appeared quite determined that I would marry today. My options were limited.'

How to damn with faint praise. Haful supposed he deserved it. Her way of reminding him their marriage was the only option left. 'Glad to be of service, my lady.'

She put her hand over her mouth. 'Apologies. My mouth runs in front of my brain. I am grateful and for the fact that we have travelled here tonight, rather than having to endure a Mercian wedding night.'

'Gratitude is something to build a solid marriage on.'

'All marriages have to start somewhere.' She clicked

her fingers at her dog, who stopped investigating a spot in the rushes and trotted obediently to her side. 'And ours starts here. At least we will not have Pybba to contend with tonight.'

'If Pybba wants something, he rarely gives up quickly,' Hafual said, and willed her to understand the danger was not yet over. 'I don't suspect he plans to start now.'

She raised her head and met his gaze. Her lashes highlighted the blueness of her eyes. 'I'm not afraid of a man like him. He is all bluster. I've faced down worse, much worse, and survived.'

He knew she was thinking about the time she'd faced the Danish raiders who were intent on killing her and the men she travelled with.

'I know you have. I arrived several days afterwards and helped rescue you and Nerian. It is where I first came to respect that man's courage and his skill with his sword.'

She ducked her head. 'I remember. I would never forget that. You must think me the most ungrateful wretch when I only mean to say that you mustn't think of me as some wilting flower. I can stand on my own feet as well as either of my sisters. You do what you have to do.'

He used a finger to lift her chin. He could see the fierce determination in her eyes. She was also the sort of person who would not have stood a chance against someone like Pybba. She would have been a butterfly broken on a wheel. 'Pybba and I have a history which goes back to that first summer when I saved Ceolwulf's life. I have always considered that he knew more about the attack than he let on. But I lacked any proof and the queen refused to hear anything against one of her favourites. Nevertheless, I refuse to allow you to suffer the consequences of our enmity. He is not the sort of man I'd trust with any gently born lady.'

'Should I trust you?'

Hafual opted for a smile and ignored the sudden pounding in his head. Hadn't she felt the hot flames when they kissed earlier? All he'd wanted to do was to drown in her mouth, but the noise from the crowd had reminded him where he was, and he'd pulled back from the precipice. 'I gave my word.'

Something akin to disappointment flickered across her face. But then she straightened. 'I wanted to let you know that I understand about your overwhelming grief for your late wife. I've no wish to take her place.'

Of course she thought she knew about his marriage to Svala. To the outside world they had seemed like the ideally matched couple. He knew how much he'd failed his late wife. He wasn't anyone's idea of a husband— far too cold and selfish—wasn't that what Svala had called him during their last quarrel when he refused to bring whatever trinket she desired from court and she'd dangled Narfi over the fire? He pushed the memory from his mind. He'd been the one at fault in the marriage, never where he was wanted, always asking too much of Svala and giving too little.

'Do you wish me to whisper sweet things and pretend it is a love match, Elene?'

'I've no need for pretence or false flattery. I'm not a child to be tempted by a taste of honey.' Elene lifted her gaze to meet Hafual's. She had to get this right. Her entire future hinged on this, not some silly custom of being carried over the threshold. She knew she could never replace his late wife, but she wanted to be respected and not indulged.

Hafual's gaze raked her from the top of her crown of braids to her slippers, lingering on her curves for that one breath longer than propriety allowed. 'I would only ask a grown woman to be my wife, Elene. Therefore, we must conclude I consider you to be one.'

Elene tried to ignore the growing butterflies in her stomach at his honeyed tones and his intense gaze. 'My father arranged both my sisters' first marriages. It worked out for Cynehild, but Ansithe was very unhappy in her marriage.'

He inclined his head and looked at her with hooded eyes. 'I would point out that you are different from your sisters, and I am not either of your sisters' first husband.'

'The hour is late,' she tried again. 'Exhaustion is poor company for seduction.'

'Seduction? How little you know me.'

'I thought—'

'How someone else behaved has no bearing on how either of us behaves.' His teeth shone in the glow from the embers of the fire. 'Stop judging me, Elene, before you get to know me.'

Elene twisted the belt around her hand. Her head pounded. She had already been far too blunt when she told him the truth about her options being limited. The last thing she wanted was to get her marriage off to the wrong start, not when he was being kind. She dreaded to think what Pybba would have been like on a wedding night.

'I remain grateful for your quick thinking about why we should come here.'

'Pressure from strangers is the worst way to start any sort of marriage. Always.' He captured her hand and raised it to his lips. A warm tremor went down her arm.

She drew her hand away and resisted the inexplicable urge to cup her palm against her cheek to see if her palm was truly that warm. He might not be attracted to her, but she could feel the desire building within her and she knew where that led and what had happened to her with Nerian. She had given him her heart and he'd trampled all over it.

'What are you saying?' she asked, tilting her head to one side and trying to regain some sort of control over her body. She was not about to proudly declare that she wanted time, to turn around in the next few breaths and demand that he sweep her into his arms again.

'We may have decided before the wedding that it was to be in name only, but then we shared that kiss. Something is there, Elene.'

'And if I say it was for the benefit of the others?' She knew the question was too quick and a complete lie. She'd given in to that kiss because she'd wanted to.

'Far be it from me to call my wife untruthful.'

He traced a finger around the outside of her mouth. She tried to rid her mind of the heat from that kiss they had shared in her father's hall and how his heart had thumped against her ear when he carried her in. She wrapped her arms about her waist. 'No repeat demonstration is necessary. I accept your assessment of the situation.'

He gave her a hooded look which seemed to reach

down to her soul. 'It is up to you to decide if you wish to invite me into your bed. I have never forced a woman and have no intention to do so with my wife, but I did marry you with the intention of it being a proper marriage. For your protection as much as mine.'

'You are willing to give me time? Not force a seduction tonight?' Elene sank down on a bench and laid her head back against the rough wall. She had never considered that he might agree or rather be willing to see her point about waiting. All her carefully thought-out arguments, the ones she'd considered on the ride over, when she was trying not to think about the possibility of Pybba's men attacking them, were superfluous.

His eyes reflected the glowing embers of the fire. 'Until you are ready to be my wife fully, I will refrain from seducing you.'

'And if I am never ready…what then?' she asked in sudden inspiration.

'Telling the future never did anyone any good.' He inclined his head. 'Are you challenging me to seduce you tonight, Lady Elene? Which do you want—a proper seduction? To be wooed and won? Or to have the choice taken from you?'

Elene bit her lip, remembering what Nerian said after they had lain together and how he made it seem like it was all her fault. 'Nerian said I wanted that.'

His nostrils flared. 'Are you tempted to pretend I'm Nerian?'

'Nerian has no part in this marriage,' she said before she confessed the truth.

'On that we agree.'

She cleared her throat and tried to move away from Nerian and how inadequate he'd made her feel. He had said that it was what she wanted, but after it was over, she'd felt soiled. And she failed to understand why people found it enjoyable. 'For now, we should keep this platonic and see if we are compatible. There is more to a marriage than a roll in the hay.'

His eyes danced. 'Speak plainly, then. How do you wish to be wooed?'

'No, I'm saying a wife should be more than a concubine.' She stopped, searched for an excuse and smiled as she saw an abandoned wooden sword on the rushes, the sort of thing little boys loved. 'To see if your son accepts me as his mother and is not afraid of me. There is someone else to consider. I, too, had a stepmother for a brief period, far from the happiest period of my life.'

The firelight highlighted the harsh planes of his face. 'My son has no influence on my choice of partner. He will accept any woman I marry as his new mother.'

Elene kept her face completely still. Hafual might be a great warrior, but it was clear from his confident pronouncement that he knew little about children. She wanted Narfi to like her, not merely accept her. 'Indeed.'

'Tell me the truth, Elene, what frightens you about a man and a woman joining?'

She kept her mind away from the pain, the empty feeling and the disappointment she'd suffered after her last experience. 'Nothing frightens me. It can be very pleasurable, or so I'm told.'

'I've given you the choice and my promise. We go at your pace.' He gave an exaggerated yawn and she noticed that he did not press her on how she knew. 'For the sake of the servants and any spies, we will share my bedchamber.'

Elene stilled. 'Spies? What spies?'

He put a finger to his lips. 'Servants have ears. If Pybba bribed Ecgbert and his wife, he may have bribed one of my servants.'

'I had not considered that.'

'We share the chamber. We want people to think this marriage was our choice, not foisted on us through circumstance. King Ceolwulf will be more inclined to forgive that if he thinks it to be a true love match.'

'Do you think this is the end of Pybba's machinations? Truly?'

He clasped his hands together, stood up, towering over her. 'I promised to protect you and that includes from all threats. Now does propriety demand I carry you to the chamber or will you spare my shoulder that?'

She rose also. 'Tell me the truth rather than giving a polite lie—who don't you trust amongst your servants?'

'Did I say that I didn't trust them?'

'I am not about to faint or behave like some foolish maiden. I used to hate it when my sisters or father kept things from me because they thought I was too young or foolish to understand. I am capable of holding more than two thoughts in my brain.'

'The kitten has claws.'

She ground her foot into the floor. 'I'm not a kitten or a cute and cuddly creature to be indulged and dismissed. I am a woman who is now your wife. Treat me as such.'

'I stand corrected.'

Rather than replying, she lifted a brow and waited. The silence between them seemed to stretch.

'What do you want to know?' he asked with a new, humbler tone in his voice.

'How great is the danger from Pybba? Surely he has departed in peace and he knows his scheme has failed. He knows we are married. Yet, you thought the owl might be an attack, same as I did. In fact, you were expecting an attack which is why you had me on the horse while you were on the ground with your hand on your sword, ready for any disturbance.'

'The danger remains until the king gives his consent. Pybba will be watching as he knows there will be a reckoning with me.'

A shiver went down her spine. It had been far too simple to think that the danger had simply passed because they'd married. Maybe he had a point in calling her a kitten. She would not make that mistake again. She needed to think beyond the now, something Cynehild often accused her of forgetting to do.

'Then he will have to know we are stronger not weaker for the marriage.' She banged her fist on the table. Bugge opened one eye from where she lay by the fire. 'Baelle Heale will never be his.'

'It depends on if your father's estate was his actual aim, or if he wanted to use it as leverage against me and my influence with King Ceolwulf. Time will tell.'

'What are you going to do now? Go to court? It is less than a day's hard ride to Tamworth.' Elene named the royal residence which King Ceolwulf favoured.

'It is far too early for such a conversation about where Ceolwulf will be. Tonight, I intend to enjoy my sleep. Pybba and his machinations are but distant problems.'

'Enjoy your bed? Oh, blow.' Elene took a step backwards, nearly tripping over Bugge in her haste. Despite her hopes, Hafual was proving to be precisely like

Nerian and all the other perfidious men she'd known—promises which barely lasted a night were easy to give.

'You are easy to tease, my lady.'

She stopped. 'You are teasing me?'

A dimple flashed in and out of his cheek. 'The lady is not for distracting. Pity, as it would be very pleasant to distract you in bed or out of it, my lady, but I have given you my word.'

She breathed easier. He was attempting a joke. 'A threat or a promise?'

'I will leave you to decide.' He lit a reed and held out it to her. 'Your eyes grow shadowed, my lady wife. The bed, the one which used to be mine, awaits.'

Elene took the reed gingerly, avoiding his fingers. 'If you will give me a little time…'

He bowed. 'Of course. You have my word on it.'

Elene sat on the iron-bound trunk, waiting for the smallest sound which would indicate that Hafual had finally decided to come to bed, watching the reed flicker and gutter in the unused goblet and trying to ignore the massive carved bed piled high with furs and pillows. It was probably the most luxurious-looking bed she'd ever encountered and the sort of bed that practically begged to be slept in, but Elene refused.

The image of her waking up curled into Hafual refused to go from her brain. She knew what it was like to wake up in a man's arms and how close his face would be to hers. The intimacy would make her vulnerable like it had with Nerian. She refused to make the same mistakes.

Instead of dwelling on the possibility, she made up a bed on the floor with several of the spare furs and pillows. Bugge had lain down on top of it and growled when she came near.

The enormity of what she had done hit her—married a man she barely knew, one who appeared to have planned this seemingly unplanned wedding. She did not believe for a breath that it was all his sister's doing. Asida was one of the most disorganised people Elene knew.

In her mind she could hear her sisters laughing at her predicament and how Elene always did leap before she looked. She hit the pillow with her hand. 'I will make this work. Cynehild and Ansithe do not get to laugh at me. I will make this into a good marriage.'

A tiny light appeared in the doorway, allowing her to make out Hafual's outline but little else. Bugge rose and moved away from the furs, settling instead down near the foot of the bed.

'Elene? Is everything well? You are not in the bed.' He moved in the room, filling up the space.

'Bugge thought the furs I put down were for her and refused to move. She growled at me when I came close.'

He glanced towards Bugge; the traitor hid her nose with her paws. 'She appears well settled.'

'And you?'

'Until you expressly invite me into that bed, I won't invade it.'

Her stomach did a loop. She'd expected his words to be a way to get around her defences. But he was prepared to give up a comfortable bed. 'And if I don't go?'

'My patience has limits, Lady Elene. In bed with you, or I will carry you there. And all promises will end.'

Elene swallowed hard. 'I… I understand. We have no idea what tomorrow will bring.'

'Quite.'

She walked with as much dignity as she could muster and dove under the furs. Two more slithered onto the floor as she wriggled out of her gown.

She tried to ignore the sounds of his clothes hitting the floor before he lay down on the furs.

'Wonderfully cosy,' he said. 'I've blown out the reeds, my lady, so you need not worry about that.'

Next time, she would ensure she was sound asleep long before he came into this chamber. But tonight, she suspected her dreams would be full of broad-shouldered Northmen.

Hafual lay cocooned in far too many furs, waiting for the sound of the first cockerel when he could legitimately rise. Despite the crowded chaos of the day, sleep was far away.

He listened to the unfamiliar sounds of Elene's breathing and tried not think about how he'd once failed badly at being a husband.

This time, he would be better. He would keep his wife from danger and attend to her needs. He would not make the same mistakes he had with Svala. He'd rushed her into an intimate relationship which she had never enjoyed and she'd blamed him for everything which went wrong in her life, starting with the baby who failed to stop crying. He'd tried to make things easier in the run-up to Narfi's birth, but she had grown more fractious and worried about the birth. He knew he'd found reasons to stay away. In the end his desire for her had shrivelled up under the weight of unspoken accusation.

He wanted to think this unexpected alliance was

a second chance. It bothered him that this marriage meant something to him. Until it happened, he had been certain his life was going to take another path.

He liked crossing wits with Elene, and the knowledge frightened him. It was like his body was waking up from a long slumber, but he also knew what he'd done and how he had failed in his last marriage.

He rolled over on his side and encountered Bugge's wet nose. The dog gave a soft woof before licking his hand.

'I know. I know. This time I will do my duty. I will protect your mistress and protecting her will have to ensure a proper marriage.'

The dog tilted her head to one side and gave him a knowing look.

'And you are right. I do want to feel her mouth move under mine. I want to explore the contours of her body. I've been too long without a woman and your mistress is very beautiful. Desire, nothing more. But with this wife, I will ensure she enjoys my touch and wants me as much as I want her.'

Chapter Eight

Elene woke the next morning with a distinct feeling that someone was staring at her. Her dreams when they finally came had been confused ones, featuring a very broad-shouldered Northman who picked her up and held her tight, keeping her safe when everything around her was falling apart.

She had woken with the distinct feeling that she wanted something more from their relationship. She wanted to see if there was indeed a raw power in his kiss. Was Hafual watching her sleep? Had he in fact moved into the bed? Or was he going to be like Nerian, only interested in a warm body and someone he could conquer?

She rapidly sat up. Maybe it had not been all her fault that she had failed to hold on to Nerian. Maybe this time she could hold her man. Maybe that was what her dream was about.

She was all alone in the heavily carved bed which was piled high with down pillows and soft furs.

Hafual had disappeared off somewhere. The goblets and flagon of ale remained on the iron-bound trunk. A pile of furs lay neatly folded at the bottom of the bed. But a little boy with a mop of ash blond hair and the largest blue eyes Elene had ever seen solemnly watched her.

He slowly removed his thumb from his mouth and tilted his head to one side. 'Far?'

Elene held out a hand and the pile of furs slid onto the floor with a loud thump. 'Narfi, you remember me, don't you? Elene? Your friend from Baelle Heale? I've come to live here with you and your father. I've brought my dog with me.'

Ignoring her hand, Narfi stuck his thumb back in his mouth and continued to watch her with solemn eyes. Bugge had obviously accepted the child as she barely lifted her head from where she lay beside the bed before settling her nose back down on her paws.

'My lady,' the serving woman said, rushing up and scooping the squirming child up. 'Lord Hafual said you weren't to be disturbed for any reason. I am so sorry. Lady Asida normally insists on looking after him so I can get on with the weaving. We are behind, you see, with the new sail for Lord Hafual's boat and I thought why not do some? I didn't realise he'd slipped out from underfoot and come in here.'

'The weaving hut is some way from the hall.' Elene frowned, remembering how her nephew had once gone down to the lake when he was a little older than Narfi. No harm had come of it, but Cynehild had been frantic, something which Cynehild told Elene repeatedly before she had left on the journey to her late husband's lands to lay his sword, the one where she met her new husband. The tale was to impress on Elene the need for vigilance. Like most of Cynehild's lessons, Elene had already learned it long before. 'He could have gone anywhere in that time.'

The woman's cheeks reddened, and she smoothed her apron down, muttering about a complicated pattern. 'I think he came looking for his father, his "Far" as Lady Asida tells Narfi to call Lord Hafual. Not like the old days let me tell you. What sort of name is Far?'

'The one he presumably uses for his father.'

The woman compressed her mouth to a thin line as if she thoroughly disapproved of everything connected to Hafual and his family but was holding back the words for the sake of politeness. 'The weaving, my lady. His Lordship was most insistent when he returned. He wants it to go to the market at Ludenwic as soon as possible. No one wants to get on the wrong side of Lord Hafual's temper.'

'I see.' Elene doubted that anywhere was ever up to date with the weaving. The production of cloth always took up much of the women's time at Baelle Heale. And that Hafual could be short-tempered was far from news.

'Unlike the last lord of Wulfhere's Clearing,' the woman continued on, seemingly oblivious to the fact that Elene had known her neighbour and thoroughly disliked him. He had lost his lands because he had plotted with the Danish warlord who had kidnapped Elene's father and Cynehild's first husband.

'Leave Narfi here with me. My dog is used to children.' Elene gave the impudent woman a hard stare. Not the sort of person she'd trust to look after a young child ever again.

The woman's eyes bulged. 'My lady, are you sure? You are a bride.'

'Leave Narfi with me. I will answer to Lord Hafual and Lady Asida should it come to it. But as you say, that sail must be woven properly. Good weaving takes time.'

The woman's face creased into a wreath of smiles. 'Bless you, Lady Elene. You will be good for this place. I can feel it in my bones.'

'I intend to try.'

'When you are ready, there is a pot of porridge hanging in the kitchen. I made extra, you see. Lady Asida asked me to before she left. She's funny like that, always predicting things which turn out to be true.'

Elene lifted a brow. Ansithe was like that as well—pretending that she knew things when in fact all she did was guess logically and hope that people would only remember the times she had guessed right. 'Asida appears to have thought of most things.'

The woman curtseyed and hurried off, leaving Narfi sitting amongst the furs on the floor. Elene clicked her fingers and Bugge perked up her ears. Elene pointed to Narfi. 'Go see if you can make a friend.'

Bugge gave a small woof as if to say that she understood what was required of her. Narfi let out a cry of pure joy and threw his arms about the dog's neck when Bugge gently nudged him. Bugge lay down and let Narfi clamber all over her while Elene dressed. He sat babbling about the horses and men to Bugge while Elene refashioned her braid and tucked it under a couvre-chef.

After tiring of that game with Bugge, the little boy took great delight in hiding his face in the furs and peeking back up at her, before hiding his face again. They played the game for a little while until his infectious laugh rang out.

The muscles in Elene's neck relaxed. One hurdle overcome and no harm done, but she would find a proper nurse for Narfi for those times when she and Asida had to be somewhere else. She suspected Asida would be horrified when she learned about the laxness of the servant.

Once fully dressed, she knelt and held out her hand. 'Narfi,' she called softly. 'Come and see me. We need to find some breakfast, Bugge and I. Bugge loves porridge. Do you?'

She waited until Narfi came over to her and put his warm hand in hers. His smile could light a thousand suns. 'Pretty lady. Dog. Hungry. Eat now.'

'Very neatly done. And I can't disagree with that assessment, young man. Even though I have to wonder why you've given your nurse the slip again.'

Elene looked over Narfi's head to where Hafual lounged against the door frame. Her breath caught in her throat. Hafual's dark blond hair sparkled as if strewn with diamonds. And his tunic opened to reveal the strong column of his throat. The memory of her earlier vivid dreams flooded through her. She wanted to ask how long he had been there, watching her and his son play. A large part of her suddenly wanted him to think her pretty when she knew she was anything but this morning.

'I take it that it is raining,' she said instead and disliked how breathless her voice sounded. She coughed slightly. 'Your hair is wet. You don't want to catch a chill.'

He shrugged, making his tunic tighten across his chest. 'More mist than rain, or perhaps it is the dip I had in the lake.'

'You always get up early to wash in the lake?'

'As a roll in the bed wasn't on offer, I made do with a cold dip.'

She glanced down at her hands. His ring weighed heavy on her ring finger. 'Unnecessary.'

'I apologise for any offence. I was attempting to be amusing and failed.' He ran his hand through his hair, scattering the droplets of water. 'I wanted to get the smithy up and running properly. After I'd done that, I was covered head to foot in soot. It seemed the simplest way.'

'You fixed the smithy this morning?' Elene winced. He'd been up and about, and she had lazed in bed. Not the best way to start her tenure as mistress of this hall.

His eyes slid away from her. 'My sister tells me that she dislikes making decisions while I'm not here. There was an issue with the anvil and several items which need to be mended. When I was young, I used to operate the blacksmith's bellows…before I learned to be a warrior.'

'Your son came in here asking for you.'

'Did he?' A flash of pleasure flickered across his face before his brow lowered and he held out his massive arms. 'Narfi, are you going to greet your father? Properly?'

Narfi flinched slightly as if Hafual's booming voice bothered him and did not move from where he sat beside Bugge. 'Dog. Me.'

After an awkward pause, Hafual's arms dropped to his sides. His smile appeared awkward with far too many teeth. 'Aren't you going to greet me, Narfi?'

Narfi hid his face in Bugge's fur.

'He is a kind boy, your son,' Elene said while Hafual's smile faded. 'I suspect he is tired and hungry. We are about to go in search of porridge after such a fun game of peekaboo.'

At the word—peekaboo—Narfi lifted his head, smiled back at her and quickly hid his face in Bugge's fur again.

'See. He is playing.' She clapped her hands and played another round. 'Your turn, Hafual. Shall we play peekaboo with your Far, Narfi?'

During the brief game, Hafual avoided looking at the boy.

'This is foolish. Time for your food,' he said in a voice more suited for the practice yard than a bedchamber. 'Narfi, come along now.'

'Are you going to tell me that it isn't an appropriate game for him?' she asked, trying to discern his mood. In her experience little children often did not perform when directed to. Her nephew used to stick out his tongue at her father and stamp his feet, often going into a full-blown temper tantrum. She'd learned that playing a game with him and distraction was the surest way to avoid trouble of that sort.

'I've little idea.' A flash of something like pain flickered over Hafual's face before it settled into its more familiar planes. 'Asida has looked after him ever since his mother died. You will have to ask her when she returns. But he screams like a fury when he is hungry. She sometimes shoves the spoon in his mouth to make him be quiet.'

'Asida is no doubt setting my father's hall to rights,' Elene said, scooping Narfi up. The boy put his arms about her neck and hugged her tight. His little-boy scent filled her nostrils. 'Porridge time.'

Hafual gave a sudden laugh. 'I've married a managing woman.'

'Is there something wrong with that?'

'Not at all. What do you intend to do after porridge?'

'*We* need to solve the problem of Pybba and his intentions. I doubt he will give up if he truly wants my father's estate.' Elene looked over the top of Narfi's head.

Hafual's face became inscrutable. 'You and my sister have become close. You share confidences. Shall we speak about those instead?'

'We visit every now and then as one does with one's neighbours.' Elene liked the woman. And she noticed how he was attempting to steer the conversation away from Pybba's intentions. Maybe Svala had not been interested in such things, but she had learned pretending a threat did not exist did not make it go away any quicker. 'I found Asida full of practical sense. It was why I was making my way here the other day. To seek her advice…and hide away.' Her laugh sounded contrived to her ears. 'Maybe I should have listened to her advice instead of coming to my own decision.'

'My sister often schemes. She was the one responsible for the goblets and ale last night.'

'I had wondered about that. Perhaps she had thought you and she would share a glass when you returned.'

He drew his top lip down over his teeth. 'A habit from her childhood, I'm afraid. She likes to pretend that she can see the future.'

'As if anyone can. I suspect she is a good guesser like Ansithe.'

'Precisely, but I worry she will get herself into trouble through overreaching.'

Elene stilled. No doubt Father Oswald would have

tutted at the revelation, but Elene knew Asida did not have a mean bone in her body. And there were many around the area who also looked for signs and portents even though the church officially advised against the practice.

'As long as the schemes do not involve me, we are fine. I've no wish to know my future until it happens. Thank you very much.'

'Another of your rules?'

'Rules keep you safe. Isn't that what you said?'

'Sometimes I talk too much.'

Narfi clapped his hands and repeated his father's words in a lisping tone. Hafual burst out laughing, but the sudden loud voice made Narfi's face crumple, and he turned his face into Elene's shoulder. Over Narfi's golden curls, Elene glimpsed a deep sadness in Hafual's eyes.

'You see this little man agrees as well,' she said very quickly, putting Narfi down. 'We allow Asida her good guesses but treasure the times when she makes a mistake.'

Hafual regarded her from under hooded eyes. A knowing glint replaced the sadness. 'You are used to sisters.'

Elene rose and took Narfi's hand. His little fingers curled about hers and he tugged as if he were dragging her towards the door. 'This young man wants his breakfast and has waited long enough.'

'How can you tell?'

'He woke me up and his stomach rumbles.' Elene knelt down so that her face was level with Narfi's. 'No more peekaboo until you have eaten some porridge, young man. Maybe your father will join us. I was told that there was more than enough. Your sister's orders.'

'My sister is very presumptuous.'

'More for Narfi.'

Narfi's stomach obligingly gurgled. The boy burst into another bout of infectious laughter. Hafual's mouth turned down at the corners.

'I doubt he has control over his stomach. I don't,' Elene said before he started shouting.

'My sister encourages him to be rude. She finds it funny, but I don't. I've no wish for a child of mine to be considered ill-mannered.' His voice rose on the last words.

The boy leant against Elene, half hiding his face. Elene put a hand on Narfi's shoulder and squeezed it. His little body trembled. Elene knew with a sudden certainty; the boy feared his father's loud voice. 'Time enough to learn. Children become grumpy when they are hungry. Do men as well?'

Hafual turned towards her, his face full of cold fury. He looked her up and down. Elene was conscious that her hair was done in a simple braid and that her gown was horribly creased. His gaze turned even colder. 'What do you know about young children or men for that matter?'

Elene refused to wilt like some cowering lady from court. 'I've looked after my sister's son. Little boys and strict rules make for trouble. They need love and guidance.'

'I know how I was brought up and it didn't do me any harm.'

'Wulfgar used to hate shouting and loud noises when he was that age. He used to put his hands over his ears and scream. It drove both my sisters mad, but I discovered if I spoke to him in a pleasant voice, like as not, he'd stop screaming. It can be hard when you are small and Narfi is little more than a baby.'

'I had never considered that.' Hafual rubbed the back of his neck. 'Even still he shouldn't have been rude.'

'Unintentionally is different from deliberately.'

Hafual shuffled his feet. 'It looked differently to me. I'm his father. I want you to feel welcome here.'

'Will you speak softly to him and tell him that everything is fine?' Elene knelt beside Narfi, who had continued to cling to her skirt throughout the exchange. 'Your father misunderstood our game. That's all.'

The boy gave an uncertain nod. 'Far too loud. Angry.'

Elene rocked back on her heels. 'Not angry. See how he smiles. He wants to be your friend.'

The boy gave an uncertain smile as his stomach rumbled again. Elene decided the maid was not going to be looking after Narfi again. The woman could certainly spend all the time she wanted in the weaving shed. Hafual rolled his eyes and gave what could only be called a grimace.

'See, Narfi. Your father smiles.'

'I will go now.' From the way Hafual edged towards the door, he wanted to be gone. Her idea earlier that he had returned because he harboured some sort of wish to deepen their relationship was simply wrong.

'Would you like to join us? Your servant indicated that there was plenty of porridge left.'

She prayed she was right because the last thing she wanted was another confrontation. Someday, though, Hafual would have to get to know his son better.

'The smithy needs checking, to make sure everything runs smoothly.'

A stab of disappointment hit her. 'You didn't intend to have breakfast with us?'

He shook his head. 'I merely wanted to check that you were awake.'

'Your son has been entertaining me.'

He nodded. 'I shall leave him to do it.'

He turned on his heel and left. Narfi's face fell but he put his hand in Elene's and asked for his porridge.

Elene pursed her lips. Hafual had avoided looking at Narfi. Was there some problem between them? She knew his late wife had had a terrible accident when the boy was a few weeks old. Svala had been a private person who seemed bowed with a secret sorrow, but what little Elene knew of her she'd liked.

She would find a way to bring them together. If she let him, he'd find a reason to go away. He had not wanted to talk about the potential threat from Pybba. The only way to solve it was to confront King Ceolwulf with their marriage.

'You'd like to go with me to court and see the warriors with their big swords, wouldn't you?'

Narfi nodded enthusiastically and babbled about swords. He even went and fetched his wooden one, waving it about in the air, looking precisely like a miniature Hafual.

Elene put a hand on her stomach. She had to be careful. She did not want to go losing her heart again. Hafual had made it very clear that theirs was a practical marriage and she had overstepped by instructing him on his parenting skills. She clenched her fists. Criticis-

ing him was not the right way. She had to find a way
to help him connect with his son.

'I will do it, Bugge,' she said. 'I will make him see
that his son is important. I will make him see that I
should be consulted about threats to this family. I'm
not merely decorative, whatever my sisters might say.'

Bugge sank down and covered her nose with her
paws.

Hafual strode out of the now working smithy and
took great gulps of air, trying to steady his nerves.
Banging out his frustration on a piece of metal had
done little to calm his thoughts. Far more satisfying
than scaring the child and putting him off his food. Little boys needed to eat. He knew that. He hadn't needed
Elene to tell him and Narfi ate better when he wasn't
there. Asida had implied that often enough.

He went down to the lake and watched the sunlight glinting off the water, rather than going back to
the hall.

Elene was being kind. He knew precisely how Asida
would have reacted—letting him know that he was a
useless father and had no business being around his
son. Useless as a father. Useless as a husband as well if
he believed Svala. And he wanted to be good at both.
He had had so many dreams about being a better father and husband than his own father ever was. Right
now, it appeared that he was far worse.

Had he done Elene a disservice by marrying her?
Pybba would have been a disaster for him, his lands
and the people who worked those lands. He could still
be if the truth about the marriage being in name only
was discovered.

Instead of waiting, he needed to act decisively. He knew that from the battles he'd fought. He would have to find a way to seduce her and make the marriage real. Then he'd confess about his first marriage and his failings, but he wanted both his son and his new wife to look at him with admiring eyes for a short while first.

He bent down and picked up the stone, before tossing it. It landed with a satisfying thump. Several of the servants turned to look at him. He forced a smile and started to walk towards the stables.

'Did you want any porridge? You forgot to say.' Elene came out of the kitchen, carrying a wooden bowl, halting him in his tracks. His eyes took in the golden highlights in her hair, the length of her slender neck and the way her gown flowed over her curves. His gaze travelled further down her form. A sudden heat flowed through his body, and he wanted to gather her in his arms and explore her curves. He managed to retain a narrow grip on the rising tide of desire. He was a grown man, not an overeager un-blooded lad. She'd asked for time. He had to give it to her.

'Your feet are in thin slippers. It is cold out.' He forced a half-smile. 'And you said you were sensible.'

The rose in her cheeks grew. 'My slippers are more than adequate.'

'Cold feet will never do.' He gestured towards the door to the kitchen. 'Go in. I will be along directly. I will not have my wife freezing.'

He smiled inwardly, proud that he managed to scrape some more time to sort his thoughts out.

'I doubt anyone will notice.'

'I noticed.'

'But did you notice your son?' She put her hand to her mouth. 'I'm sorry. I didn't mean…'

'My failures as a father are renowned.' Hafual forced a shrug. He'd refused to detail his failures as a husband when he was married to Svala as well. He knew with bitterness in his heart that he was the last person who should be a father or a husband. Except here he was attempting to make the best of the circumstances which were forced on him.

'Are they? You will have to enlighten me. Thus far, I've seen you speak too loudly but that will come in time. Your boy looks up to you.'

An unaccustomed sense of hope rose within him. Maybe one day Narfi would look up to him. Maybe he could prove that he was a worthy father. Then he thought about finding Svala's broken body, and knew if he had been a better man Narfi would not be growing up without his mother. 'Asida insists I keep to the rules and let her feed him without distraction. It makes it easier for everyone concerned.'

'I'm in charge of the rules now. Watching your child eat is allowed.'

He tilted his head to one side and indulged in a spot of teasing to see how she'd react. 'A forceful woman. Am I supposed to like that?'

She ducked her head, but not before he caught a rose-coloured hue invading her cheeks. 'Too late for you to do anything about it.'

'I will try to remember that the next time you need rescuing.'

Elene wrinkled her nose. 'I will put your bowl on the table. Have it when you like, but a word of warning— cold porridge tastes like congealed daub.'

'Does everyone think that?'

'Bugge loves it cold.' She turned back towards the door, paused and pressed her hands together. 'Your son would love to see you when you have time to spare. He wants to play swords and I suspect you will be better at that sort of thing. I'd appreciate your doing that as my morning gift. Before we left last night, Asida whispered I must be sure to ask you for something as you'd forget.'

A little thing like that as her morning gift? Elene was very different from other women. 'Did anyone ever tell you that you were beyond stubborn?'

'Frequently, but the accusation never made me change my ways. Pray save your breath and stop trying.' She curtseyed and left him standing, alone in the yard. Her skirts twitched as she walked back towards the hall, revealing the slender curve of her ankles. Hafual watched until she disappeared.

Bugge sat next to him and gave a soft woof.

'I'm keeping to my word, dog. Giving her time to adjust. It is harder than I thought it would be.'

Bugge shook her head and buried her nose under her paws as if he'd said precisely the wrong thing.

'You think I should go to her?'

The dog barked sharply.

He pressed his lips together. Maybe the dog was right. Unlike Asida or Svala, Elene had not taken the opportunity to detail his clear failings as a father or a husband, rather she had given him an opportunity to do something with his son disguised as a gift to her. A pretend sword fight. A great longing to do that with his son swept over him. 'You might be right.'

Chapter Nine

With most of the women in the weaving hut at this time of day, Hafual discovered Elene and his son alone in the kitchen. Hafual stood in the doorway and silently watched. Elene was coaxing him to eat but much to the unbridled delight of his son, porridge kept dropping on the floor. Elene's dog rushed over and gobbled the splodges up.

He cleared his throat. The spoon hung in midair before Narfi caught it and threw it to the ground with a clatter. Narfi clapped his hands and shouted for more.

'It would appear my son has particular manners concerning his food.'

Elene rapidly reached for a cloth and wiped Narfi's face before turning to face him. Two bright spots had developed on her cheeks. 'Hafual, I didn't see you there.'

'Obviously.'

'Narfi finished his breakfast. His manners have been lovely.'

'Until I arrived.'

She rubbed the back of her neck. 'You said that, not me.'

'He appears to be feeding the dog.' The instant the words were out of his mouth Hafual knew they were wrong. When had he started to sound like his father? He had intended them as a joke rather than a condemnation. And he did have a peace offering. 'I've come for that sword fight, but if the boy is busy, we can leave it until another time.'

He put down the wooden sword he'd fashioned.

'Your father is here, Narfi. He wants to play swords with you if you have finished your food. Bugge will eat anything you don't want.'

Narfi stuck his thumb in his mouth and stared at him with those big blue eyes full of silent reproach.

Hafual turned his head to stare at the simmering pot of pottage. 'We can play later.'

'Good to know there is no time limit on your playing with your son.'

Hafual watched Narfi feed the dog again. 'Is he supposed to be doing that?'

'Something wrong with feeding Bugge at the table? My nephew used to do it.' Elene asked, tilting her head to one side and peeping out at him from under her lashes.

'Nothing wrong. I was trying to make conversation.'

'I see.'

He suspected she did see, far too clearly. He shuffled forward and placed the pieces of worked leather on the table. 'I brought you some leather for your new boots and for Narfi's as well, even though Asida hasn't mentioned it. I reckon little boys grow quickly.'

'Will wonders never cease?' She wrinkled her nose, unaware that porridge had migrated to her cheek. He itched to remove it and see if her skin was rose-petal-soft. 'New boots as well as a sword fight with Narfi? I'm truly blessed this morning.'

'You need to have warm feet. Your slippers might do for court or a feast, but they will fall to bits in the mud around the yard. My wife must reflect my importance. Choose the piece you would like.'

'I didn't mean to imply…' She put a hand to her mouth. 'My tongue can be sharp sometimes.'

'Only sometimes?'

She dipped her head, but he caught the twinkle in her eye. 'New boots would be lovely. I've been bothering my father ever since my last pair developed a hole in the sole. How did you guess?'

He wanted to punch the air in triumph. He'd done something right. 'Sometimes I can see things with my eyes.'

He rapidly spread the leather out, explaining about the different weights and possibilities.

'You did the right thing in bringing up so much leather,' she said. 'Little boys do have a habit of growing quickly and Narfi's boots appear to pinch his toes.'

Hafual glowed under the unexpected praise. Something else Asida had overlooked.

'You choose and I will get the boots constructed. It should take no more than a day or two.'

'You will make the boots?'

Hafual shrugged and rearranged the selection on the table, secretly pleased at how well the small peace offering appeared to be received. Elene lifted Narfi up so he could choose first. The boy chose a soft rabbit one with a butter yellow colour before wriggling to be put down to toddle after Elene's dog.

Hafual watched the pair quietly play a game of fetch the wooden sword.

'Boot-making has a certain amount of satisfaction. I've done more boot-making than carving lately.' He gestured to the beams in the kitchen. 'I had intended on ensuring that these were all carved with vines as Svala wanted. Never found the time. Asida swears I never will.'

'I like how your hall looks—not overly ornate,' Elene said, dishing up a bowl of porridge from the pot.

'My son is far happier with you. With anyone but me, it would seem,' he said to her back.

'Your son is far happier now that his belly is full.' She set the bowl in front of him. Hafual started to eat, surprised at how hungry he was. Immediately a sense of well-being came over him.

'He talks about you all the time,' Elene said when he had finished his second bowl.

Hafual clenched the spoon until his knuckles shone white. 'He does?'

'Yes, he does. Far this and Far that. You are a great warrior, according to him.' Elene removed the bowls. 'I'm surprised Asida never said.'

'Your dog and my son appear to be fast friends,' Hafual said, nodding towards where Bugge and Narfi continued their game of fetch. Narfi gave an infectious laugh which warmed Hafual all the way through. Narfi seemed to be a different child.

'Bugge is used to children of his age. She and my nephew used to play together a great deal.' Elene put a hand on her chest, highlighting the expanse of her bosom. 'Your son will be safe with her, I promise. Cross my heart.'

'I know he will.' Hafual ran his hand through his hair and tried to concentrate on something other than the way her bosom rose and fell. 'Narfi and I...we haven't been around each other much. Asida keeps telling me that it is my fault that we don't get on.'

Elene tapped a finger on the table and her eyes flashed fire. 'Why would anyone think that?'

'It is the way he looks at me. He reminds me... reminds me of my late wife, particularly when she was disappointed in me.' The words came out in a rush and hung between them.

She tucked her head into her neck and the light went out of her eyes. 'I'm sure that wasn't very often. Your devotion to her was legendary.'

It was on the tip of his tongue to explain about the marriage and how all was not as it seemed, but Hafual held back. Why should he soil Svala's memory for Elene when he knew how much he was to blame for Svala's death and what a good friend she'd considered Elene to be? He could still hear her breathless voice explaining at how much she enjoyed the woman's company. Some things should remain private.

A tiny voice in the back of his mind questioned who he was trying to protect—Svala or himself? Would Elene think less of him if she knew the truth? He feared that she would.

Elene looped a strand of hair about her ear. Hafual realised that he was staring at the curve and shape of the ear and not paying much attention to what she said, allowing her soft tone to wash over him. 'Do you miss her that much?'

He started. 'Yes, I was devoted to her. How could anyone question that?'

The words came out more forcibly than he intended. A reflexive action, too quick and too defensive. One day he would have to explain the whole sordid story about how his love had turned to disdain and then cold fury with Svala and the games she insisted on playing. What she had done to Narfi and how he'd failed them both on that fateful day.

Elene's mouth trembled. He steeled himself for the inevitable hurt look.

'Svala was a good neighbour,' she whispered, but then her voice grew in strength. Her eyes became fierce. 'I'd hoped in time that we would become good friends. She used to listen when I spoke of my sisters and how I missed them.'

'She always considered you to be a friend.'

'I'm not trying to take her place.'

Hafual firmed his jaw; confessing about his sometimes troubled relationship with Svala became nigh impossible. He refused to destroy Elene's memories of a kind person who had listened.

'Svala has been dead for over a year.' He nodded decisively and hoped she'd accept the subject finished. It was kinder to everyone that way.

She raised a brow. 'Except you can't look at your son because he looks far too much like your late wife. You need not look so surprised. His eyes remind me of hers.'

'It is more complicated than that.' Hafual wondered how he could explain about his growing attraction to her without confessing everything that was wrong with his first marriage. 'You must trust me, Elene.'

She placed her hands on the table and stood. 'This is about trust? We are speaking about a little boy, your son who loves you but whom you spend as little time as possible with.'

He shook his head. 'My son, not yours.'

She sighed and started to clear away the breakfast things. Hafual watched her, noting the narrowness of her waist and the way her skirt moved, little things he had not bothered with before.

His hand brushed her arm as she passed. A jolt of recognition went through him. She instantly halted. He leant forward so that their breath interlaced. The longing to taste her mouth again swept over him.

'Is there something you require, Hafual?' She looked at his fingers.

'Give me time, Elene. Help me with my son.' He put his hand on his forehead. 'Later, I will play swords with him. I promise, but right now I…'

Elene scooped Narfi up. 'This young man and I are going to see about the weaving. Once he has new boots, he will be able to run better. Running can be important when you are playing with swords.'

'I will start to work on the boots.' Hafual took the leather. 'My first priority.'

'As you say, cold feet are unwelcome.'

She whispered something to Narfi, who waved goodbye enthusiastically. Hafual tentatively waved back and Narfi's wave grew stronger and his smile broader.

With a lump in his throat, Hafual watched them go. His son had waved to him. To him, not to someone else, and with such a smile. A start.

They were perhaps the most exquisite boots Elene had ever seen, sitting there on the iron-bound trunk the next evening. And next to them was a smaller pair which could easily fit Narfi. She put her hand over her mouth. When Hafual offered, she hadn't really expected anything because as the youngest of three she was used to getting the hand-me-downs.

'Do you like them?' Hafual asked from where he sat on the bed. His hair shone golden in the torchlight and his tunic was undone at his neck, revealing a shadowy hollow.

'Yes.' She wet her lips and realised she was staring at him rather than at the boots. Her proclamation of not being attracted to him was rapidly being shown to be what it was—a lie. She was attracted to him but her experience with Nerian had taught her to be wary and to distrust her reactions. If she had not given in that day, would Nerian have formally offered to marry her? She had seen the change in him immediately afterwards and had known it was her fault. Somehow, she'd been less than what he anticipated.

But despite knowing all that, she'd kept thinking about Hafual and the way his eyes crinkled all during the day when she was playing with Narfi and supervising the women.

'Your son has gone to sleep so he will have to wait for his present. I fear my dog has altered her allegiance.' Narfi had asked for Bugge to stay with him while he slept, and Elene had readily agreed. The boy and the dog appeared made for each other, something she had not anticipated. When she had agreed the boy had flung his arms about her neck and hugged her tight. He was very easy to love.

'A good thing?'

'They think so. It is something to be so easily sup-
planted in Bugge's affections.'

'She only wants the porridge.'

'And someone to throw a stick for her. Narfi seemed
to really enjoy doing that.'

She tumbled into his gaze, forgot how to breathe and
belatedly realised she was staring at the way his chest
filled his tunic. 'There are things I should be doing.'

He motioned towards the shoes. The little smile on
his face reminded her of Narfi's smile after Bugge had
brought the stick back and settled down at his feet.
'Time to try the boots on. See if the sizing is right or
if adjustments need to be made.'

Elene slipped the nearest one on. The fit was nearly
perfect, and the white fur warmed her feet. 'You managed to do it quickly.'

The warmth of his smile was enough to make her
knees feel weak. 'I started to make them when I remembered a nearly made pair. It made my job easier.'

A sudden stab of jealousy went through her. Those
boots had been made with love and care for someone
else. Hand-me-downs again. 'Svala's?'

She hated that she risked opening up that particular wound again, but it was like a scab she found difficult to resist picking. The woman had been a friend
and died in horrible circumstances. Why did she resent
Hafual's regard for his late wife?

He shook his head. 'I forget the reason. I wanted
to see how the leather would work, I believe. A lucky
coincidence.'

She allowed the lie. They were the sort of thing
a man made for someone they loved, rather than for
the bride they had to marry. Giving them to her was

because it made things easier for him. A piece of her argued that he'd seen she had cold feet and had gone about solving the problem quickly.

She forced a bright smile. 'For my personal morning gift. Asida said that I would get one, but I thought she might be mistaken.'

He drew his brows together. 'I have already agreed the morning gift with your father—the farm which lies next to Baelle Heale. We have both added land to it. It will do if anything happened to me. I wanted you to have something for you to live on, something your father could not take away.'

'Thank you. And unexpectedly generous.'

'I can be kind.'

'I know you can be.' She stopped and examined her hands at the teasing lilt tone.

'Go on, put the other one on.'

She started to put the boot and discovered the toe was blocked. She reached in and pulled out a set of intricate gold and garnet brooches. They were a good match for the necklace she'd worn at the feast. 'For me as well?'

'A woman always needs something of her own as well as land for her morning gift.' His mouth twisted and his eyes became shadowed. 'My mother taught me that. She was my father's third of five wives.'

'Did your father have them all at the same time?'

'Pretty much. Unlike the Mercians, it is not uncommon for a sea king to have several wives and concubines at the same time. It helps bind his men to him.'

Elene stared at the boots. Wives and concubines at the same time, a reminder that the North was a very different place to Mercia. Hafual may have grown up in the North, but he was Mercian now.

'Do you remain a man from the North?'

'My oath is to Mercia, and I have become an ealdorman, rather than a sea king.' The corners of his mouth twitched. 'One wife at a time is enough for me if that is what you are asking. I learned from my father's mistakes.'

'Your mother would be proud of what you have achieved.'

'Kind of you to say. My mother was disinclined towards praise.' He bowed his head. 'I regret you had to wait a little before I gave them to you. Remiss of me. Hopefully the gift will return the smile to your face.'

'Thank you for them as well.'

Elene stared at the brooches. She'd been annoyed with him earlier when he'd obviously been trying to avoid Narfi, but he had more than made up for that with his gift of the boots which were now warming her toes. But her moods were not dependant on the gifts she received. 'I wasn't expecting anything. It is not really expected in Mercia. If I seemed out of sorts earlier, everything is new to me.'

'My manners were lacking, and I apologise.'

Elene firmed her mouth. It wasn't his manners about the morning gift she had objected to, but rather how he had treated his son. Or if she was being honest, how she thought he had reacted to Narfi. It seemed clear that his heart was in the right place. He needed more time to get to know the boy instead of leaving to go off on another mission for the king. She was the one jumping to conclusions, something her sisters complained about.

'The brooches will be good to wear when we next

have a magnificent feast. Everyone will marvel at them.' She reached into her pouch and held out a small jar. 'I made some ointment for your shoulder. Not the same as the brooches or the slippers, but you might find it useful.'

He tilted his head to one side. 'Are you offering to put it on?'

Her palms tingled at the suggestion. 'I suppose I am.'

'Since when did you become a frightened rabbit afraid to touch a man?'

She straightened her spine. She had nursed many men before. Hafual would not be any different. 'Take off your tunic.'

His eyes deepened to a midnight blue. 'As my lady requests.'

'More than requests—orders.'

He winced as he lifted the top. Stopped and then started again. 'Sometimes my shoulder is stiff. Doesn't bother me none.'

'Allow me to help.'

She took his barely perceptible nod for agreement. Elene went over and took the tunic from him. His body was covered in a network of silver scars but rippled with muscles before tapering down to his slender hips. She swallowed hard and set about putting the strong-smelling ointment on his shoulder, taking care to rub it in. His flesh was warm and pliable under her fingertips. Her hands stilled and her mouth went dry.

She rapidly took a step backwards and nearly tripped over her gown. 'Finished.'

He put his hand beneath her elbow and stopped her from falling. 'Careful. I wouldn't want you to trip over your new boots.'

'Your shoulder is far worse than I'd considered. You will be having the bed. Sleeping on the floor will not be doing it any good. You should have explained.' She busied herself with gathering up the furs. 'You have the bed tonight.'

'No.'

She rolled her eyes and held the furs in front of her like a shield. 'Shouldn't I get to decide? Someone needs to ensure you look after yourself.'

'We can share if you insist, but I will not allow you to sleep on the floor while I take the bed.' He lifted his brow and gave an exaggerated stretch. 'Unless you feel unable to control your desire. I, for one, intend to keep my promise to you.'

She tightened her grip on the furs. Unable to control her desires? He made it sound like she was panting after him, or worse, that the attraction was entirely on her part. She peered at the carved wooden bed. 'You are right. The bed is big enough for both of us. Why should I be afraid that you might break your promises? We are both good at keeping to the rules.'

'My shoulder thanks you. The ointment has improved it no end, taken away the dull ache.' He kicked off his boots and gave an exaggerated yawn before plumping up the pillows and turning firmly away from her to face the wall. 'Sleep will come easily for me tonight. We will speak in the morning. The best way to demonstrate my intentions is to keep my word.'

Elene stilled. Sleep might come easy for him, but for her... Last night had been hard enough, with dreams of broad-shouldered warriors who carried her off and played her body like a well-tuned lyre. All she would have to do was reach out a hand and...

Banishing the image from her brain, she blew out the reeds and rapidly undressed to her under-gown before settling into the bed, being careful to keep well away from the now softly snoring Hafual. How hard could it be? She turned her back to him and began to think about what needed to happen next, what things she needed to do to ensure that Baelle Heale remained safe and Pybba could no longer threaten them. It was far easier to occupy her mind with that than to think about Hafual's warmth and her growing attraction to him. But she also was aware of his bulk and how easy it would be to accidentally roll towards him.

Chapter Ten

Hafual woke in the early morning grey light to find Elene snuggled in the crook of his arm with her hand intimately splayed across his chest and her curves moulded to his body. Her faintly floral scent of rosemary and buttercup tickled his nose. And he ached to the point of agony. Another dip in the ice-cold lake loomed. The acceptance of their physical relationship had to come from her. But he'd almost forgotten what it was like to hold a sleeping woman gently in his arms. It took all his willpower not to tighten his arms about her, kiss her awake and ease his agony that way.

'Elene,' he whispered close to her ear. 'I must move, or I won't be held responsible for what happens.'

She murmured something in her sleep which he could not quite catch and pressed her body closer to him, her breasts firmly hitting his chest, and his body thrummed anew.

Sighing, he eased her away from him. Learning that he kept his promises was far more important right now. Anticipation would make her eventual acquiescence that much sweeter. Slow and steady. He was not going to repeat the mistakes of his first marriage. Then they had both been far too young and too impatient.

He moved the hair from her temple and placed a soft kiss. 'Soon you will see what I have in store for us both. In this marriage I want a partner who takes joy in our joining, not someone who does her duty. I know what that sort of marriage is like.'

She murmured something, moving into the place which he had vacated.

He took one last look at her sleeping perfection and sprinted towards the lake's cold watery embrace.

Elene sleepily moved towards a warm hollow in the bed. She reached out a hand but encountered empty space. She allowed her hand to fall back amongst the heavy furs, opening an eye. She was alone in the bed and Hafual had kept his promise.

It was for the best. If Hafual had been here, she would have been tempted to kiss him and allow things to go from there. It would have been easy to give in like she had done with Nerian. She'd resisted for a long time, permitting no more than a few chaste kisses on her hand and forehead. Then the last time he'd visited something had been different. There had been a new urgency and she'd given in to his pleas, naively thinking he would go straight to her father and make a declaration. Instead, he'd gone straight to his horse and ridden to Wessex to marry another.

'Rules keep you safe. Always.'

A sharp bark answered her.

She glanced over and saw Bugge's nose poking around the door. Narfi must be up. Elene hurriedly dressed, shoved her feet into her new boots, but did not stop to do her hair up. She whispered a prayer to St Hilde and any saint who was listening that he was not in any mischief.

'Take me to Narfi, Bugge. Now, before something worse happens.'

With an imperious bark, Bugge led the way to the kitchen. Her feet skittered into each other. With the fire blazing, Hafual calmly spooned porridge into his son's mouth. After the spoonful, Narfi clapped his hands and demanded another, opening his mouth like a little bird. Hafual missed the target and deposited it on his chin. He dabbed the boy's face with a cloth before getting the spoon in properly.

'I need to get this right, son, or I'll be in trouble with your new mother.'

She stopped in the doorway and put her hand to her mouth. Hafual was with his son, and they were having a good time together.

'Are you able to manage?' she asked.

Hafual looked up with a guilty expression on his face.

'I encountered him when I was coming back from my swim. Narfi was hungry.' Hafual leant over and wiped some more porridge off his son's chin. 'I took a guess that the servants would have put the soaked oats out. I even managed to find him some clean clothes.'

'You were able to dress him?' Elene staggered over to the bench and sat down heavily.

'I used to be a boy myself.' His gentle laugh caused Narfi to laugh along with him. He immediately stopped in wonderment. And tears filled his eyes. He blinked rapidly but gave a huge smile. 'You should see your face, Elene. The servants helped me, but I wanted to see if I could feed Narfi. And the women wanted to get busy with the weaving. My sister must have put the fear of God into them.'

'You appear to be doing a good job...with the feeding.'

Hafual casually ruffled Narfi's hair. The boy beamed up at him. 'Praise from Lady Elene is high praise indeed. I took your advice and avoided making loud noises. It has worked wonders.'

Narfi ate a few more bites and then wriggled, asking to get down to play with Bugge.

'I assume Bugge has had her porridge as well.'

Hafual pointed to an empty wooden bowl before the fire. 'How else could I get Narfi to eat? The dog comes first.'

'A man of hidden talents.'

'Don't you want to hear my news?' he asked, not moving from where he sat. 'What I've decided. I had hoped to speak of it last night, but other things were on my mind.'

Other things on his mind. Had he come into their room to seduce her?

She concentrated on the boots which fit so well on her feet. She should have known there would be a but or an addition to the morning gifts he'd given her last evening. She knew she should be grateful to Narfi and his wandering. Hafual might have returned, and matters could have taken a different course. Somehow what he was about to say would have been harder then. She half guessed from things Asida had said—he seldom stayed at Wulfhere's Clearing for more than a week.

Her father had done such things—giving her treats or trinkets to sweeten the blow. He was going to leave.

It was why he was getting things done like ensuring the anvil was working. Their marriage was going to be distant. She'd have her sphere of influence with the domestic. She'd wanted that less than a day ago, but now, staring at those shoes and having woken up with his faint lingering warmth beside her, she knew she wanted something more. She wanted to see if they could make something of the marriage. And she was willing to fight for it.

'Are you going to court to let Ceolwulf know about our marriage?' she asked, injecting a light note into her voice. She'd learnt with Nerian not to make a fuss. She'd screamed and cried when they parted. A clinging vine he'd called her the last time they had met. 'Are you going to ensure that Pybba cannot do any damage either to you or my father? Sensible.'

The twinkle in his eyes increased and he looked precisely like Narfi before he gave Bugge a hug. 'I won't be going alone.'

She froze. 'Really? Won't it violate one of your rules?'

'If Pybba has run to the court, Ceolwulf will need to meet you and be reassured that you want this marriage. Rules must be obeyed, Elene, and that includes ensuring Ceolwulf is seen to approve of our marriage. You see what I've done there?'

'Invented a rule?'

'Elaborated on a custom.'

Her stomach tightened. He wasn't abandoning her. He wanted her to go with him to court. He'd even made up a rule to ensure it would happen.

'Narfi must come as well,' she said quickly, wrapping her arms about her middle so that she would not be tempted to throw them about his neck in relief. She wasn't going to be one of those wives who were never at court. 'The journey to Tamworth is short. An introduction to court, and it will show everyone your peaceful intentions.'

Hafual drew his brows together. 'Ceolwulf is in Ludenwic for a meeting with Alfred, the King of Wessex. Are you certain Narfi can travel that far? It will be about three days along the Watling Road in a covered cart.'

Elene contemplated. The Wessex court would be there as well as the Mercian one. She might have to encounter Nerian and his new wife. Her stomach tightened. The last thing she wanted was to see pity in anyone's eyes. And she was bound to see it if the whispers started about her and Nerian again. What had passed between them seemed to belong to a different part of her life, fading into insignificance beside the few kisses she had shared with Hafual. Whatever was happening between them was too new.

'I thought the court was to be at Tamworth for the Christmas season,' she said and hated the desperation in her voice. 'Surely we should consider travelling there then.'

'Delaying will give Pybba a chance to increase his influence.' His mouth became a thin white line. 'Ceolwulf wants certain matters settled with Alfred before the Christmas season. The governance of Ludenwic has long been a thorn in both Mercia's and Wessex's sides. Ceolwulf had asked that I travel there once I settled matters at Wulfhere. I was supposed to take all the time I needed.'

'Which means you were supposed to leave as soon as possible.'

'The demands of a king can be heavy,' he acknowledged. 'He thought I could be instrumental in achieving peace but reluctantly agreed I should take the time to see my son and visit my estate.'

Peace with Wessex? She'd believe that when she saw it. Wessex always wanted to dominate Mercia and had fought wars over their border. But the fact they had been at each other's throat had assisted the Great Heathen Horde in conquering most of England, leaving only Wessex and the smallest portion of Mercia free. Although her brothers-in-law were good men, Elene knew some of the invaders were not. 'It is good that Ceolwulf thinks so highly of you.'

Hafual frowned. 'Nerian is currently a close advisor of Alfred's. We have been working together on achieving a lasting peace. Our friendship and mutual regard have assisted.'

'I am sure you remain friends.' Elene was proud of how even her voice sounded. She wondered how much Hafual had guessed about the nature of her relationship with Nerian. Or if Nerian had mentioned how lacking she had been in bed. 'Will Pybba go to Ludenwic? It is what I would do.'

'I suspect Pybba will go to Tamworth as he is quite friendly with Ceolwulf's wife and put his case that way.' Hafual gave a half-smile. Elene risked a breath. 'The current Lady of Mercia distrusts most Northmen. She has seen the war's destruction first hand and blames the Great Heathen Horde.'

'But she trusts you.'

'She is grateful I saved Ceolwulf's life and that I helped to contain the Hwicce. Beyond that I don't press her. What I do know is that we have peace with the Five Boroughs and will hopefully have peace with Wessex soon.'

'Best to get to Ceolwulf first.' Elene tapped a finger against her mouth. That settled it. She might not want to encounter Nerian again, but neither did she wish to hide away. Her only flaw had been believing the easy promises of a love-struck warrior and she'd hardly have been the first woman to do that. 'I can brave Ludenwic and Nerian.'

An unaccustomed stab of jealousy went through Haful. He had witnessed her blossoming relationship with Nerian of Wessex that summer. Everyone had expected them to marry. Nerian had once confided that it was his lack of prospects which had held him back from making a formal declaration, but that Elene was the perfect woman for him.

'How long will it take you to pack for a journey like this?' he asked, pushing the thoughts away.

Elene rapidly listed various things they would need and why. With each new addition, his respect for the woman grew. She had obviously considered about the intricacies of court life in a way he had not even appreciated.

'Impressive.'

The colour in her cheeks became infused with a rose hue. She peeped at him from a forest of thick lashes. 'Do you think so? My father tells me that my mouth gallops away before my thoughts can catch up, and I keep thinking about things which might not come to pass.'

'Better to be safe.'

'My view entirely. Is there anything I have forgotten?'

He laughed. 'You have done an admirable job. When did you first start thinking about this?'

'When I started feeding Narfi porridge yesterday, my mind began to work overtime. Wool-gathering, my sisters call it. But we need to go to court instead of cowering at the hall, waiting.'

'Is that what we are doing, cowering? Here, my sister said that we were on our wedding journey. Good to know the difference.'

She peeped at him under her lashes and then her smile broke through. The muscles in Hafual's neck relaxed. She'd understood his attempt at a joke rather than bristling as his sister or indeed Svala would have done.

'Journeys are usually moving somewhere.' She sobered. 'Going to court is the only way to ensure we prevent Pybba from causing harm, but you must not shut me out when we are there.'

'Do I shut you out?'

'You expected trouble the other night. It is why you had me on the horse. I'm not a child, Hafual. I deserve to know when danger lurks.'

He tilted his head one side. The morning sunlight filtered in through the door, highlighting the gold in her hair, the sweep of her neck and the delicate curve of her bottom lip. 'Do I get a kiss to seal our bargain as you are not a child?'

She put a hand on her hip. 'A kiss? Are you trying to distract me?'

Hafual shrugged. He refused to promise something that he might not be able to keep. Keeping his options open was necessary. He refused to put her in harm's way. 'We have agreed that I will not keep danger from you, surely that is worth a kiss.'

He waited to see if his hunch from earlier was

correct—that she was attracted to him and that she would welcome a deepening of their relationship.

'You are incorrigible.' Her laugh rang out. 'Worse than your son, who flirts unmercifully. I now know where it comes from.'

'I'm pleased that my son and I have something in common—an eye for pretty ladies.' He inclined his head. 'Is this getting me any closer to my kiss? Right here. Wish me good morning.' He tapped his cheek. 'We will want people to think our marriage has meaning if we are going to Ludenwic.'

A kiss on the cheek? What harm could it do?

She darted forward and went to kiss his cheek, but he moved his mouth at the last breath and their lips met. His mouth tasted like cold small beer on a hot summer's day. She was tempted to linger but he let her go.

'You see, no harm done from a simple good morning kiss.'

A simple kiss? Anything but. Her breath came in little puffs and a great tingling went through her veins. Her body had responded to his and if he hadn't pulled away, she would have deepened that kiss. She knew it, but what was worse, he knew it. His smile showed that he was intimately aware of yesterday's lie about her disinterest in a physical relationship.

She concentrated on her hands, on the heavy gold ring which now sat on her left ring finger. 'I had thought you meant on your cheek.'

His laugh sent a series of warm pulses up and down her spine. 'Good morning kisses must always be on the mouth.'

'Another of your rules?' She risked a peek up at him

and immediately wished she hadn't. The intensity of his eyes stole her breath away.

'Clarity makes for a contented marriage.'

A contented marriage, not a passionate one or even a loving one. A small stab of disappointment hit Elene. She quashed it. She was through with all romantic nonsense. The heartache was too great when she'd discovered that her dreams had been only clouds in the sky. If contented was all that was on offer, she was going to accept that.

'We should get ready to depart as soon as possible,' she said, changing the subject. 'I shall ask my father if we can borrow one of the maids. The woman your sister used will be far more use here working on the weaving. She does not seem to understand the nature of little boys.'

He put his hands behind his head and closed his eyes. 'Your wish shall be fulfilled now that I have had my kiss. Fair is fair.'

'You mean to exact payment in kisses?'

'An intriguing proposition. Will we have to work out how many kisses I get for each item?'

'You are being impossible.' She hated the breathlessness in her voice. 'Kisses indeed!'

'I will take that for a yes.'

Elene stood up and busied herself with clearing the dishes. Hafual in this mood was very hard to resist, but she knew what had happened to her before, when she'd trusted far too quickly. This time she was going to keep her heart safe.

A dog bark pierced the quiet calm. Elene dropped a wooden bowl. 'Bugge. Something is wrong.'

Hafual had already started to move. 'We go now.'

They both raced to where Narfi sat in the dirt by the doorstep with a graze on his cheek and a surprised expression on his face. The tension went out of Elene. The boy was fine.

'That dog of yours is better than any nurse could be,' Hafual said.

'I do believe she is.'

Narfi held up his hands. In one hand he held a feather which he'd obviously captured from one of the hens who pecked about in the soil. 'Kiss. Elene.'

'A boy after my own image.' Hafual laughed and scooped the boy up, holding him so that Elene could kiss him.

'Is he coming to Ludenwic, then?' she asked after Narfi had wriggled down to go play with Bugge again.

The twinkle in Hafual's eyes deepened. 'As long as I get a kiss or three at the very minimum.'

Elene's heart lurched. 'That might be able to be arranged.'

Chapter Eleven

'Are you certain you wish to take Narfi with you to Ludenwic? Is it wise?' Asida asked with a supercilious expression on her face when Hafual confronted her at Baelle Heale. 'Wulfgar has been regaling me with stories about Elene's mishaps at court. Her ability to irritate King Ceolwulf is quite the Baelle Heale joke.'

After briefly greeting Asida, Elene had gone to pack the remainder of her things and speak to several of the maids, giving Hafual the opportunity to speak with his sister alone and ensure that she understood why she needed to behave.

Wulfgar, Hafual noticed, remained closeted with his steward.

'Are you questioning my decisions, sister?' he asked, attempting to control his temper.

Asida worried her bottom lip. 'You two should have a wedding trip, alone. Somewhere other than court. And Narfi might become unsettled in a new place. He has never travelled.'

'Narfi is my son. It is long past time that he met Ceolwulf, his godfather by proxy. Some day, Narfi will serve in his household, all being well. And the king will find Elene charming. You underestimate her. The entire family does.'

'But that is not for years. You and Elene should do this together.' She pinched the bridge of her nose. 'I know I said that I refused to look after Narfi any more, but maybe I didn't mean it. Maybe I wanted you to beg me.

'Ceolwulf only reluctantly allowed me to return home. He values my insight.'

'The threat of your sword arm, more like.'

'This will show that I can attend to his wishes and my family. I can also see to the outfitting of my ships. There is a profit to be had in the markets of Frankia and beyond. Once I have done one voyage, the entire court will see and clamour for the opportunity to sell wool that way.'

Asida hung her head. 'I will miss him.'

'It will give me a chance to get to know him. He is my son, Asida, and I need you here, looking after Wulfgar and ensuring all is in order with the hall.' He patted her awkwardly on the shoulder. 'Being at Baelle Heale seems to have put the roses back in your cheeks.'

Asida's smile was like the sun peeking out from behind the clouds. 'You are right about that. I'm enjoying pitting my wits against the steward's wife. It turns out that Wulfgar is partial to a game of *tafl*. He is not nearly the frost giant I thought he was—merely a lonely old man.'

Hafual raised his brow that his sister had dropped the formality in referring to his new father-in-law and apparently had changed her mind about him. But if Asida manged to oust any influence the steward's wife had, so much the better. 'I will keep that in mind and thank you.'

Asida scrunched her nose. 'That is the first time you have voluntarily thanked me in a long time. I suspect marriage is good for you.'

'Ask me again after I return.'

Asida put her hand on his sleeve. 'Brother, one last thing—make sure you properly bed Elene before you arrive at court, before people can whisper.'

'I don't have time for your fantasies, Asida.'

Asida jabbed a finger at him, punctuating each word with another stab. 'I can tell you haven't, and if I can tell, others will be able to as well. Keep us all safe, Hafual, do the right thing.'

Hafual gritted his teeth until his jaw ached. Do the right thing as if that was a good reason to make love to Elene. He wanted her to the point of aching, but it had to be because she wanted it to happen, not because she feared the consequences of it not happening. And certainly not because it would keep people from guessing at court. And the last person he wanted to be involved in his dilemma was his half-sister.

'The state of my marriage is not your concern. Ever.'

Asida jabbed the air with her finger. 'Wrong, it is everyone who lives in this area's concern. You swore to protect us. Think on that as you travel to Ludenwic.'

'You are lucky you are my sister, Asida. I allow you to make statements that others wouldn't dare to.'

'Maybe they should.' Asida marched away, with her skirt twitching.

'I won't have you peeking into my future.'

She stopped and turned. 'No need to peek, Hafual. All I did was look at your face when she was close by.

When are you going to admit you are human and not a dead man walking through life?'

'Do you wish to stay in the covered cart, or do you want to walk awhile with me?'

Elene looked up from where she sat beside a now sleeping Narfi and drank in how Hafual appeared in his travelling clothes with his short cloak barely concealing his broad shoulders and the faintly bashful expression on his face. Her mouth went dry. All practical thought about supplies vanished, leaving only the consideration of his mouth's bow-like shape.

Even though they had barely started, a small pain had developed between her brows, and she felt vaguely sick from the swaying of the cart. Narfi on the other hand was rapidly proving to be an excellent traveller, particularly with Bugge riding in the cart next to him. When it came to it, Hafual had decided that boy and dog should remain together. Good for each other was the terse explanation.

Her father appeared younger than he had for years and had insisted that their departure would not cause any problems. He volunteered to look after Lady Asida until they returned. Something Asida readily agreed to. Elene dismissed the thought that Asida might have designs on her father as her mind working overtime.

'Elene?'

'I can walk,' Elene said, eager to get out of the stifling cart. She'd forgotten how tedious travelling in a covered cart could be. Watling Street was one of the main highways in Mercia and had been around since time first began. It was kept in a reasonable state with not too many ruts but even still the cart travelled at little faster than walking pace. 'Narfi is fast asleep and Bugge will bark or the maid will give me a shout when he awakes,' she added with a smile. 'Or otherwise, he could walk with us.'

'This one is a much better nurse than the last one.'

'Particularly as she has Bugge to help her. I don't know if I should be pleased or annoyed that Bugge has become besotted with Narfi.'

'Bugge understands that you are safe with me.' Hafual put his hand under her elbow to help her down but managed to slip Bugge several pieces of dried meat as he did so, much to Bugge's delight.

His fingers curled about hers once she had landed, sending a tingle of awareness up her arm. She swallowed hard and concentrated on the plump brambles which were at the side of the road, rather than turning towards him and demanding a kiss. 'It is a pleasant autumn day.'

Elene concentrated on breathing steadily. There had been something slightly different about Hafual ever since they had returned from Baelle Heale with her travelling trunks. She could not put her finger on it.

She realised that her fingers remained loosely in his grip. She rapidly let go. The twinkle in his eye deepened. 'Yes, it has been surprisingly dry, but you can tell winter and the season of mud will be here soon enough. Travelling is not difficult at a time like this. Narfi—'

'Narfi is a better traveller than I thought he would be. Thank you for agreeing to a walk.' He motioned to the men to go on. 'I want to show you something that I think you might like.'

Elene tilted her head to one side. A faint fluttering started in her stomach. 'You want to get me alone?'

A smile trembled on his lips. 'Guilty.'

'Intriguing.'

He led the way to a rise and pointed. 'If you look over there, the top of the large oak at Wulfhere's Clearing is visible. This is where I always I go when I am leaving or returning home. I make the promise to return.'

Elene stood on her tiptoes and peered in the general direction of Hafual's pointing. It was a stretch to say you could see an oak at Wulfhere's Clearing or even Baelle Heale. The trees all blended to one. 'I will take your word for it.'

'I wanted you to know what I do. Will you promise with me?' His eyes turned serious and seemed to bore into her soul. 'That we will return. That this land will be ours for our descendants to hold.'

A shiver went down her spine. Despite what Pybba had claimed, Hafual was Mercian and his kinship to the land was far greater than hers, even though she'd been born here.

'Yes. We will return,' she said, pushing the vague sense of disquiet from her. 'An easy promise this time, not like when you go to fight the Hwicce. I refuse to allow Pybba any sense of satisfaction. He will not destroy you or my father. Trust me.'

Giving in to temptation, she put her hand to his face and felt the roughness of his stubble under her fingers.

His arms went about her and drew her close and then his mouth claimed hers. This kiss was different from the other ones and called to something deep within her. She opened her lips and drank him in. Their tongues tangled.

She put her arms around his neck and held him there.

'I think you made that promise up,' she said.

He rained little kisses on her face. 'Why do you say that?'

'Because I like to think that you wanted to get me alone.'

His loud very masculine laugh rang out, making a warmth curl about her insides. 'Astute, Elene.'

'You don't always have to kiss me in secret,' she said. 'We're married.'

He caught her hand and raised it to his lips. 'I wanted you to know that I intend to hold these lands, no matter what Pybba might do. I may not have been born a Mercian, but I intend to die one.'

The breeze whipped his hair from his intent face. A shiver went down her spine. Hafual meant what he said. He had turned his back on the North and had become a Mercian.

'I trust you and your sword arm to hold these lands as any Mercian lord should.' She knew when she said the words that she had failed to put in to words how much his declaration meant. 'We should get back to the cart or they will worry.'

'No good having Narfi wake and you not being there.'

'There's hope for you yet,' she said.

'For me as what? A father?' His gaze narrowed. 'I know how badly I've failed in the past.'

Elene tilted her head and pretended to consider. 'The father whom Narfi needs and wants is you and no other. Someday you will believe that.'

'You see the good in people, Elene.' He raised her hand to his lips. 'I hope to prove myself worthy in due course, but you must not expect too much of me or our marriage.'

Prove himself worthy while she expected too much. The words reminded her of something Nerian had once said to her and how she was always pushing and asking for far too much.

She withdrew her hand. She couldn't rid herself of a suspicion that every time they became closer, Hafual erected some barrier. She could never see who he truly was. She mentally shook her head. Had her experience with Nerian ruined her? Why couldn't she accept the growing attraction between them? And that his heart belonged to his late wife entirely and there was no room for anyone else. She could have kindness, friendship after a fashion, but not love. Chasing after rainbows led to disappointment. 'We need to be going back.'

The cold seeped into his eyes. 'As my lady desires.'

'Why are we stopping here?' Elene asked when Hafual called a halt to the journey in the late afternoon. They had made decent time, but all her bones now ached from being in the cart and Narfi had decided to become cranky, pulling Bugge's ears and generally demanding. She'd been looking forward to a quiet evening at the abbey.

'Good a place as any.'

'There is an abbey a little further up the road,' Elene said, trying to keep her voice reasonable. There was something about the place which made her feel uncomfortable. 'My father has often stayed there. The abbot maintains guest rooms. They lay a good table.'

Hafual's eyes slid away from her. He started to undo

the packs. 'The abbey is further than you think. We would not arrive until well after dark. The gates will be locked and barred.'

'But wouldn't it be better to travel there and see?'

'Are you questioning my decisions, Elene? Narfi has spent long enough in the cart for today!'

The sound of his voice caused Narfi to start crying.

Hafual winced and ran his hand through his hair. 'I didn't mean to shout. I know the abbey you mean, but I must balance reaching it with the needs of our party, including Narfi's.'

'Narfi seems to agree with you.' Elene handed the boy to his father. Narfi instantly stopped crying and started tugging at Hafual's hair. 'Here, amuse him for a little while.'

Hafual hugged the boy.

'Where are you going?' he asked in a quieter voice.

'To stretch my legs with Bugge.'

Beside an old oak, Elene put a hand on her forehead. She had to stop thinking about the outlaws and seeing trouble around every turn. Hafual was right. Narfi needed to be out and about. And he knew the road better than she did. If he said the abbey was too far, then it was.

She certainly had had enough of the swaying cart for the day. She had to trust him to keep her safe. He was not Ecgbert or indeed Nerian.

She put her hand against her stomach. It frightened her that she wanted to believe in him and that she wanted to believe that the kiss they had shared showed his attraction to her. Could she trust him or more importantly herself with her body and possibly her heart?

* * *

Elene woke in the dark with a start, uncertain of where she was. Her pounding heart resounded in her ears as she sought out the familiar. She struggled to a sitting position and breathed easier when she spied Bugge's nose resting against her paws.

Her dreams had been confused about being chased and people pointing fingers at her before she found safety in a strong set of arms which clasped her to a broad chest and carried her away from the noise and mayhem.

Slowly her heart returned to normal. Her hair was plastered to her forehead. Naivety had dogged her every move. She could still lose everything if people learned her marriage remained unconsummated. The knowledge could be used against her. King Ceolwulf was unlikely to look kindly on attempting to cheat in that way and she had no real idea of Pybba's power. What if she was asked to swear that she had a real marriage?

She could hear Narfi softly snuffling in his sleep near her and the maid. Hafual had declared that they should sleep in the covered cart, and he would make do on the ground. The ointment had made his shoulder that much better.

She grabbed a shawl, pushed her feet into her boots and peered out into the dark. Was it worth trying to settle her thoughts with a quick walk? She gave a wry smile. Who was she trying to fool? She wanted to see Hafual and explain her concerns. She motioned to Bugge to stay with Narfi. The dog settled her nose back down on her paws.

A figure sat hunched beside the dying fire, drawing with a stick in the dirt. A tremor of recognition went through her.

'Hafual?' she called out.

'Elene.' Hafual turned towards her. 'Did something disturb you? All is quiet.'

'I had trouble sleeping.' Elene gave a half-shrug. 'Always happens when I travel. Because of…because of when we encountered the other band of outlaws. They came first at dusk and then we were hunted over several days.'

'They were not outlaws, but warriors in the pay of that Danish warlord Moir killed. Bandits are mostly cowards, Elene. They seldom attack groups of warriors.'

Elene looked up and tried to control her emotions. She knew instinctively he was trying to make her fear go away with his reassurances, but it remained like a hard knot in the pit of her stomach. The trees made dark silhouettes against the star-spangled sky. 'Seldom is more than never.'

'Come sit with me. Talk to me.' Hafual patted the stone next to him. 'I could do with the company and the night remains young.'

'Your thoughts bothering you?' Elene pursed her lips together. There was another reason for them stopping here, something she couldn't quite put her finger on.

'I already know my thoughts. I don't know yours. My sword will protect you.'

She remained where she was. Going and sitting next to him would mean confessing her fears about being caught out about the marriage and her growing sense that she had to do something about it. She had not the least idea where to start, how she'd explain about her mistake with Nerian. The last thing she wanted was for Haful to bed her out of pity. 'My thoughts are very simple—how safe are we, will Narfi sleep through the night, will we have time for hot porridge in the morning before we continue on to the abbey where we are going to spend tomorrow night.'

'Much more interesting thoughts than mine. You've little idea how tiresome my thoughts can be.'

'I'm quite willing to listen to your thoughts.'

He reached forward and stirred the embers. 'Not worth the spit it takes to say them.'

'But they disturb your sleep.'

'For that reason, I've no wish to disturb your sleep.' He gave a half-smile. 'Not in that way. There are other ways I could, and which would prove pleasurable for the both of us.'

A warm pulse went down her spine. This was the time to tell him about Nerian and the mistake. She wrapped her arms about her middle. 'Haful—'

'You are trembling from the cold. Come here and get warm. I must insist as your husband, Elene. The last thing I require is for you to get a chill.'

She swallowed her words, went over to the dying fire, and he put his cloak about her. The heavy fur-lined cloak which smelt of woodsmoke and something indefinably him instantly made her feel more secure. She settled down on the rock next to him. Their shoulders lightly touched. Neither made a move to get away from the other but equally neither leant into the other. Elene debated returning to the cart after the idle chatter about where they were headed tomorrow faded away.

'How much longer is your watch?' she asked, breaking the awkward silence which had settled over them as she searched for a way to bring up the subject again.

He reached for the stick again and stirred the fire, causing the sparks to fly up into the sky, sparkle and die. 'For a little while yet. I rarely sleep well. Too many thoughts.'

'I wanted to thank you for marrying me,' she said quickly before her nerve failed her. 'But you should know about Nerian and me. What he was to me.'

'In the past.'

'Yes, of course, in the past.'

'It has no bearing on our present.' He sighed and ran his hand through his hair. 'I know you were close, Elene. And enough of the North remains in me not to care about the details. It is in the past.'

'Very much so,' she said.

'Our marriage has you and I in it.'

Her stomach tightened. He didn't care about what had passed between her and Nerian. She pressed her lips together and hoped it did not mean that he wasn't interested in her and was simply going to do his duty. 'I was wrong the other day about wanting an uncon-summated marriage. Ceolwulf is sure to ask. Lying to my sovereign will be difficult.'

He completely stilled. 'My sister made a similar observation.'

Elene stared at the embers of the fire. What else had Asida said? 'Your sister spoke about it? How could she know? Did you tell her?'

'I told her to keep her long nose out. Our marriage is our business. I will make it right with Ceolwulf should it come to it.'

'I see.' She started to move away while shards of her dignity remained. To think she'd nearly begged him to make love to her with such a pathetic excuse as not lying to his king. And he didn't care about Nerian. Was that because he didn't desire her? Had she misread the kisses they'd shared? He reached out and captured her hand.

'Fear is a poor excuse to take a woman to one's bed, particularly one like you. Should anyone ask, we can truthfully answer—you have shared my bed.'

She gave a crooked smile. 'Always best to tell the truth.'

He put a finger to her lips. 'Wait here.'

Hafual put the stick down and stood up. He went over to one of his men and woke him for watch duty. The man good-naturedly agreed. Hafual handed him a thick cloak to keep him warm and told him to keep sharp. The man sleepily agreed.

He held out his hand to Elene. 'Come for a walk with me. I will not leave people without protection, but I will speak with you alone. There is a lake not far from here and the moonlight will provide more than enough light for us.'

Elene stood up, ignoring his hand. If she returned to the relative safety of the covered cart, she might never discover if what she was feeling was her being unsettled about the possibility of Pybba or if it was something more. 'A walk will settle my errant thoughts. A short one, mind. Getting lost and causing alarm would be counterproductive.'

'A short walk to the lake, it is.'

When the lake shimmered silver in the distance, she missed her footing and softly swore, grabbing his arm for support. 'I'm always doing that!'

'Elene,' he whispered before his mouth lowered on hers and claimed it. This was no gentle kiss designed to make her feel at ease, but one designed to steal her breath away. A warm curl of heat wrapped around her sides and coursed through her.

His hands slid down her back and pressed her closer to him so that the apex of her thighs encountered his hard arousal. The knowledge thrummed through her— he wanted her. Nerian had wanted her too until he'd had her. The knowledge spread through her like cold water. 'I… I…'

'The reason I want you has nothing to do with fear of Ceolwulf, Pybba or anyone,' he growled in her ear. 'And everything to do with desire.'

She leant back against the circle of his arms and tried to see his face. The moonlight had turned it into a contrast in silver planes and shadows. 'Desire?'

He took her hand and placed it over his groin. 'Do you doubt the evidence of your own touch, your own eyes? I want you, Elene.'

His mouth captured hers and his tongue penetrated its innermost secrets while his hand pressed her more firmly over his groin. She allowed her tongue to play with his—tangling, retreating and moving forward, while all the while, he grew ever harder against her.

He placed little kisses along the line of her jaw. 'Well?'

'I believe you,' she whispered and drew back.

'Are you stopping the play?' he growled against her ear, sending a fresh tingling down her spine.

She pretended to consider, pressing her hands against the broadness of his chest. She could feel the tautness of his nipples under the linen cloth of his tunic. 'Is that what this is—play?'

He half closed his eyes and threw back his head,

revealing the strong column of his throat. 'Be careful or this will be over before we truly start.'

Her fingers stilled. A sense of power roiled through her. Her touch excited him and was sending him teetering on the edge.

As suddenly as the thought came, it vanished. She'd enjoyed this teasing play part when she'd been with Nerian. It had been the coupling where she'd failed. The words stuck in her throat, as a little voice whispered at the back of her brain—Hafual was different, and she should take the chance. 'What might this be?'

'The lady requires a demonstration.' His hand moved her hair from her temple before he gently kissed it, sending little flames radiating outwards. 'Very well, shall we begin?'

His mouth returned to hers and suckled before moving along her jaw to nibble at her earlobe. Round and round until she looped her arms about his neck to keep from falling. His hand held her firmly against him, pushing their groins together. Each new touch sent a fresh wave of heat thrumming through her, causing her back to arch.

His hand gently pushed her down on a bed of soft and dry leaves. 'Better here on the ground.'

He loomed over her, taking off his tunic. The scars on his body were silver-white in the starlight. His hands undid the cloak before skimming the contours of her body over the linen under-gown which she wore, a feather-light touch which quested rather than demanded. Her breasts arched forward to meet his questing hand. When he encountered her hardened nipples, he made a satisfied noise in the back of his throat.

He slowly traced the outline her breast, fanning out

from the nipple and then circling around back to it. She went completely still. His thumb and forefinger returned to the nipple and rolled it until it hardened to a point. Then he lowered his mouth and suckled, his tongue lapping the nipple over the linen. The cloth turned translucent, revealing the rose hue. He turned his attention to the other breast and repeated the exercise. When her back arched upwards, the damp cloth rasped her sensitised skin, sending a fresh wave of heat through her.

She twisted her fingers in his hair as his mouth returned to her nipples. Her body bucked upwards seeking his hardness and relief. She moved against him and the cloth which was between them. Round and round went his mouth until she exploded in a haze of stars. She heard a cry and knew it came from her throat.

When the world righted, he skimmed his hands further down her contours until he reached the bottom of the gown. Understanding her mute plea, he drew it gently upwards, stroking her skin with the back of his thumb until the heat built within her again and she knew she wanted him inside her, not just over her and against her.

'Please,' she whispered, tugging on his shoulders and then his trousers. He gently pushed her hands away, undid his trousers and shucked them off. His arousal sprang free. Large and rampant. She put out her hand to touch his velvet hardness and then remembered the coupling pain. 'Will it hurt?'

'Not if you are properly prepared.' He placed a finger against her mouth. 'I want to make it right for you. I want you to enjoy this.'

'I want to.' She forced her body to still, digging her

fingers into the dirt as she remembered what Nerian had said to her about not moving.

'Move against me. I like it,' Hafual rasped in her ear, capturing her hand and raising it to his mouth.

'You do?'

'You have a lot to learn, wife of mine.'

His fingers hovered over her nest of curls at the apex of her thighs and then plunged into her innermost folds. Stroking her. Slowly and then increasing ferocity until all she knew was those questing fingers.

'Put me where you want me,' he said in a hoarse voice, his breath tickling her ear. 'I can feel your wetness. You are ready and so am I.'

She nodded and opened her thighs.

The tip of him nudged her and drove deep within her, filling her entirely without the slightest hint of pain. Slowly she began to move with him. The world around her exploded as they rocked back and forth.

He finally gave a cry and collapsed down on her. She brought her arms about him and held him tight. Now she understood why her sisters appeared to enjoy the act.

What had passed between them was a world apart from what she'd experienced with Nerian. Then it had been frantic with him fumbling at her clothes and pressing into her until she wanted to weep with pain. He had taken her cries of agony for enjoyment. She silently prayed that Hafual would not turn away from her as Nerian had done because she knew she wanted to experience this again.

Hafual slowly drifted back to earth. What he had experienced rocked his very being. He had not expected it to be like that. He'd guessed she was not a virgin from the gossip which had swirled about her. From her earlier skittish reactions, he suspected Nerian had taken her too roughly. He wanted to murder Nerian for disappointing her and he also wanted to wipe all memories of the man from her. The fierceness of his feelings surprised him.

He brushed Elene's hair back from her temple before rolling off to one side of her and staring up at the black branches silhouetted against the sky. He took several steadying breaths. This marriage was not going to become like the one he'd had with Svala. This time he was not going to utter he loved her over and over again until the words had no meaning. He could still hear Svala's taunt—*'If you truly love me, choose me, not the changeling child'*—and then her running out of the hall with Narfi's scream of terror as he tumbled towards the glowing embers. He'd chosen to save his son from harm, rather than follow her. Later he'd found her broken body at the base of the cliff. Everyone said she slipped. He allowed them to think that and sometimes he even believed it. He locked the thoughts down deep inside him. He would keep his past from her. 'We should go back.'

'Must we?'

'I don't want you to catch cold.' The excuse sounded pathetic. To make up for it, he ran a hand down her flank. His body began to stir again, but he could see the streaks of grey in the sky. Dawn would be coming soon and they would have to go back. 'Next time, I promise you a soft bed, rather than leaves on the ground. More enjoyable, I promise.'

She raised herself up on her elbow. Her hair fell over

her face, hiding her expression. 'No one can say that this marriage wasn't properly consummated.'

He tilted his head to one side. Something panged within him—was this all that joining was to her? A consummation. A stab of jealousy went through him. She harboured feelings for her old lover, Nerian. He wanted to wipe all memory of the man from her. He didn't know what was going to happen when she encountered him in Ludenwic. He frowned and forced the thoughts away. This was supposed to be a simple meeting of bodies, but there was something more to it. He screwed his eyes, hating that sense of vulnerability. 'Was anyone ever going to say that? Would I have allowed that?'

She hugged her knees to her chest. Her blond hair had worked free from its braid and splayed out around her like a shimmering curtain. 'I suppose not. An irrational fear. Must do better.'

He put a finger under her chin and raised her face so he could see it in the dim light. 'I refuse to allow my wife to be humiliated. Ever.'

'I understand.' She wrenched her chin away and smoothed her gown down before wrapping the cloak about her body. 'We should go. Narfi will wake soon.'

He sensed her pulling away but knew he'd said too much already. Everything was far too new and raw. All he knew was that he enjoyed her and wanted to spend more time with her. He could not commit to more than that. He knew where overcommitment led.

Svala's pale face rose in front of him and her accusations about ruining her life rang in his ears. It was on the tip of his tongue to explain. He wanted to think Elene would understand that Svala had destroyed much that was good and caring within him. He had little left to give.

'Yes, Narfi will wake soon.'

Neither moved.

A distinct bark rang in the air, followed swiftly by a howl. Hafual grabbed his sword, debating whether he should leave her there. She'd be safe enough in this glade.

'Bugge, right on cue.' Elene laughed. 'Something has upset her. Narfi has probably woken up and she is worried. She takes her duties seriously.'

Hafual put a hand on her sleeve, silently cursing that he'd allowed his desire for her to overcome his duty to the men. He knew the risk of bandits, but he had thought they would attack before now, if they were going to attack.

'Is there something wrong, Hafual?' She put her hand against his cheek. 'You are looking very serious suddenly. I swear to you it will be Bugge calling me to look after Narfi.'

'I don't like that sound,' he admitted and decided to give her a small version of his fears. 'Caution is necessary in these circumstances.'

Her eyes became big in the grey light of dawn. He wished there was an easier way of putting it. He wished he hadn't dismissed her fears earlier.

Another unearthly howl filled the early morning air. Something had gone terribly wrong at the camp. And it was all his fault. They could have pressed on and arrived at the abbey after dark. He could have taken the chance that they would open the doors to a Northman and his family. He should have listened to

Elene's counsel that Narfi was a better traveller than he seemed to be.

'What are you saying?' she said, putting a hand to her throat.

'I think there might be trouble which will require my attention.'

Chapter Twelve

The sound of rough unfamiliar voices, demanding to know where the gold was hidden, echoed in Elene's ears as they approached the clearing where Hafual had insisted they make the camp. The knots in her stomach grew. Her worse fears were true. Somehow, the guard had been overpowered and Hafual's men were under attack, or rather, from the rough Mercian voices, they had finished fighting and were now being robbed.

'Bandits don't attack well-armed war bands.' How hollow Hafual's earlier boast sounded. And she knew better. She knew the strength of the war band Nerian led years ago.

But she'd been the one to draw him away when his sword arm was required. For what? Her desire to consummate the marriage. If he'd been there, those bandits would now be dead and Narfi would be safe. She'd seen him fight before and knew he was one of the best warriors in Mercia. Everyone said so.

She bore some of the blame for this debacle. She'd agreed to go with him, neglecting the fact that her first duty was towards his son. And she wanted to put it right. She needed to make sure that Narfi was fine.

A loud crack of metal hitting flesh followed swiftly by Bugge giving a spine-chilling howl. Her knees went weak, and she wanted to run in the opposite direction except she also knew she had to get to Narfi. She had to keep the boy safe. She started forward but Hafual shook his head and motioned for her to stay where she was.

'What is going on?' she whispered.

Hafual shook his head. 'Bandits, I think. A disturbance of some kind. My men appear to have been caught asleep. A basic error.'

'But you woke that man up. You said—'

'Turns out I can make a mistake, my lady.' He inclined his head. 'You must forgive me, but I will wait for the lecture until after we have ensured the safety of my son.'

She was back to being a lady and she searched his features for any sign of softening or warmth. 'He was supposed to be a good warrior, wasn't he?'

'He may wish he'd obeyed my request before the night is out. Or else he might be dead, cut down in the first attack.' His brow furrowed. 'We don't know, my lady. It is useless to speculate.'

A shiver went through her. How many others might be dead? Or wounded? Or worse? And all because she wanted to lie in Hafual's arms. 'Don't say that.'

'I thought you wanted the truth, my lady. Always.' His lip curled. 'Or is it only when I mouth pretty things?'

Elene noticed the formality. The intimacy of only a few breaths ago had vanished, just as it had in a different way with Nerian. She closed her eyes and willed the disappointment to go. 'The truth is preferable. I'm surprised it happened. I had thought...'

'Bandits are known to operate in this area, but I took a calculated risk as I had not had trouble with them before.' He stilled and listened again. 'The night watchman will never hear the end of this. These are amateurs.'

Amateurs? He was trying to calm her down.

'We could have made the abbey if we tried.' Elene hated how her voice rose on the last word. 'Don't deny it.'

'Abbeys have refused me sanctuary before if I have arrived after dark. I had no wish for that to happen when I was with my wife and child.'

'Why did you take me away from the camp?'

He put a hand on her arm. 'I wanted to seduce you because your kisses intoxicated me. Easier in the green wood than with churchmen nosing about.'

'I see,' she said, trying to ignore the hard lump of fear in her stomach.

'You had my sword arm. You were in no danger. You are in no danger. Currently you will be in no danger if you obey me.'

'But your son might be in danger and that is all that matters.'

He stood still for a long breath. 'Thank you for reminding me. Undoing time is beyond my capabilities, my lady. Please understand that.'

Elene heard the heavy irony in his voice which failed to mask the pain and fear. He was as worried as she was but was trying to comfort her.

She put her hand on his arm. 'We will save him, Hafual.'

He shrugged it off. 'Don't start predicting the future. Please.'

'We need to think straight. That is what Ansithe said

before we faced the raid.' She attempted a feeble laugh. 'You are probably wishing you had her here instead of Useless Elene as she and Cynehild used to call me.'

'She has the reputation of being a good fighter, but you have other talents.'

Elene's stomach knotted. 'The only weapon I have is my eating knife.'

'It is good that I brought my sword with me.'

'Did you think this would happen?'

'I dislike getting caught out. I've learned my lessons, my lady. However, my men have obviously ignored them.' Hafual crouched down and drew a rough plot of the campsite in the dirt. 'Luckily, the bandits will not know we are here. We have the element of surprise on our side. Depending on what we see, we split up—you rescue any of my men who were bound while I distract and try to take on their leader.'

Elene swallowed hard. 'The last time... I had to go on the run...'

'Last time, your opponents were warriors disguised as outlaws, sent deliberately to stop you. This time it will be something different.' He used a finger to lift her chin, forcing her to stare into the deep pools which were his eyes.

She swallowed hard. He was asking her to trust him. Something she found difficult to do, even after what they had shared a little while earlier. 'You sound very certain.'

'Stop borrowing trouble. My men are excellent fighters, their skill honed this summer in fighting the Hwicce, if they have the chance. The key to success is giving them the chance.' He gestured towards the map. 'Do you want to help, or do you wish to remain here, safe?'

He was giving her the option again. If she remained here, she wouldn't know what was going on with Narfi. She had a duty towards that little boy. And she wasn't going to think about Hafual.

'Safety is a matter of perception.' Elene crouched beside him and stared at the rough map.

'Leave it to the warriors to finish the job once you have freed the men.'

She shook her head. 'Once I free the men, I will go to Narfi. Your boy matters. I won't have him frightened or held hostage. I suspect with all the barking, Bugge is holding them at bay.'

'They won't want to tangle with Bugge's teeth.'

Silently she prayed no one had harmed the dog. 'She's a brave dog. She will be worried, but she knows her duty. As do I. Ne—' She stopped and decided speaking about Nerian would be awkward. 'I'm scared.'

Hafual squeezed her hand and noticed how cold it was. His estimation of Elene went up. 'Trust me?'

'I want to.'

'Trust my sword arm at least.'

Her lips moved upwards. 'I can do that.'

He resisted the urge to kiss her. Tonight, he'd been far too intent on seducing Elene. Now his son was in danger. He'd failed the mother and now he was continuing to fail the child. The knowledge tasted sour in his mouth. He offered a prayer up to any saint or indeed any god who might be listening that Narfi would be spared and that Elene would not suffer either. His growing feelings for her frightened him far more than the handful of outlaws who had managed to overpower his men.

'Thank you. Keep low and keep out of sight. Do not

go to the covered cart until there is a lull.' He mentioned several other things he suspected she knew about keeping safe, particularly during a sword fight, before drawing a breath.

Her lips turned up into a sweet smile. 'I am hardly likely to put myself in the middle of a sword fight but thank you for caring about me.'

'Narfi would be upset if something happened to you,' he said carefully.

Elene cocked her head. 'What are they shouting about now?'

Hafual heaved a sigh of relief. She'd pointedly changed the subject. His feelings towards her could remain hidden for a while and perhaps for ever. He knew how Svala tried to manipulate things with appeals to his great love for her until what had been love had become something else.

'Asking for gold and for someone to remove the savage wolf from the door or they will do it for them.' Hafual shook his head.

'They still gained control of your men. Be careful, Hafual.'

His lips turned up into a smile which made her knees feel weak. 'Go steadily, Elene. Much depends on your stealth.'

Elene attempted to move around the outer perimeter of the site without cracking any twigs or stumbling over any rocks, in general doing something which caused the bandits to realise that they no longer held an upper hand. Her stomach hurt from the knots. She tried to concentrate on the task at hand, rather than thinking about how she'd failed Narfi or indeed everyone. She'd been the one to take Hafual away.

Her foot stepped on a twig. She froze, glanced over to Hafual, who gave her a thumbs up and gestured for her to move on.

At Hafual's gesture, she slowly moved closer to the campsite. Hafual's men were corralled into a small group at one side with their arms bound. One of Hafual's men, the man whom Hafual had said to take the watch, lay on the ground, clearly injured and possibly dead. The five bandits regarded Bugge, who was guarding the covered cart, alternately growling and lunging at the motley group of men if they tried to get near the cart's single opening.

In the rose-tinted dawn, Elene made out the maid-servant carrying Narfi behind Bugge. She heaved a sigh of relief. The little boy appeared unhurt. Her arms ached to hold him.

'Easy now,' the leader of the outlaws said, turning his face with a great purple scar running from his jaw to his temple towards the cart. 'Do what I say, and no one will get hurt. Give me the gold and we will be nice and easy like.'

He attempted to go around Bugge, who lunged forward, snapping her jaws, nearly connecting with his leg. Elene silently cheered Bugge on. 'I want that wolf dead. Do I have to shoot it full of arrows myself?'

The members of the gang guffawed, and someone handed him a bow. Elene gritted her teeth and continued to make her way around to where Hafual's men were, rather than going to Narfi or Bugge's aid. She had to trust Hafual.

Stepping on a twig in the undergrowth, she froze and held her breath. One of Hafual's men half turned towards her. She put a finger to her lips and withdrew the eating knife. He nodded and held out his bound wrists. She started to cut through the rope, all the while praying that Hafual could rescue Narfi before it was too late.

'Give me another arrow. The damned wolf won't stay still,' the scar-faced leader said with a snarl. 'We have wasted enough time here. We are going to take whatever gold is in that cart now.'

Hafual roared, crashing through the undergrowth with his sword held aloft. The man froze. Hafual continued his run, swinging his sword. With one slice, he knocked the bow out of the man's hands and sent the arrow flying up into the trees where it stuck in a branch. 'Not today, you won't.'

The man's mouth dropped open. 'Who? What?'

Hafual kicked the man's legs out from under him and sent him sprawling on the ground. 'You are making it too easy.'

'It's a Northman,' someone shouted and started to run. 'We are in for it now. Told you that something didn't seem right about this here set-up. It was like they wanted to be attacked. A trap. How many times have I told you…get in and get out.'

'There's only one of him. The rest are otherwise occupied. We outnumber them. Hold fast, boys,' the leader called from where he was on the ground.

'Next time, you should ask before you attempt to rob one of King Ceolwulf's men.' Hafual charged forward and engaged the leader, kicking him to ground, and pointed the sword at the man's neck. 'Who dares me to finish you off?'

Bugge barked loudly and surged forward, snapping at the men. And the man twisted to the right and grabbed a sword as Hafual lost concentration for the blink of an eye.

'Seems like that dog did me a favour.'

'Shall we have at it, then?' Hafual swung his sword.

Elene quickly cut the knots and managed to get the first man's arms undone. He rapidly started on the others while the outlaws' attention was turned towards Hafual and the fight.

Hafual pivoted and blocked a charge from another assailant, knocking the axe out of the man's hand but not before the axe had connected with Hafual's shoulder. Elene could see why Hafual was respected at court. He was magnificent to watch.

'Two against one is hardly sporting.' He brought his sword hilt down on the leader's arm, causing the man to drop the sword. Hafual kicked it away towards one of his now free men.

The leader immediately cowered. 'I didn't mean… I didn't know… This was supposed to be a simple robbery. One single covered cart, hardly any guards.'

'You should study the land better before you attempt such a thing.'

His men roared and, freed from their bonds, joined the affray. The outlaws did not appear to know what had hit them. They started scrabbling and then rapidly surrendered.

Elene went over to the covered cart where Bugge licked her hand. Bugge appeared none the worse for her adventure. She took Narfi from the trembling maid and buried her nose into his skin, savouring the little-boy smell.

'Your Far is doing an excellent job,' she whispered.

Narfi clapped his hands and crowed with delight.

Hafual made rapid work of the remaining would-be assailants, ensuring their surrender.

He dispatched three of his men to go to their lair, telling them it was their chance to redeem themselves after the pitiful performance. The men bowed low and took the youngest bandit with them to lead the way. Elene sensed an eagerness in their eyes before they departed. The men pledged to return victorious. Surprisingly the bandit was eager to cooperate, claiming in a loud voice he'd been held against his will.

The unfortunate night watchman appeared to be near death. Elene handed Narfi back to the maid and retrieved her medical supplies, intending to help.

'My lady, I was so worried when I woke and you weren't there,' the maid said, catching her sleeve.

'Lord Hafual and I went for a little walk.' Elene narrowed her eyes. Hafual was holding his shoulder in an awkward position while he directed the clearing up of the incident. The leader now lay on the ground, next to the night watchman. Hafual gestured to her to come over when she held up her medical supplies.

'It doesn't look good for either of them,' he said.

'You want me to save the man who tried to kill you?'

'He should face justice, but work on my man first.'

She knelt beside the hapless night watchman. He had lost a lot of blood but remained breathing. Drawing on her training, Elene worked on binding up the wounds. She rocked back on her heels. 'If we can get him to an abbey where there is a hospital, he has a chance of healing properly.'

'More than I deserve.' The man groaned and apologised again for falling asleep and putting everyone in danger.

Hafual put a hand on the man's shoulder. 'An error you won't make again.'

The man pledged his loyalty and Hafual explained that he should look to healing first. Elene was impressed that Hafual kept his voice low and spoke in a reasonable tone. The man's face became wet with tears, and he called out for blessings on Hafual's head.

She'd half expected him to take his anger out on the man and his near-fatal lapse. She could remember how angry Nerian had been after they were running for their lives. Mentioning him though would not be a good idea. Hafual might have thought she was comparing him with Nerian, and while the Wessex warrior was competent, she knew Hafual had been the only one who could have saved them today.

Something of her confusion must have shone on her face because Hafual smiled. 'Why should I punish this man when he will relive this night every day of his existence? My son is safe. My men are safe. We have rooted out a band of dangerous criminals in the bargain. A good morning's work when you stop to consider it.'

'I'm surprised. I know about your reputation as a hard warrior.'

'Mercy is important, Elene,' Hafual said in an undertone. 'I learned that the hard way. This man, provided he heals properly, will want to repay his life debt and I intend to give him that opportunity.' He gestured towards the bandit leader, who now lay still. 'I've no pity for the real culprit but will see the body is disposed of.'

After the men had returned laden with silver, jewels and swords from the bandit's lair and the remain-

ing bandits were secured, Elene brought Narfi over to
Hafual, who was finally sitting down on a rock, staring out at the scene rather than speaking to one of his
men. 'Here is someone who wants to say thank you.
He has been saying your name over and over.'

Narfi clapped his hands and kicked his legs, crowing about his Far beating the bad men.

'Give him here, Elene. I want to see him.' Hafual
held out his hands and Elene passed the boy to him.

Hafual took one of the brooches which the bandit
had worn and fastened it to Narfi's tunic. 'Because you
were brave, my son.'

Narfi put his arms about Hafual's neck and pressed
his face with great sloppy kisses. 'Far kill bad man.'

'That I did, son. That I did.' Hafual blinked rapidly
and hugged him to his chest for a timeless breath before holding him out to Elene again.

'Have him back before I drop him. He wriggles. I
don't want him to get injured on my account.'

'Little boys do like their freedom.'

Elene took the boy back; he wriggled free and toddled off towards where Bugge sat, lisping all the while
about his Far and the bad men. He proudly showed the
brooch to the maidservant, who clapped her hands.
Bugge barked along with Narfi's song, adding a joy-
ful counterpoint noise. The effect lifted Elene's spir-
its no end.

'He loves that brooch. Such a kind thing to do.'

'My blood ran cold when I think of what nearly
happened to him.' Hafual ran a hand through his hair.
His right shoulder was hunched up far higher than his
left. He crossed his arms as if daring her to mention

that he might have been injured in the fight. 'Maybe Asida was right, and I should not have brought him.'

'Being at Wulfhere's Clearing is hardly any guarantee of not being raided,' Elene said quietly before he suggested returning to Wulfhere's Clearing and leaving them there. If he did that, they would be back to the same problem of Pybba's potential influence over King Ceolwulf.

'True.'

'If we had been here instead of out there on a walk…' she said.

He put his fingers over her mouth. 'There is no telling what could have happened. We could have been captured. You can drive yourself insane if you start worrying about what might have been. Put your face forward and stop second-guessing about things which did not happen. We saved people because we went for a walk together.'

Elene forced a smile. Hafual spoke a certain amount of sense, but she kept feeling like she should have been there. She knew how quickly these things could happen. 'Now you are trying to make me feel better.'

'As a leader, you have to be able to delegate. The man who failed in his watch has paid a high price for his failings.' Hafual circled his right shoulder, wincing as he did so. In the rose light of dawn, Elene could see a distinct paleness about his lips. Whatever he'd done to that shoulder, he was overdoing it.

'We will get him to the nearest abbey and medical attention.'

'The ealdorman in these parts will have some explaining to do. Ceolwulf takes a dim view of banditry on the Watling Street Road.' Hafual frowned. 'Before I left, Ceolwulf swore to me that the problem was solved thanks to Pybba.'

She signalled to the maid to look after Narfi and Bugge. The maid stopped talking to the men and went over to the toddler.

Elene gestured towards the cart. 'Before any of that, I am going to see about your shoulder.'

He shrugged, but his lips were blue. 'Other people require fussing first. I know what I am doing with it. I've dealt with such injuries before.'

'Even so, it needs tending to.' Elene stepped in front of him and prevented him from moving. 'You are carrying it awkwardly. I must insist as...your wife.'

'I do like a masterful woman.' He slid his good arm about her waist and dropped a kiss on her lips. Elene noticed everyone was looking at them but pretending to tidy up the campsite in preparation for departing.

She put her hand on his chest. 'What are you doing?'

'Obeying you but with a little added reward.'

She rolled her eyes. 'You are trying to distract me. It won't do. I am resolved to examine that shoulder before I do anything else.'

'I refuse to apologise.' He sobered and his arm released her. 'What we shared should not be only for one night. Next time we will be in a bed without bandits to interrupt.'

She bent her head, aware her cheeks burned bright. 'You are doing this deliberately.'

'Deliberately? Are you asking for another kiss, sweet Elene?'

'It won't stop me. I will examine your shoulder. You are not getting away from it through flirtation.' She led the way to the covered cart and had him sit down. Under the cloak he wore, a bloodstain showed on his tunic. Parts of the cloth stuck to his back, and she cleaned the wound with the herb treatment Father Oswald and she had developed. It appeared straightforward enough and not very deep, but it was the same shoulder he'd complained about before. He needed a few weeks of rest.

Hafual winced when it went on. 'Stings.'

'Doing its work, then. I fear you will be adding another scar. But no training or sword fights for the next few weeks. You have to give it a chance to heal properly.'

'I will try to remember that for the next time the bandits come calling. "Sorry, boys," I'll say. "My wife has proclaimed I'm not to fight today."'

'We shouldn't run into any more bandits. Not in Ludenwic. King Ceolwulf has better control of the countryside than that.'

'A king is only as good as his comitatus.'

'Which is why you must rest that shoulder.'

Hafual reached for the clean tunic she retrieved from one of the trunks and put it on. Clothed, his back did not appear as twisted as it had done. But it remained injured. 'Now that you have finished fussing, can you let me go? We need to get my man to the abbey.'

'You have lost some blood, Hafual. One would think you are little older than Narfi with the way you are acting. Ignoring a problem doesn't make it go away. This should have been dealt with sooner.'

He rolled his eyes. 'There is too much to be done. These bandits are not quite the amateurs I considered them to be earlier.'

She set the ointment down. 'Do you think they were sent to attack us?'

He shrugged. 'Even Pybba could not have known where we'd stopped.'

'We should have pressed on to the abbey and stayed in the guest house.'

'It was too far for Narfi. If we were being followed, they would have taken advantage of the dark road closer to the abbey and the gates would have been shut.' He caught her hand and raised it to his lips. 'Admit it. You enjoyed our night under the stars.'

A flash of anger went through her. He seemed to have a pat answer for everything. 'We are married. We are supposed to share such things.'

The lights danced in his eyes. 'We did and very satisfactory it was too.'

'That is not what I meant. You are trying to distract me. The abbot would have opened his gates to us.' She slammed the bandages down. He was treating her like she was simple-minded. 'I deserve the truth, not flirtation.'

He turned on his heel. 'I expect unquestioning loyalty in all things from my wife, Elene.'

'And I expect my husband to trust me,' she called back.

'Sometimes trust has to be earned.'

Elene concentrated on putting her medical supplies away and tried to ignore the growing pit of anger in her stomach. There was being loyal and then there was blind obedience when she had no idea about the truth. She could do the first, but not the second.

Chapter Thirteen

'You bested the bandits who have been terrorising this area? Truly?' Abbot Wilfrid's eyes bulged, and his hands stilled on his rosary beads. The abbot sat like an inquisitive owl on his overstuffed chair in the abbey's antechamber. 'How?'

'Bandits are seldom a match for trained warriors,' Hafual said, tensing his body for rejection as he explained what had happened.

The abbot was sure to refuse his request, and despite counselling him on what to say, Elene was being less than helpful. She'd declared her intention to remain in the cart with Narfi until Hafual explained matters to the abbot. The priest in charge of the infirmary refused her leave to go to the infirmary until after he had sought Abbot Wilfrid's permission.

It would take less time if he went alone was the message she sent back when he'd dispatched one of his men with instructions for Elene to come into the abbot's antechamber with him.

The stubborn woman was forcing him to do this interview alone while she stayed in the cart, looking after

Narfi. Punishment. Expecting him to go on bended knee and beg for her help when he made a mess of things like he normally did with priests. He could never find the words, despite Brother Palni giving him help time and again. *Ask for forgiveness.* What had he done this time which needed forgiving?

Normally Hafual would rather gouge his eyes out than discuss matters of this nature with an abbot. He found such men to be condescending, often treating him as if he were all brawn and no discernible brain, only to be tolerated because of his proximity to King Ceolwulf. In the past he'd always sent Brother Palni or Father Oswald to request accommodation or assistance from any abbey or monastery. But this time, he had no one else. One more reason to be annoyed at Elene and her stubbornness. There was a certain order to things.

'A little matter, Abbot. All in a day's or in this case a night's work.' Hafual gave a laugh which sounded very forced to his ears and silently cursed having to deal with difficult priests who judged and found him wanting.

'You might consider it a little matter, Lord Hafual,' Abbot Wilfrid said with much sucking of his teeth and the infernal clicking of the rosary beads he carried. 'But we here at the abbey consider it a matter of great import. I, for one, should like to inspect the bodies, to make sure.'

'We brought the bodies for burial…they are in the courtyard whenever you are ready,' Hafual said before Abbot Wilfrid started to lecture him on the Christian way to do things. Those men had been intent on robbery combined with murder. 'I…that is, my wife explained even though they were imperfect men, they should have a Christian burial.'

'Your Lordship mistakes me.' The abbot's laughed boomed out. 'Cross purposes. I and the rest of my brothers have been praying for months for relief from those who prey on churchmen. Our ealdorman promises but is far too busy in Ludenwic with the court to do anything. I want to be certain that these are the men. The leader is an ill-favoured fellow with a great scar across his cheek. He delights in removing churches of their offerings and holy water.'

'The corpse does have a scar across his face. You are more than welcome to confirm his identity.'

Hafual led the way to where the bodies were laid out. Abbot Wilfrid crossed himself and said a loud prayer for the repose of the bandit's soul.

'But I suspect he will burn in hell,' the good abbot said with an overly pious look on his face. He then winked.

Hafual noticed Elene's blue eyes watching him from the cart and retained control of his features. Priests like soothsayers were men set apart. He would never be able to understand them or their humour.

'Something has been done,' he said, gesturing to the corpses. 'They need a burial as I was disinclined to leave them for the crows. Neither did I wish anyone to doubt what had happened in that clearing.'

The abbot rested his chin on his pressed together fingers. 'We are very grateful, Lord Hafual, but I must confess I expected no less from you. We have followed your exploits, particularly this summer with the Hwicce.'

'I had no idea you knew who I was.'

'King Ceolwulf mentioned you the last time he graced us with his presence. Your friend Brother Palni is a great friend to the abbey. He always stops on his travels. I would hate to think you might feel that this house would be unhospitable to you and therefore I must conclude you put yourself and your family in danger to save us from this scourge. The Lord works in mysterious ways, Lord Hafual.'

'Mysterious ways indeed.' Hafual clenched his jaw. He'd been an idiot—putting everyone at risk because he'd considered the abbot would refuse him like others had before when he'd arrived late, tired and footsore. He always asked to be treated like an individual and now he was guilty of doing the same thing to the abbot. He'd never given the abbot the opportunity to say yes.

'If I might leave my man here at the infirmary...' Hafual gestured to his injured man and then produced a handful of silver. 'I am happy to pay. I've no wish to burden the abbey.'

Abbot Wilfrid threw up his hands. 'We are happy to do our duty with your man. A Mercian warrior in need will be looked after here. Our pleasure.'

Hafual put the silver in a pouch. 'Nevertheless, I will leave it at the church before we depart. Consider it a donation to your church. Use it to pray for my son's soul.'

The man watched him from under hooded eyes. 'You and your party must stay the night. Brother Palni says that we have some of the best mutton this side of the Dane-law country. He seems to think no one can cook like they do up North.'

'Always the joker, Brother Palni.' Hafual tugged at the suddenly tight neck of his tunic. The abbot and the monk were friendly? There was something wrong which he couldn't put his finger on. Something important about Palni and mutton.

'My husband and I would be delighted to stay, Abbot Wilfrid,' Elene said, materialising at his side. She gave him a brilliant smile. Hafual ground his teeth. She'd obviously been listening to the entire exchange, waiting for the opportune moment. 'Today has been an eventful day and your hospitality is legendary.'

'You are far too kind, my lady.' Abbot Wilfrid and Elene spoke for a little while about what was happening with Father Oswald and the community at Baelle Heale before she asked to be shown to the infirmary so that she could speak to the monk in charge and leave specific instructions for the injured guardsman's care.

Abbot Wilfrid expressed surprise that she wanted to be involved, but she explained about her training with Father Oswald. As they left, she glared at him as if daring Hafual to forbid it.

He watched the swaying of her gown which revealed her backside's gentle curve with hungry eyes and knew there had to be some way to heal this rift between them. The way he'd always done with Svala was through the trinkets she'd always hinted that she wanted. He was going to have to find another way with Elene.

'Thank you for the lovely meal,' Elene said, rising from the abbot's heavily ladened table. The combination of the soot from the fire and the heavy meal made her eyelids feel heavy. But she beat back the tiredness. Duty towards her patients had to come first. 'I will leave you men to discuss the latest news while I go check on the state of things in the infirmary.'

The abbot banged his goblet on the table and made a pointed cough. 'Lord Hafual, we discussed this.'

Hafual cleared his throat. 'The priest who oversees the infirmary requested that he be allowed to heal the patients as is his custom rather than having outside interference.'

The abbot made murmuring noises confirming the edict. He was sure that Elene would understand the delicacy of the matter. Elene pressed her hands on the table and struggled to contain the heavy weight which had settled on her soul. Hafual should have told her before supper.

'They belong to my household. I have a responsibility.' She hated hearing the slight trembling in her voice. Anyone who knew her well would realise how close she was to collapse, but Hafual and the abbot appeared unmoved. 'Are you asking me not to do my duty?'

'I'm sorry.' The abbot bowed his head and refused to look at her. 'Discipline must be preserved in this house.'

'Shall I go?' Hafual asked. 'I can report back to you, my lady. Put your mind at ease.'

'What say you, Abbot?'

The abbot waved a hand. 'Lord Hafual may go. They are his men.'

'You mean the priest only mentioned women visitors.'

The abbot's smile increased. 'They have proved a nuisance in the past.'

'Some people are very short-sighted,' Hafual said in a firm voice. 'Personally, I know how much my lady contributed today.'

Elene swallowed her scream and forced her fists to

relax. Hafual was trying to be kind in the face of obstinance. Someday the abbot would have to see that women could do things. 'I will check and see how Narfi and the maid have settled.'

'An excellent suggestion. But you appear to be very tired. You must sleep, Elene.'

'Bowed down with exhaustion, my lady Elene,' the abbot said, pouring himself another glass of mead. 'You must be proud of the way your husband rescued everyone single-handedly.'

Hafual, rather than defending her, merely took another sip of his mead.

I helped. She wanted to scream, but drawing on her years of training she held her tongue and marched out of the room. The abbot's ears were closed to the truth.

She clung on to her temper until after she had seen Narfi and the maid, ensuring they were well settled in the chamber the abbot had provided for them. Even in his sleep, Narfi clung to the brooch which Hafual had given him.

When she returned to the guest chamber she was supposed to share with Hafual, she gave full vent to her temper and threw her couvre-chef down on the bed before sitting down hard and kicking her boots off. One nearly missed the ewer and shocked her to her senses.

What was wrong with her? Why did she keep wishing for things she could never have? Why was it wrong that she hoped for support?

Elene paced the guest chamber where a distinct chill and musty smell had crept in. She suspected it had not been used for a long time. The furnishings were very fine but dusty.

'I helped too,' she muttered, taking off her gown and

placing it carefully on the stool. The hard knot in her centre grew. And she knew what the real trouble was— Hafual was behaving in a similar fashion to Nerian. Was she that awful at the physical act that men only required her once? Had their joining been simply to ensure they were truly married after all? It had meant more to her, much more.

The room tilted and righted itself as another wave of exhaustion passed over her. Elene pinched the bridge of her nose and tried to concentrate but none of her thoughts made any sense. She knew there was no finer feeling involved in the marriage and that his heart was buried with his late wife. His behaviour shouldn't hurt but it did. All she knew was that she wanted to be held and she didn't dare ask Hafual for that. She had her pride.

She stumbled over to the bed, curled up into a ball and waited.

Hafual stood in the doorway of the private guest chamber at the abbey, the one which was normally reserved for the bishop or visiting dignitaries. Elene lay sound asleep on the bed, her knees tucked into her chest.

Sleep healed most things. He knew how hard the day must have been on her and how well she had coped.

Ever since their disagreement this morning, he'd avoided speaking with Elene alone and concentrated on finding a way to avoid repeating that scene or worse in front of everyone. He wanted everything to go smoothly at the abbey and now she was even angrier at him because the abbot had made an idiotic decree about women in the infirmary. Surely Elene had to understand that he could not contradict the man in his own abbey even if he considered the ruling short-sighted.

He watched her sleep for a little while. She murmured something in her sleep which he couldn't quite catch but which he feared was her former lover's name. Hafual frowned. Another stab of jealousy hit him. He wanted Elene to be dreaming of him and what they had shared earlier.

It would be very easy to return to the stables and sleep there. He had done that sort of thing with Svala in the end to avoid the accusations and the fits of temper. He wanted it to be different with Elene though.

He closed the door with a soft click.

Elene's eyes blinked open, and she raised herself up on her elbow. A small frown appeared between her perfectly arched eyebrows. 'You returned. How are the men?'

'Everything is under control at the infirmary. It seems a peaceful place. The father who is in charge did take it upon himself to shout at me when I was leaving. Apparently, he will not have his charges overexcited.' His nerves tensed to see how she would take the news. Earlier, she seemed like she was about to burst into tears for no clear purpose. Svala had done that—swinging from laughing hysterically to weeping wildly, all the while making ever increasing demands of him.

'The good father objected to me earlier as well.' She pushed the braid to one side. Her eyes were less sunken in the flickering tallow light, but they retained the fragility he'd noticed at supper. 'I was only getting in the way. As if I hadn't been the one to staunch the blood and bandage him in the first place. The words hurt even though I know they shouldn't. I tried so hard.'

'The monk who is looking after the patients said what a good job whoever had patched him up to begin with had done. Probably saved his life. Different people have different views.' He watched with wary eyes, waiting for the scene.

'Not totally useless, then.' Her voice was light and carefree, but Hafual heard the raw note of pain.

'Elene—' he began, intending to tell her that she had to stop judging her worth on what others said, and then stopped. He gritted his teeth. The least said, the soonest mended. It was how he'd done his marriage with Svala—allowing her temper tantrums to subside and going forward. He'd learned the hard way that Svala mainly wanted attention, rather than any actual explanation about why things could not happen.

'He'll live and I've spoken to Abbot Wilfrid again. His gratitude seems to know no bounds, particularly as I had him look over the treasure from the hideout and it would seem they were in the habit of robbing churches. Most of it belongs to him.'

'Godless, then.'

'He's been trying for ages to get the ealdorman interested but always there was an excuse as to why he was busy. I will see if I can interest Ceolwulf into investigating if the ealdorman received bribes.'

Her eyes widened. 'Did you tell Abbot Wilfrid that? You don't want to create enemies, particularly with Pybba likely to cause trouble.'

'Deeds, not words, I said, and left at it that.'

Elene looped her hands about her knees. Her loosely braided hair fell over her shoulder. Hafual's fingers itched to undo the braid and run his fingers through the silky smoothness again. 'The ealdorman could have done more. We both know about your predecessor at Wulfhere's Clearing and what he did. We should give the recovered treasure to the abbot. I think he understands the value of coin more than most.'

'Your words, not mine.' Hafual shrugged. 'But I do agree with you. The brother in the infirmary has agreed to tend to my man until he has healed properly in exchange for a small donation like you suggested.'

Her smile trembled on her generous mouth. 'You see, I do have good ideas. Sometimes.'

His hands itched to gather her to his chest and kiss the puckered frown from between her brows. Doing that with Svala had always resulted in huge sighs and great wailing that he made her life a misery. He kept his hands rigidly at his sides. 'More than sometimes. Are you rested? Or shall I go? We have a long way to travel tomorrow.'

'You may stay.' Her voice was barely a whisper. 'I'd hardly like the abbot to remark on our strained marriage if Pybba should chance by. He would not put it down to the strange ways of the Northern ealdorman. He would use it to harm you.'

'What are the strange ways of the Northman ealdorman?' He tilted his head to one side. 'My pride can take whatever slurs you wish to confide.'

'Must you make a joke of it?'

'I'm used to them. I normally prefer it when they insult me to my face. Do you think my ways are hopeless and crude?'

'Your ways are different, not strange. I keep trying

to tell people that. You are Mercian in your heart and in your deeds.'

He went over to her and gathered her hands within his. She did not pull away. His heart lurched.

'Am I forgiven?'

'Have you done something wrong?'

He knew then he had to take a chance and explain about what truly happened earlier and why he'd insisted on stopping. 'I should have told you that I feared a bad reception and that was why I stopped early rather than pressing on. I didn't want to have to beg my wife to attempt to get the abbey's gates open. I feared how you and my son would see it. My arrogance nearly cost me many things. Please don't let it have cost me you and your arms about me tonight. Please forgive me, Elene.'

Elene listened to the humble note in Hafual's voice. He was apologising and explaining why he had decided to stop where they had. And he had been right— travelling to the abbey last evening would have taken too long and they could have been caught out in the dark.

Her body thrummed. He did want to put his arms about her. She had not completely failed when they made love. He thought she was angry with him. He wasn't turning away from her because of her limitations in bed. 'You were right though. It would have been too far for Narfi to travel. The bandits might have struck in the darkness when we were on the road and that would have been far worse.'

'Being from the North does not always make for a welcome reception, even when one is an ealdorman. Like Pybba, there are some who are waiting for me to fail. My oath is worth less than a Mercian's because I was born in the North. Therefore, I need to work harder to prove its worth.'

Elene stilled. She had not even considered that he might worry about how he was perceived, particularly as a man formerly from the North, an outsider. He always appeared confident and in charge. But it made his words yesterday more poignant. Except Hafual had proved himself worthy.

'Then you will have to keep showing them that they are wrong. Luckily, that is easy for you.'

Hafual bowed his head onto her hands. 'I thought you might be angry with me.'

'You were right—you can fight. You rescued everyone instead of running away.' She wrapped her arms about her waist, trying not think about how frightened she'd been.

'Sometimes running is the right thing to do. I am sure Nerian made the right decision when you last faced bandits.'

She held out her hand to him. The last thing she wanted to do was to discuss Nerian and what had happened that summer. Her feelings for that man seemed to belong to another time.

'We have a bed,' she said. 'And I doubt very much we will be interrupted. I think we should take advantage of the situation.'

He tilted his head to one side and gave one of his smiles which made her tingle all the way down to her toes. 'Are you making me an offer, my lady? I thought you were angry with me.'

'It seems to me that a bed will be softer than a cloak spread out on the ground. Can't have your shoulder being further injured.'

He came over to her and caught her hands, raising them to his lips. 'My lady becomes demanding. I like that.'

The warm curl started at the base of her spine. He wanted her. 'I should examine your shoulder.'

He wrinkled his nose. 'Aren't you going to trust my judgement?'

'Sometimes I want to see. Let me undress you.'

She lifted his tunic. The bandage stood out white against his skin. 'No more blood. That is a hopeful sign. I will put some ointment on it in the morning.'

'I believe you said that you wanted to undress me,' he rasped in her ear. 'There's more to undressing than simply taking a tunic off. My shoulder is much better.'

She pressed her palms against his back. His flesh was warm. 'I will take your word for it.'

'Shall I show you?'

'I would hardly like you to hurt your shoulder again.'

She moved her hands along his flesh, exploring the ridges and sinews of his body until they reached his trousers. Her hand skimmed his bulge.

He groaned. 'Shall I?'

'When I need your help, I will ask for it.'

'A masterful woman.'

She worked on the trousers tie, fumbled slightly, but managed to undo it. She pushed them down, allowing him to spring free.

She feasted on the sight of his engorged erection. She reached out her index finger and stroked him. His flesh was hot and silky smooth.

Giving in to impulse, she knelt before him and tasted him. Her tongue went round and round the head, savouring the salty sweetness of him. She opened her mouth further and took him in.

'Elene,' he rasped, burying his hands in her hair.

She glanced upwards and saw his eyes were half shut in ecstasy. A surge of power went through her. She had done this to him. She had brought this powerful warrior to his knees with her touch.

She rocked on her heels and toyed with the end of her braid. 'Shall we try out that bed?'

'You are overdressed.'

He pulled at her garments, undressing her until she stood before him in her nakedness. Finally, he undid the ribbon of her braid, fanning her hair out to become a shimmering curtain between them which allowed him tantalising glimpses of her skin. He gently pushed so that she tumbled down onto the soft bed. He stood over her, his eyes devouring her loveliness.

She used a hand to cover her nest of curls.

A very masculine smile crossed his lips, and he shook his head. 'None of that between us. No secrets. No hiding. Allow me to savour you.'

She nodded. Slowly he moved his mouth over her body, stopping to linger at her breast while his hands began to play in her nest, slipping in and out of her innermost folds, stroking her innermost nub. She became slick with longing.

Her back bucked upwards, seeking him and the release only he could give. 'Please,' she whispered.

He moved his mouth lower still. His tongue circled and probed her belly button. The ache within her thrummed to fever pitch.

His tongue followed his fingers and inexorably went lower. He drew figure eights against her innermost folds. The intensity rose and rose until she thought she'd shatter into thousands of pieces. 'Please. I need you in me.'

He slowly moved up, positioned himself between her thighs and drove forward. Her body sighed and enveloped him fully.

They began to move together, back and forth. The intensity kept building until her entire body convulsed in wave after wave of pleasure.

Slowly Hafual settled back down to earth. Elene was sound asleep in his arms. Her blond hair was spread over both their bodies. He wrapped a tendril about his finger.

Tenderness, almost akin to love, rose within him. He never expected to feel that sense of contentment and satiation that came when one intimately joined with the one person who mattered in one's life.

He struggled to breathe. Elene mattered to him. Truly and unexpectedly mattered. Not as a bride towards whom he owed some duty of loyalty but as a person who commanded more and more of his heart. The thought terrified him. He'd failed Svala and he had not been able to be the sort of husband she required. How could he hope to be the sort of husband Elene needed?

The saints and all the angels knew that Narfi deserved a better father, even though he could not bear the thought of losing that boy. His little song and the clapping of his hands about his father defeating the bad men echoed in his heart.

'Perhaps there is hope for me,' he murmured. 'Perhaps this time I can make it work.'

Elene sighed in her sleep and moved closer, her now familiar soft curves nestling against the hardened muscles of his body.

He half fancied she used the word *love* in her dream-filled murmurings. The fear which hovered on the edge of his mind clenched around his heart, making him ache.

He ran his hand down Elene's flank and wondered if he trusted her with the truth about his relationship with Svala and it made him undeserving of hoping for any part of her heart. He knew after today that he did have growing feelings for her.

He could see even now that she wasn't fully over Nerian. She'd mentioned his name in connection with the raid several times. And it was clear the hurt he'd caused remained raw. He knew better than most that there was a fine line between love and hate. But he wanted to tear his old friend to pieces for what he'd done to Elene and how he'd destroyed her dreams of love and marriage.

He closed his eyes and tried to conjure Svala's features. She was no more than a ghost to him. Instead, her features were overlaid with Elene's far more sensuous ones. He groaned.

'Tell me about her.' Elene's hand stroked his cheek.

'Svala?' he asked, his voice rising in dismay. He frantically tried to remember if he had said any of his thoughts out loud.

'You are thinking about her. I can tell when you do. You go all still.'

'Why would I be thinking about her? I made love to you.'

Her hand touched his face. 'Because I heard you

sigh the same sigh that you give when you think no one is watching you with Narfi.'

'I didn't realise I did.'

Her hand fell away. He winced. The words were far too quick.

'You can talk about her to me. I liked what I saw of her. I wished we'd been better friends.'

'That's the problem,' Hafual answered truthfully. 'Everyone liked her. They saw what she wanted them to see.'

'Except you? Behind closed doors, you saw something different.'

He watched her form in the dark and knew he had to tell her the truth. Lying to Elene was impossible after what they had shared. 'Svala was far from an easy person. She gave one side to the world and saved a far crueller side for her family...for me. It became worse after Narfi was born.'

He settled an arm about Elene and knew the words needed to come out. He needed to explain to her why he could never love her the way she deserved to be loved and why he would always fail as a husband.

'Hafual?'

Slowly and steadily, he explained about Svala, how they'd married and how the marriage unravelled after the baby died at sea. How she accused him of forcing her to have another child far too quickly. And she kept demanding reassurance of his undying love for her until he didn't know what to do or say any more, so he'd taken refuge in his work for the king. When he did return, Svala became like another person, capable of unimaginable cruelty. She would say things to get his attention, telling him that she'd tossed their baby screaming into the sea because she couldn't stand the storm gods, couldn't stand the noise, or Narfi wasn't theirs but a changeling which the wolves had left, demanding that he go out and search for the actual baby.

'A changeling? But he looks like you. He has Svala's eyes.' Elene's voice held the same confusion he'd had when Svala first proclaimed it.

'In the North, some would claim a witch had cast a spell on her, but I wondered if it was something deeper,' Hafual admitted. 'Just when I thought I had calmed her, she'd look at me and tell me that it was all a joke to see how I'd react. And that if I truly loved her, I'd understand.'

'Sometimes women have funny notions after giving birth. My stepmother did,' Elene said in a low voice. 'My sisters and I discovered her standing in front of the open door with her gown soaked with water. She caught a fever and died. Then the baby died shortly after.'

'On the day Svala died, she threw Narfi in the firepit where the embers smouldered, before running out the door, telling me to choose who I loved most—the changeling or her. By the time I'd rescued Narfi, she'd vanished. I found her body, but to this day, I don't know if she fell or if she threw herself off.'

Elene moved away from his encircling arm, and he felt like his heart was being torn apart. She had judged him. 'She did what?'

'We quarrelled over the fact I'd forgotten to bring her a trinket from court. She claimed my love for her had waned and I needed to prove my love to her. I failed, Elene.'

The simple words seemed to hang in the air and

damn him for all of his failures on that day. He bowed his head and attempted to gain strength to continue with his story.

'Brother Palni said that the earth must have given way and she slipped. Father Oswald had no hesitation burying her in the churchyard,' Elene said in a low voice.

Hafual raised his head from his hands. 'I like to think she had an accident.'

'I know she did and I'm sorry that I never knew about…about the other things.' She gave a helpless shrug. 'I was busy. Cynehild was away. I'm sorry. I didn't know about her troubles. After my stepmother, I should have thought.'

With her kind heart, Elene misunderstood his point entirely. He wasn't asking for her help or absolution, merely explaining why he had no love left in him.

He smoothed a strand of hair from her temple. 'No apologies ever. You did nothing wrong. Svala had no wish for company in her final days.'

'But—'

He put a finger on her lips, silencing her and any expression of guilt. The last thing he wanted or required was Elene taking any of the blame for what happened. 'Very few people know. I never even told Asida when she arrived.'

'You never told your sister about what happened?'

'How could I tell anyone?' he asked. 'It was as if Svala had been taken and someone else was there in her stead. I kept hoping that somehow it was all a terrible dream and I'd wake up to the family both Svala and I thought we'd have. And I did love her once.'

He choked on the last few words and his cheeks became wet. Elene held him for a long time while sobs racked his body. He didn't know why the tears poured from his eyes. Until that moment, he'd never been able to cry for her or the imagined life they'd both looked forward to back in the North country, just before he'd join the *felag* and she'd been pregnant with their first baby. He had often thought the inability to shed tears was a fundamental failing on his part, something missing in his character which proved all Svala's accusations of his extreme heartlessness correct.

Eventually the storm passed. He put Elene away from him and regained control. It was wrong of him to seek comfort when he was attempting to explain why she must never expect love from him like Svala had. He had no wish to make Elene unhappy; the last thing he wanted to do was to hurt her by making the same sorts of promises that he had made to Svala.

'Hafual,' she whispered, reaching her arms out to him. 'I—'

'Now you see why I never wanted to marry again,' he said before she could say anything about caring about him or attempting to give him absolution for what he'd done. 'I'm bad at loving, Elene. Do not ask me for more than I can give. Not for you or for Narfi. Don't make the same mistake Svala made.'

Her hands fell to her sides. 'What are you saying?'

'I don't want you to have a false idea about what we share.' His stomach ached and his heart screamed that he was making another error. He ignored it. He was doing the right thing for both of them. He refused to make any promise he could not keep. 'Promise me.'

'I promise,' she said. 'My heart remains where it has always been.'

The words thudded against him, hurting him more than he thought possible. She was trying to tell him gently that Nerian still commanded her heart. He should be glad of it, but the man most certainly did not deserve her regard.

'Then we should sleep. Morning will come all too soon.' The words were hard and callous to his ears, but necessary to keep from clutching her to his chest and demanding that she care for him. He rolled onto his back and stared up at the ceiling.

In the silence which followed, Elene stared up at the ceiling and listened to his soft breathing. After his confession, she understood him better and why he'd feared bonding with his son initially and why it had become a habit he struggled to break.

In the dark, she wondered if his heart was indeed too wounded ever to love again. Instinctively she knew he was trying to protect it, rather than her, by telling her not to love him. In nearly all ways, he might as well still love his late wife because his heart was lost to her. The knowledge hurt more than she'd like it to. And she knew she'd told an untruth about her own heart being the same as it ever was.

Right now, her heart felt like it had shattered into a thousand pieces, along with her half-formed dreams of the life they would have together. She hadn't realised how much she cared for him until he told her not to.

'Somehow I will make this marriage work,' she whispered. 'Somehow I will ensure things do not turn out the same way. I won't love you and I'll never ask you to love me or prove you love me but maybe I can carve out my own place in your life and you will learn to value me.'

She ignored her heart which screamed she already did love him and each day was giving him more of her heart. She cared about him more than she thought she would. The lessons she learned from her earlier experience with Nerian taught her that he must never guess. She was going to remain independent. She was no longer a clinging vine. She wasn't going to ask for things he could not give, but already her heart whispered she lied.

Chapter Fourteen

'Ludenwic moves to a different beat,' Hafual said when they arrived in the town after a couple more days of travel. 'Something always seems to be happening.'

Elene peeped at him from under her lashes trying to assess his mood. Since his confession two nights ago, their conversations had been mundane and orderly to the point of extreme politeness. Each avoided the subject of Svala or anything in the past.

At night, their joining was passionate, but each time, Elene was left with a nagging sense that there could be something more. She wanted more than simply desire because she knew how quickly such a thing could fade. 'I look forward to exploring the town. It has been a long time since I last visited. My father preferred to go to the royal residence at Tamworth.'

He stopped the covered cart and motioned for her to disembark. 'Easier to explore Ludenwic on foot. The streets are a regular warren and deeply rutted. But trade is the lifeblood of this place. It is why both Wessex and Mercia claim her.'

With the sun having burnt away the early morning mist, Ludenwic teemed with both Mercians and people from Wessex in the late afternoon sunshine. With the sunlight sparkling off the Thames, the entire village bustled with purpose. The market stalls were crowded with housewives buying their food, and merchants seeking to trade. The presence of a great many warriors showed that both the Wessex and the Mercian court were in Ludenwic.

Elene concentrated on the muddy ruts leading to the bustling centre around the sandy stretch of beach. The Wessex court would be staying over the river and using ferrymen to get themselves across each day if negotiations were happening. There was a legend that there had been a bridge once, but that bridge had fallen down years ago. The waterway served as a boundary between the two countries.

There was no reason why she should come face to face with Nerian. She didn't fear seeing him, but he was an added complication which she didn't need.

The strand heaved with boats and their cargo from timber and wool to more exotic goods like amber. The entire town had grown immeasurably since the last time Elene had visited. Several streets had been added and it was easier to be confused completely.

She had enjoyed the journey with Hafual and Narfi. The dull ache in her heart had ceased. With each passing day, she found another reason to appreciate Hafual. Theirs might not have been a love match but the desire was there. And she had the growing hope that she could find a way of carving her own place, and being satisfied with that, instead of wishing for the moon like her sisters always used to do when they were young.

'Will we be able to find somewhere to lodge?' Elene asked Hafual.

'Ceolwulf promised lodgings would be readily available for me when I last spoke to him.' Hafual nodded towards the strand. 'If all else fails, one of my ships will be pulled up on the strand. One of many. The spit of sand is the main reason why Ludenwic continues to be such a thriving market, despite the war. It is an easy place to land cargo. Ships come from Frankia and the North as well to trade.'

Elene shifted Narfi onto her other hip. 'How many ships do you have?'

'Ceolwulf has seen fit to allow me to trade as well as serving under him. Timber and wool mostly. These things are much needed in the North.'

'Surely they have their own sheep in the North.' Elene shook her head. 'What are you really trading in?'

'How much wool do you think it takes to make a sail? How much wood? The land is poor in the North but the hunger for ships is great. I can get better prices for these things in Birka or Hedeby than here, so I operate the ships and Ceowulf gets a percentage of the profits.'

Elene tilted her head to one side. 'Are you planning on leaving soon?'

'The year draws to a close. I will do a voyage in the spring, before the Hwicce cause trouble again, should the king permit it. Currently, I'm buying the stock in, getting ready for the turn of the seasons. I have several warehouses further off the strand. The spring markets often yield the most gold.'

She stared at him, suddenly realising that she knew very little about the man who had become her husband.

She had assumed that he was like her father—a warrior with lands—but now it seemed he controlled ships and was a merchant as well. He was in the process of building an empire.

'I'd never thought about how much wool might be needed in the North,' she admitted, trying to fathom out his mood as it had suddenly turned dark.

'Now you know. I will be gone in the spring, Elene.'

Elene glanced up into his face, trying to read his mood, but the shutters had come down over his eyes and he was back to the remote warrior, rather than the tender lover who had held her most of last night. He told her not to care about him, but she did. 'What's wrong, Hafual?'

'Why should anything be wrong, Elene?'

She shrugged. 'A feeling.'

His eyes narrowed. 'Do not start acting like Asida on me. The thing is that people only remember the times that the feelings came true, not the times that they didn't.'

'You mean I've become better at reading you and you dislike that.'

Hafual tilted his head to one side. 'Maybe I don't think you will like the answer.'

'Narfi and I are in no danger here but we've no idea if Pybba is in town or if he waiting spider-like in Tamworth,' she said. 'We should go to the royal residence and see King Ceolwulf straight away. Before we have changed out of our travelling clothes.'

'A breach of protocol.'

'But I sense this would be the correct thing. I've not seen Pybba or anyone wearing his insignia. Maybe our luck has held.'

'If it has held this long, then it will hold that much longer.' He took Narfi from her and put him on his shoulders. The little boy crowed and pulled Hafual's hair. 'See, Narfi agrees with me.'

At the sight of his simple pleasure in his son, Elene choked back the urge to say that she was falling in love with him. It was far too soon for that.

He'd explained why love was out of the question and she refused to allow him that sort of power over her. She remembered how Nerian clasped her to his chest, giving her easy promises when she'd whispered the words after their coupling. Hafual never broke his promises, her heart argued. She ignored her heart, as experience proved it very untrustworthy.

'The lodgings, it is,' she said around the proud lump in her throat.

The gatekeeper shook his head at the royal residence which they had gone to after settling Narfi in the lodgings. The royal residence was built on the stone which the Romans had left. The place was an assortment of new wood buildings combined with the old stone.

The king had gone out for a boar hunt with his courtiers shortly before. The gatekeeper had no idea when they would return. He suggested Lord Hafual return in the morning as the king's temper was uncertain after the chase. Hafual and the gatekeeper both laughed at the private joke which Elene understood to be about how well Hafual could hunt.

'Maybe your instinct was correct,' Hafual said, putting his hand under her elbow. 'We should have gone straight to the royal residence rather than getting Narfi settled in the lodgings. Next time, I will yield to my lady wife who knows what to do at court.'

Elene felt her cheeks burn. High praise from Hafual. 'My sisters always say that I make a pig's breakfast of it every time I go. Family legend.'

'Legends can be altered. Up to you to decide.' He raised her hand to his lips. 'I believe in you, Elene.'

A courtier came up and engaged Hafual in a conversation about wool and its prospects. Elene took a few steps away from the pair to give them privacy.

'Elene, it is you!' The deep voice sounded behind her, and a heavy hand descended on her shoulder as she turned towards it. 'You are a sight for sore eyes. How goes things at Baelle Heale? Same old tumbled down loveliness that I remember so fondly? Managing to stay out of trouble at court? Of course you are. You haven't had time yet. Never fear. I'm here.'

Elene froze at the sound of Nerian's butter-smooth tone. His words were singularly hurtful. Tumbled down indeed! Baelle Heale had been worn at the edges when he visited, but they had improved it.

She concentrated on breathing and had the sudden realisation that the man held little attraction for her. His voice had not caused her heart to beat faster or sadness at what might have been to well up like a great wave within her. He and what they shared belonged to her past, not her future.

'Nerian of Wessex, an unexpected pleasure. I understand congratulations are in order. Is your wife with you?'

She delicately shrugged, hoping he'd remove his hand from her shoulder. The man wore his tunic too tightly and had a specific look in his eye. She could see now what she hadn't before—he was the sort of man who had a penchant for the ladies, and it didn't matter which lady as long as her mouth was soft and her body warm. Unfortunately, Hafual continued with his conversation, oblivious to her predicament.

She twisted slightly and Nerian finally released her. 'I look forward to meeting your wife,' she said, dropping a heavy hint.

He bowed his head but slid his hand down her waist. 'Unfortunately, my bride died of a summer fever. Bad air from the marshes shortly after our wedding.'

'My condolences,' Elene said, automatically falling back on politeness while trying to twist away without causing a scene. 'I'm sure you must be heartsore at her loss.'

Nerian's eyes held a hooded look, but speculation was also there, like a hawk sizing up its next meal. 'Yes, yes, I am. She was a timid creature. We rarely had a cross word. Is your father well? And you must tell me all about Baelle Heale. I've often thought of its rustic charms and my time there.'

His eyes blinked rapidly. She doubted if he had ever understood how much she loved the place.

'My father continues to prosper. You'd hardly recognise Baelle Heale with its new barns. It is amazing what can happen when determined effort is put in. Our wool yield has gone up considerably.'

'I must take the time to visit him, then.' He captured her hand and held it for too long in his grasp, his thumb stroking the inside of her wrist, a gesture she'd once thought of as their secret signal but now suspected was something he did without thinking. 'You've only grown in your beauty, Elene. It amazes me that your father allowed you to come to Ludenwic, this notorious town. Unaccompanied.'

Elene forcibly removed her hand from his paw. The man was eyeing her up to be the second bride. Not in her lifetime. She refused to be second best for anyone. 'You may remember Lord Hafual of Wulfhere's Clearing. I believe you were friends.'

Nerian's lip curled slightly, and he gave a peremptory nod. 'Yes, one of the Northmen. A member of Moir's old *felag*. He won his estate through saving King Ceolwulf's life. Fortune smiled on him that day. How I wished that I'd been the one to rescue a king. Pity his wife died.'

Elene kept her chin up and paused dramatically. 'Hafual is my husband.'

Nerian's eyes widened. 'I had understood you remained single, Elene, waiting. We…that is…or rather there was something, but I thought it was how courtiers speak. You gave me your word, you see.'

Elene narrowed her eyes. The man had a supercilious smile on his face. All the days she'd wasted on him. As if all he had to do was snap his fingers and she'd come running. Her and her dowry. 'Why would I be waiting for anything?'

Nerian gave a careless shrug and what could only be called a calculated flirtatious smile as he leant towards her. 'A feeling I had. We were good together. I've been thinking about our time lots recently.'

Elene ground her teeth. She refused to create a scene and confirm to any courtier who might be watching that she remained unruly and incapable of displaying the correct decorum. 'It took some doing to convince my father of the merits of the match, but he approved of my choice in the end.'

'Hafual was your choice? Not foisted upon you? A marriage of convenience and unconsummated?'

'Very much consummated.'

Hafual slipped his hand about her waist and hauled her against the hard planes of his body. His mouth grazed the top of her head. Her body thrummed with anticipation, even though she knew the gesture was for Nerian's benefit and not hers. She had to wonder how much of the conversation Hafual had overheard.

Nerian raked his hand through his hair and rapidly stepped away from her. 'My mind must be in the clouds today.'

'You will give us your best wishes,' Hafual said, his face becoming all planes and angles.

'Yes, yes, of course. My best wishes. Delighted to.' Nerian hurried off into the crowd of courtiers.

Hafual's mouth twitched as if he couldn't decide whether to laugh or frown. 'An interesting encounter.'

'That man.' Elene stopped and tried to get control of her temper. 'That man used me and was going to use me again. As if he could crook his little finger and I'd fall into his arms like an overripe plum.'

'He obviously doesn't know you very well if he thinks you an overripe plum. You may pretend to be agreeable to all, but you are fiercely determined when it is required.'

Hafual's eyes crinkled at the corners. A warmth developed in Elene's middle. They were friends. And friendship in a marriage while it might not be the romantic love her heart desired was something to cultivate. Hope sprang in her breast. She could carve something out and be content with it.

'We can't be sure if Pybba has arrived or not,' she said, firmly moving the subject away from Nerian and his behaviour. 'Pybba would have made sure that everyone knew about our marriage.'

'How do you know? Nerian's remarks about our marriage were strange, and Pybba might wish to keep the union a secret until he has time to use it as a weapon.'

Elene shook her head. She was missing something vital. 'I think I may have it wrong. It wasn't that he didn't know. He was surprised that we appeared to be happy.'

'Nerian is far better as a warrior. And he made a mistake with you. He appeared to think that he could re-enter your life. You put him straight. Our marriage is more than one of convenience, something I concur with.'

Elene made a curtsey. 'I try.'

Hafual lent close so that his lips brushed her ear. 'You do more than that, you succeed.'

The tight knot she'd had in her stomach eased slightly. Maybe they could work things out after all if she kept from confessing her love for him. If she didn't make the same mistakes she had made with Nerian. All seeing Nerian had done was to stiffen her resolve to do things differently with Hafual. She was not going to wear her heart on her sleeve and accept excuses. But she knew that her love for the man was growing.

Elene was pleased to get back to the lodgings without making any more mistakes. While she had been out, the maid had made the place habitable, unpacking the various trunks. Narfi and Bugge appeared right at home amongst the toy wooden ships and swords which had appeared from somewhere.

The widow who had been out when they first arrived was delighted to see Lord Hafual again, filling him in on various nuggets of court gossip. He apparently had been kind to her after her husband died, ensuring that she was able to have these buildings and helping her set up her market stall.

'I see you don't simply patrol the outer reaches of Mercia,' Elene said after the woman had left.

'Ludenwic is an important port as well as being a boundary with Wessex. Only natural that I should spend time based here. Her late husband was part of my band of warriors.'

'And you forgot to tell me about this?'

The twinkle in his eye deepened. 'I was busy with other matters.'

She rolled her eyes. The attempt to get around her through flirtation was blindingly obvious. 'Your excuse wears thin. You keep too many secrets, Hafual. I'm your wife, not a brainless maiden.'

He sobered and raised her hand to his lips. 'I will try to do better.'

Before Elene could answer, the door banged. Hafual frowned.

'No secrets in Ludenwic,' Elene said in light tone. 'Our arrival has reached people's attention.'

Hafual opened to the door to reveal Brother Palni and Father Oswald. Father Oswald resembled a disgruntled hen. Brother Palni had particularly fraught expression on his face, the sort he wore when he'd been asked to do too many things.

'Here we find you! We must have been to a dozen places, including three ships on the strand, Hafual.'

'To what do we owe the dubious pleasure?' Hafual asked, his face becoming shuttered.

Elene's heart clenched. Both men together spelt trouble. She hurried to stand beside him. Whatever had happened, they faced it together. He moved so that their bodies briefly touched. She leant in briefly and then stood upright. 'Is there some unforeseen problem at Baelle Heale? Is my father well?'

Father Oswald fanned himself with his hand and explained that all was well at Baelle Heale and beyond with her sisters as far as he knew. Ecgbert remained chastened but he expected the steward would soon be back to his scheming ways. However, he seemed to be fearful of Lady Asida's sharp tongue and even sharper eye. Interestingly Lord Wulfgar would not hear a word against Lady Asida.

'Then why are you here?' Hafual thundered. 'What earthly reason could you induce you to come to this place?'

Father Oswald blinked rapidly. 'Your sister sent us. She appeared to think we might be needed. I was wasted, she said, at Baelle Heale and had to leave immediately.'

Hafual put his head in his hands and groaned. 'My sister wanted you away from there. I'm afraid she is angling for your father, Elene.'

Elene patted him on the shoulder. 'Your sister and my father? Impossible. He is old enough to be her father.'

Brother Palni shook his head. 'The lady was all but

pushing Father Oswald onto his donkey when I arrived back and stepped in. Oswald is far from a good traveller.'

'Brother Palni has served as my guard. We travelled almost without stopping. Asida believed I could do good work here.' Father Oswald's face crumpled. 'I put myself at your service, my lady, whatever that service might be.'

'Your service is greatly appreciated, Father.' Elene bade them to enter and called out to the landlady to provide some refreshment.

When the men had settled with refreshment, Hafual leant forward. 'I trust your journey was a profitable one, Palni.'

Brother Palni's brows lowered. 'I expect there is a good explanation for this...this tangle of a marriage.'

'Careful, Palni!' Hafual ground out, clinging to his temper by the barest of threads. Typical of the man seeking to take over. He had everything under control.

'Moir and Ansithe will be unhappy when they learn of it. Ansithe has always been determined that her youngest sister should marry for love, rather than for duty,' Palni continued serenely as if Hafual had remained silent. 'We were once members of the same brotherhood, Hafual. Why didn't you wait for considered counsel? I understand from Father Oswald you heaped dry timber on the flames of Wulfgar's drunken anger and forced the issue.'

Considered counsel? Forced the issue? Hafual concentrated on breathing deeply and remembering that the man was now a man of the cloth.

'You always did have a high opinion of yourself.' Hafual slammed his fist down the table. The tankards jumped. Elene gave him a warning look as Narfi had closed his eyes, curled up next to the dog. Hafual nodded to show he understood and lowered his voice to a furious whisper. 'Are you saying that my marriage has no legitimacy? That I forced Elene at sword point to marry?'

'If anyone did any forcing, it was my father,' Elene added, linking her arm with his.

'I did marry them, Palni, and what I said to you I said in confidence—one man of the cloth to another,' Father Oswald said. 'There is nothing wrong with this marriage. The roses have quite returned to Lady Elene's cheeks.'

Brother Palni growled and said something very impolite in his native tongue.

'I thought men of God refrained from such language,' Hafual said.

'I shall ask pardon later.'

'We arrived in Ludenwic today,' Elene said with a bright smile. 'You must stay here with us rather than finding lodgings elsewhere.'

Hafual made a considering noise and glowered. 'Must we? Surely they can stay at a church.'

'Your sister sent them, Hafual, for a reason. They are tired. As are we.'

'They should go,' Hafual said, drawing his brows together.

'We will go soon,' Brother Palni said. 'I'd hardly like to interrupt a newly married man and his bride.'

Hafual glowered at him.

'Father Oswald, why don't you and I discuss medical matters and leave Brother Palni to Hafual while I put this one to bed?' Elene picked Narfi up. 'I've no wish to bore Hafual but I could use some of your expertise. Hafual has injured his shoulder and is a terrible patient.'

Father Oswald gave Elene a grateful look. 'I believe I can spare a few moments before I go and greet some of my brothers at church.'

'Under pain of death do not tell Brother Palni the truth about our marriage,' Elene murmured as she passed him. 'The last thing I require is one of my sisters giving me a lecture when I next encounter them.'

'Agreed.' Hafual waited until he was left alone with Palni. 'You and Father Oswald should return to Baelle Heale as soon as possible. My sister has a capacity for mischief-making.'

Palni reached over and took a chunk of hard cheese. 'You always were grumpy. I think I shall stay in Ludenwic if it is all the same to you. Lady Asida can look after herself.'

Hafual ground his teeth. He could hardly explain to Palni what he'd witnessed earlier between Nerian and Elene. It had taken all of his self-control not to physically attack the man for touching her in the way he had. He had taken Elene back here with the full intention of seducing her and making her forget about that man.

'But I don't want you here. Why is it today that I keep meeting people I don't want to see like you and Nerian of Wessex?'

Palni gave a sudden impish smile. 'Might be unwise to say with you in this mood but having seen you and the lady together, marriage is good for you, better than the last one I'd say, but one should never speak ill of the dead.'

Hafual froze. How much had Palni guessed about Svala? 'Good for me?'

Palni leant back and took a huge mouthful of bread. 'Improved your temper to no end. Svala bears part of the blame for what happened in your marriage. Before you start on me, I knew the woman back in the North and in Mercia. What happened to her was God's will.'

Hafual stared at his former comrade-in-arms in amazement. 'You are full of compliments today. I expected insults.'

'You knew me before I took the holy orders. Now I see the miracles in everyday life, and your change is nothing short of a miracle.' Palni filled his cup with ale. 'Have you told her that she holds your heart? Or has your jealousy blinded you to an obvious course of action?'

Hafual put his hands behind his head. He'd made a mistake in mentioning Nerian. Palni was always too clever for his own good and he knew about Elene and Nerian's former relationship. 'What makes you say that she does?'

'I have eyes in my head.'

'Your eyes are clearly failing, then.'

Palni gave him one of his looks. 'Show her in the clearest possible way if you wish to get rid of the spectre of that man from Wessex. Her response might surprise you.'

'They've finally gone,' Hafual said, when Elene was sorting out the trunk in their bedchamber. She had retreated there after putting Narfi to bed. Since Brother Palni arrived, Hafual's time appeared to be taken up with problems and concerns as word spread that he'd arrived. Then it had been time for the evening meal, and he insisted on Brother Palni and Father Oswald staying. 'Father Oswald wanted to examine my shoulder before they left for the monastery.'

'Father Oswald wanted to make sure there was no infection. He worries.' Elene concentrated on the gowns in her trunk. Was this the sort of behaviour that Svala had complained about? It was not really Hafual's fault.

'You were quiet all evening.'

She turned away from the trunk. He was watching her much like a cat might watch a mouse. She shook her head. 'I kept thinking about my last few times at court and the mistakes I made.'

'You won't make any mistakes.'

She pulled the pins from her crown of braids. 'Little do you know. Father Oswald gave me a lecture from my father earlier.'

He caught her hand and put the pins on top of the trunk. Then he carefully undid each braid, making her hair fall about her shoulders. 'I like your hair loose. I've been thinking about it since we arrived.'

'You were too busy with your men, with everyone.' She screwed up her nose. 'That came out wrong. I was busy as well. I just doubt you had any time to think.'

He lifted her chin so she met the full force of his gaze. 'I had plenty of time to think and this is what I thought about—feasting on you.'

He lowered his lips to hers. The intensity of the kiss immediately inflamed her senses. She looped her arms about his neck and forgot everything in its carnality. The urgency of it called her passion. She moaned in the back of her throat and pressed her hips forward, encountering his rigid hardness. The fire within her burned higher.

'I want you,' he rasped. 'Like this, upright.'

'Upright?'

'Let me show you how good it can be.'

'I trust you.'

He took her hands and held them above her head while he unfastened the front of her gown, exposing her bare breasts. He took each nipple in turn into his mouth, suckling on them until a whimper escaped from her throat.

He undid his trousers and lifted her up, placed her on him.

She instinctively wrapped her legs about his waist. She knew he was deeper inside her than he'd ever been before. They rocked together until he came shuddering and she broke.

Afterwards, he carried her over to the fur-covered bed. Rather than diving under the covers, she propped herself up on her elbow to watch him undress. The flickering light from the tallow lamp made his skin shine gold shot with the silver scars.

'Are we finished?' she asked after he'd blown the lamp out.

'Hardly.' His soft laugh caused her insides to burst into renewed flames of passion.

He settled himself between her legs, moved her curls so that her inner folds were exposed to the air. 'That was merely the first course. Now I want the remainder of the feast.'

He lowered his mouth to her and proceeded to demonstrate what he meant by feasting. Each time, Elene thought the peak could not get any higher, but it did.

Until she finally tugged at his shoulders, and he entered her once again, impaling her. Together they reached a shuddering climax.

'Did Father Oswald say anything else about your injury?' she asked, much later when she lay in the circle of his arms. There had been an intensity to his lovemaking that she had not felt before. It was if he had been trying to brand her as his.

'He thinks, with rest, I will get the full range of motion back. I'm not supposed to practise any sword skills for the next few weeks.'

She softly hit him. 'Why did you not tell me that before? You should not have been doing what you did.'

'Would you have stopped me?'

'Probably.'

He leant so his mouth touched her ear. 'Are you being truthful?'

'I feel guilty. I would never have—'

'But the thought of doing that to you kept me going throughout the dull meetings about wool and rent. I'm not good at denying myself where you are concerned, Elene.'

'We could have found another way. I could have pleasured you.' Elene cupped his cheek with her hand. 'I don't want to be the cause you having to rest for longer.'

'It would appear I have married an inventive woman.'

'I just want you to heal.' She didn't dare say anything about Pybba and the poison he might pour into Ceolwulf's ear. How the prohibition against duels might be lifted if he thought Pybba would lose.

He pushed the hair from her forehead. 'A warrior always has to be prepared to fight. And I will if I have to.'

'Be careful because...' Elene choked back the words that she loved him. He had made it very clear that he didn't want her love or her concern. She had to hope for a small place in his life and be content with that, even though she knew she wanted much more.

He stilled. 'Because why?'

'Because Narfi needs a father,' she said before her unwanted love burst from her.

'That serves,' he said against her hair as his arm tightened about her.

She snuggled into the hollow of his good shoulder and tried not to think about the slight disappointment she fancied she'd heard in his voice. That was weaving dreams with clouds on her part.

Chapter Fifteen

The court, which lacked some of its usual sophistication without the queen and her retinue, hummed with a certain air of barely supressed tension the next morning. Hafual frowned, dismissing the notion as fanciful.

No danger lurked here at court, particularly as Nerian seemed to believe that Pybba was away somewhere. He and Ceolwulf enjoyed a cordial relationship based on gratitude and loyalty. He might not have been born a Mercian, but he had become one. Elene and Narfi seemed unconcerned. Elene was busy pointing out various things to Narfi, who kept asking why. Bugge had stayed with the monk and Father Oswald.

Hafual rubbed the back of his neck. Nerves about presenting Ceolwulf with his marriage. The king was sure to approve. He'd even mentioned that he thought Hafual should remarry. The nerves were an overreaction. He forced his shoulders down, wincing slightly.

'Lord Hafual, I must ask you to surrender your weapons,' the chief of Ceolwulf's bodyguard said, stepping forward and blocking their passage towards the hall.

'What sort of nonsense is this? King Ceolwulf has commanded that I be armed in his presence.'

'Orders, Lord Hafual.' The man shifted his weight from foot to foot. 'From King Ceolwulf, like.'

Hafual glanced at Elene, unable to eliminate the tiny prickle of concern. She nodded, seemly unconcerned about this development. He reluctantly handed over his sword.

'I expect it back without any scratch marks when I leave.' He lowered his voice. 'We will get this sorted, Elene. Ceolwulf has never demanded my sword or that of my men before.'

She shifted Narfi onto her other hip. 'They will be asking everyone, Hafual.'

'Will they?'

She patted his arm. 'Let's get this over with. Narfi wants to meet his godfather.'

Rather than greeting him as he normally did, the king remained sitting on his throne. 'Hafual, you have come back.'

'I wish to present my wife, Lady Elene of Baelle Heale. She carries my son and your godson, Narfi.'

The king's gaze narrowed. 'You married without asking permission.'

'The lady was willing, sire.'

Elene curtseyed and agreed with him, even going so far as to lean against him. Hafual in that heartbeat knew he should have told her how much he loved her last night, instead of simply making love to her. When they returned home, he would tell her the truth and offer her his heart, he resolved.

Ceolwulf stroked his chin. 'I understood your bride was promised to another.'

A prickle of alarm ran down Hafual's back. He had been overconfident. Pybba had been able to get word to Ceolwulf.

'A misunderstanding. Lady Elene chose me.'

'You chose to attack peaceful men on Watling Street.'

'Hardly peaceful. They attacked my camp and demanded gold. My son was in danger.'

The king made a temple with his fingertips. 'A man was killed, a peace-loving man who had done nothing wrong.'

Hafual stared at Ceolwulf before tapping his ear. 'Killed an innocent man?'

'Are you denying you killed a man?'

'The man I killed was a bandit. He had attacked my camp without provocation. He threatened my son.'

'So you say,' Pybba said with a sneer, coming to stand beside the king. 'So you say.'

'Yes, he does say,' Elene said, shouldering her way forward. Her entire being bristled. 'I was there. You weren't. The man wanted to rob us.'

The king regarded his wife. 'Lord Hafual, it would appear your wife is incapable of keeping silent. Perhaps she should learn the value of holding her tongue.'

Two bright red spots appeared on Elene's cheeks.

'I like my wife well enough as she is,' Hafual said, putting a hand on Elene's shoulder. He took Narfi from her. 'Seems to me that I should be the one who makes this choice.'

Pybba's face grew puce. 'I have it on good authority!'

'What, the same authority which meant you were determined to try to win Lady Elene's hand? A fit of pique because Lady Elene chose someone else is what this is. Lord Pybba has sought to undermine me since I first swore allegiance to you, sire. He wanted the estate so that he could claim injury against me. He cared nothing for the woman.' Haful glared at the man before turning to the king. 'I hope you will understand my reasoning for the marriage and the why of the bandit's death.'

Ceolwulf's face could have been carved from stone.

'Whose man is he supposed to have been?' Haful asked into the silence.

'Pybba's. You attacked him because of your undeclared war with the man. I will not have my ealdorman going to war with each other. The butchering must cease.'

'The man was a bandit!'

'Do you have physical proof?' the king asked in harsh tone. 'Can you show me that Lord Pybba bears false witness?'

'I left the brooches with Abbot Wilfrid,' Haful said in a low voice. 'We can send for them. I ask that because of the service I have given you.'

The king nodded. 'It can be done.'

'Then I shall go and arrange it. After which, Pybba will have to give way for trying to assassinate my character.'

'Why not ask Haful's men?' Elene asked.

'My lady, they are from the North. They pledged their loyalty to a Northman.' Pybba spat the last word. 'Ceolwulf agrees with me. It must be physical proof.'

'I'm Mercian,' Elene cried. 'My word must be worth something. I was there.'

'You, my dear, are his wife.' Pybba's smile turned

nasty. 'Wives are incapable of giving evidence for or against their husband. You are one with him.'

'Why must I be detained? Why can't I ride to the abbey and retrieve the brooches?' Hafual demanded.

Pybba and Ceolwulf exchanged glances. The king motioned for Pybba to go ahead. But Pybba shook his head. 'It is better coming from you, sire.'

The smug tone clawed at Hafual's innards.

'Lord Pybba fears that you will take your ships and leave. He believes you are attempting to create another army. He has shown me how you have stockpiled wool, Hafual.'

Hafual struggled to keep his temper. 'I explained what that was for. I believe I can open new markets in Frankia and beyond for Mercia. We discussed this.'

'You have gone behind King Ceolwulf's back. The wool will be used to raise more ships to invade this land! It is how Northmen behave, always trying to get things to their best advantage. You will never be a Mercian.'

'Lord Pybba has been drinking far too much mead,' Elene said in low voice under the cover of taking Narfi from him.

Hafual motioned for her to be silent. Pybba's accusations were baseless, but the mud could stick.

He swallowed hard and regained control of his temper. 'I am seeking fresh markets for Mercian wool, sire. You will receive part of the profit.'

Ceolwulf nodded. 'You said that but for now you will understand why I must keep you close until everything is thoroughly investigated.'

'Close?'

'I'm arresting you, pending enquiries. If you have

killed one of Pybba's men, he has asked for the appropriate punishment. I will, of course, send word to Abbot Wilfrid and ask him for the treasure.'

'If I give my word to stay in Ludenwic? Surely that is enough.'

Ceolwulf looked sorrowful. 'At this time, I must show Wessex that Mercia remains a country of laws, not lawless war bands.'

Red mist settled over Hafual's eyes. He took a step towards the king. 'I have given you my loyalty! Does it count for nothing? I saved your life! I saved your country and that counts for nothing? What sort of man are you, Ceolwulf?'

'Hafual?'

Elene's gentle voice cut through Hafual's fury. He took a step back from King Ceolwulf, who had shrunk back against his throne and appeared terrified, calling repeatedly for the guards to protect him from the madman. Hafual concentrated instead on breathing deeply and ignoring Pybba's smug look of triumph. The man must have done a deal with the abbot, and had no fears from that side, Hafual belatedly realised as the true blackness of his situation hit him. If called on, the abbot would twist and wriggle. He might even deny that there had been any brooches. Pybba had outplayed him.

'Elene,' he said in a low voice. 'Go to Palni. Get him to get you and Narfi away from here. Pybba is determined to have my hide one way or another, but I'm not going to make it easy and I'm not going to have you in danger.'

'Your shoulder remains injured. You will lose any fight.'

Hafual set his jaw. 'My shoulder is my concern.'

'I will find a way out of this, Hafual.' She hesitated. 'I promise.'

He wanted to believe her, but her promise was nothing more than whispers in the wind.

'Keep my son safe. That is all I ask.' He took what he knew would be the last look at her face and made a memory. There were far too many things to say, things he should have said when he held her in his arms.

She flinched like he had hit her. 'Why are you saying this like it is the end? Why don't you trust me to put things right? I'm not going to run away.'

'Yes, you are. You are going to run until you and Narfi are safe.

Pybba's men came and fastened chains about his wrists and ankles. Elene protested loudly.

'I'm innocent,' he roared, but Ceolwulf turned his back. 'Elene, leave now. Look after my son. I will prove my innocence.'

'I'll go.' Elene hugged Narfi tighter to her body, turned on her heel and strode away before Hafual could explain that he loved her with all his heart, and she meant the world to him, but he was a failure as a husband. He needed her to be safe. At the door, she gave him a terrible look which seared his soul.

'Move.' Someone jabbed him in the back, and he fell to his knees.

The world drained of colour and Hafual knew he'd lost her and the life he'd hoped to have with her. She hadn't been the one making halls in the clouds—he had been. He had known what Pybba was capable of, and he'd exposed her and her entire family to the man.

'Move, Northman.' One of Pybba's minions prodded him in the back again, harder this time, sending him sprawling to the ground. It was too much trouble to explain that he was Mercian. Instead he rose, and shuffled forward, allowing them to lead him to a damp cell in one of the tumbled-down towers. His men were led away to be held somewhere else.

The key sounded in the lock. Hafual sank down and put his head in his hands. His carefully constructed world was in ruins, just as Svala had predicted before she threw Narfi in the fire. He had lost everything. Palni would tell him to escape and start over. But here in Mercia was where he had planted his trees and where he wanted to grow old with Elene by his side. The dream tasted like ash in his mouth.

'They have Hafual. We must help him. We must before something worse happens.' Elene choked back the rising hysteria. She'd run all the way from court to the lodging, not bothering to see where they had taken Hafual. Narfi cried and shouted for his Far until people on the streets turned to look at her in astonishment. One fishmonger even accused her of stealing the child and attempted to take him from her, which made Narfi cling all the tighter to her neck.

Thankfully, the instant Narfi spotted Bugge, all the tears vanished. He struggled to get down and toddled to be with the dog. She stumbled to a bench in front of the fire.

'What's wrong, Lady Elene?' Brother Palni asked. 'Where's Hafual? Who has him?'

'Hafual is in danger, true danger. Ceolwulf has him in a cell. And his men. We must help him, but I don't know how.' She pressed her hands against her eyes. 'I can't think.'

Brother Palni came to sit beside her and gathered her hands in his. 'Why has King Ceolwulf put Hafual under lock and key? Along with all his men?'

'This makes no sense. Slowly and clearly please, Lady Elene,' Father Oswald said.

Elene withdrew her hands and fumbled for a handkerchief to wipe her eyes. Narfi had stopped his playing and was watching her with big eyes. 'Pybba accused him of killing his man when the bandits attacked. He cast doubt on if we were attacked at all.'

'Is that all?'

'He claims that Hafual was raising an army of Northmen and that is why he needed all the wool. Hafual wants to open new markets for the wool.'

'Opening new markets is a good idea. Why does Ceolwulf object?'

'Pybba has poisoned his mind. He claims Hafual murdered the bandit.'

Brother Palni's brow knitted. 'But you were attacked. I've seen Hafual's wound. His men will say the same. Has Ceolwulf questioned them?'

Elene took a steadying breath. Screaming at Brother Palni would make things worse, not better. 'I know we were. I was there. I helped to rescue the men. Ceolwulf listened to Pybba and believed him. Apparently, Hafual's men are all from the North and their word is suspect.'

Brother Palni drummed his fingers. 'What about you?'

'My word doesn't count as I am married to him. A good wife will not speak against her husband.' Elene banged her fists together. 'My temper hangs by the slenderest of threads.'

'What is the essence of Pybba's claim?' Father Oswald asked.

'Pybba claims they were his men and is asking for a trial and confiscation of all Hafual's property if he is convicted. Pybba laid his trap well.'

'It is good that you believe Hafual.'

Elene clenched her fists and counted to ten. Slowly the red mist vanished from in front of her eyes. 'My husband speaks the truth.'

'Surely you must have something to prove his innocence. Anything, Lady Elene?'

Elene kept her voice calm and explained the full situation, including the wool which was intended for markets in Frankia and beyond. Brother Palni raised his brow at the wool but agreed that attempting to sell it to a new market hardly constituted an attempt to raise an army.

'The abbot will have the gold and various items,' Father Oswald declared. 'We should go to him. Retrieve them. King Ceolwulf will give way once he sees the items have nothing to do with Pybba.'

Brother Palni sucked his teeth. 'I never liked Abbot Wilfrid. He kept the choicest bits of meat for himself and his favourites. All I ever received was the toughest mutton.'

'What does mutton have to do with anything?' Elene asked. 'Stop speaking in riddles.'

'Pybba will have done a deal with the abbot. Where do you think he learned about the incident?'

'You're right, Palni. The man would not make such

a claim without first ensuring that he had evidence.' Father Oswald positively beamed at Palni.

Each word hit Elene's heart like a hammer, reinforcing what she'd already guessed. Pybba had outmanoeuvred them and Hafual was about to pay with his life unless she contrived something special. 'But why would the abbot do such a thing?'

'It could be as simple as not liking men from the North,' Palni explained.

'The abbot likes you,' she said, trying to force the rising tide of panic back down her throat. 'He said how much he enjoys it when you visit, bringing the gossip and news.'

Brother Palni drummed his fingers against the table. 'You see that is why I distrust this situation. The abbot normally has something else to do when I am there.'

'He is a political creature, Lady Elene, blowing with the wind,' Father Oswald said in a soothing tone. 'Most abbots are. It is the nature of the job. He may not even know that Lord Pybba has made an accusation, but I agree with my brother monk, we must assume our cause will receive no help from that quarter.'

Elene regarded the heavy ring on her left hand. Only a few short days ago she'd noticed it all the time, but now it was part of her. 'The wind is currently blowing in Pybba's direction. I have to make it blow the other way. No one else can.'

'You go in demanding, and you are likely to come away with nothing, Lady Elene. Caution. You want to keep Hafual alive. Above all things. I have heard the stories about your failures at court.'

Elene stared at the dying embers. Brother Palni was right. Pybba had the upper hand. Hafual was going to lose everything that he'd worked so hard for because she had insisted they leave the treasure at the abbey. She'd been naive. She always found a way to make a mistake. In her mind, she heard Hafual's voice telling her to stop being unfair to herself and that he believed in her. She twisted the ring round and round on her finger. 'What do you suggest? Sitting here, wringing my hands, helps no one.'

'Rescue him and put him on board a ship for the North. Go with him. Start over. Hafual has gold, my lady, and contacts. A new life. Maybe in Iceland. The land is good there from what I hear. Your sisters will help you through the worst.'

An ice-cold chill went through Elene. Brother Palni was recommending running away and then throwing themselves on the mercy of Ansithe or Cynehild. 'Leave everything behind? Abandon my father? The people who work the lands?'

Brother Palni raised his brow. 'Do you want to save his life, or do you care more about your position?'

'I married him to save Baelle Heale,' Elene said, fighting back the tears.

Brother Palni shrugged. 'Pretty poor reason to marry anyone but what do I, a humble monk, know?'

Elene stared the embers. Brother Palni made it sound like she had no heart, but he didn't know Hafual. Hafual was proud of being Mercian and what he had done with the land. She doubted that he would slip away even if he were rescued. 'He loves Wulfhere's Clearing with every fibre of his being. Would he even go? Hafual is no coward who wants to slink off into the night.'

'What is more important to you—the man or the land?'

It surprised her that Father Oswald even asked. She loved Hafual with every breath, but she also knew Hafual had put roots down in this land. It was here he wanted to make a stand. He might not have been born a Mercian, but she knew he wanted to die one. Leaving would kill him.

'Hafual is more important, but he loves the land.' Elene closed her eyes and saw Hafual's face again as he pointed out the spot where he claimed he could see Wulfhere's Clearing. 'He won't go. It would be wrong of me to ask him. We will have to find another way, Brother Palni. Escaping to Iceland will not outrun any demons.'

'It is your job to make him see that he has no choice.'

She bowed her head. 'There has to be another way.'

Brother Palni slapped his hand down on the table. 'When you find it, let me know. Until then, I'll make preparations to rescue Hafual. We will get him on a ship even if I have to bind his legs and arms and gag his mouth.'

'And if he wants to fight? Surely he has earned that right.'

'Then he is a bigger fool than I thought he was. He is in no shape to face any battle. You have seen his shoulder. Explain it, Oswald. I refuse to waste any more of my breath.' Brother Palni strode from the hall.

Elene paced up and down while Father Oswald started to intone a rosary. Leaving was too easy an answer, and she knew they would both regret it in time. There had to be a way of forcing Pybba's hand and revealing the truth that Hafual was innocent. Hafual deserved to be the Lord of Wulfhere's Clearing and to be an advisor to the king. Giving in was giving up.

'Pretty. Far kill bad man.' Narfi toddled towards her carrying the brooch Hafual had given him. 'Far.'

She scooped Narfi and held him close. 'You at least believe in your father.'

The boy placed a kiss on her cheek before handing her the brooch. Elene examined it with fresh eyes. The design was unique but one she knew from years ago. She drew in her breath and wondered that she had missed its significance before. The brooch symbolised alliance to the old King of Mercia. No one who supported Pybba would dare wear such a brooch. Pybba famously hated the old king and blamed him for losing half of Mercia.

'Far?' the little boy said. 'Where?'

'He will be back soon, darling.' With trembling fingers Elene wrapped the brooch in a handkerchief and gave instructions to the maid to keep a good eye on Narfi as she had jobs to do.

Brother Palni was wrong. She did have options. 'Father Oswald, I have a task for you.'

'While you are doing that, I will be figuring out how we are going to get your man out of that place and on a ship bound for a safe haven,' Brother Palni said, stirring the fire. 'Sometimes running is the only way, my lady.'

'Sometimes a person has to fight for what she believes in and knows to be right. Hafual taught me that.'

Chapter Sixteen

'Lady Elene, you wished to see me?' King Ceolwulf looked up from his prayer book later that day in the deserted private chapel of the royal residence. 'My confessor said that you needed to see me. Most irregular, but I've no wish to put my immortal soul in peril by denying him.'

Elene risked a breath. Father Oswald had done as she'd asked and more. Immortal soul indeed. The priest obviously knew what he was on about. She took the brooch out from under her cloak. 'This is the brooch which the bandit was wearing openly. I thought you might like to examine it.'

Ceolwulf smiled gently. 'Why, will it put my soul in danger?'

'Look at it. I remember seeing brooches like that before the Northmen came. I suspect you will as well. It is a device which has fallen out of favour in Mercia.'

He turned the brooch over and over in his hand. 'Supporters of the late king wore it.'

'Lord Pybba vowed that he would slay any supporter of the late king. He blames them for his father's death. Therefore, the bandit could not have been one of Pybba's men.'

His hand closed about the brooch. 'Pybba is given to exaggeration.'

'That may be, but the man was wearing it when my husband slew him.'

'How did you come by it?'

'Hafual presented it to his son. He had little idea of its true meaning.'

'Why didn't you say this at the time?'

'I was a young girl when the last king reigned. I barely recognised the brooch. After I returned to our lodgings, I looked at it again and discerned its hidden meaning. All the other treasure is with Abbot Wilfrid. My husband felt the abbey which had suffered greatly should have some reward.'

'Why would the abbot side against your husband?'

'He might not like Northmen.' Elene tried to ignore the pounding of her heart. Ceolwulf had to agree to her suggestion. Her scheme depended on it. 'He might have been misled.'

'Are you accusing Lord Pybba of seeking to subvert the truth?'

Elene widened her eyes and fluttered her lashes. 'I believe Lord Pybba may have allowed his sense of grievance to overcome his natural caution.'

'Sense of grievance?'

'He desires above all things to humiliate my husband. There has been bad blood since last summer. Something to do with the Hwicce attempting to grab land on the border. There was some question about Pybba's loyalty at the time. My husband mentioned it in passing. Then I chose my husband, a former North-man, over him.'

Elene waited with bated breath. Ceolwulf had to see she was right.

'You are right about the disagreement. I had believed it settled but perhaps not.'

'I would say definitely not. Pybba made an offer for my hand, but I refused it having plighted my troth to Hafual. When he heard the story about Hafual killing the bandit and rescuing the entire party, he was tempted to believe a lie. A sort of madness has descended.'

Ceolwulf smiled. 'You should be a politician, Lady Elene. Lord Pybba could be mistaken. He could have used the tale to bear false witness. I accept that, but Hafual should never have tried to attack me.'

'He came to stand by you. He was attempting to defend himself against false accusations.' Elene kept her head up and knew she was fighting for Hafual's life and what remained of their marriage. 'He saved your life, King Ceolwulf. Why would he want to take it now after serving you for so long?'

His brow knitted. 'I had not thought about it.'

'Surely that deserves some consideration. Has Lord Pybba ever saved your life? Has he ever put his body in front of a wild animal for you?'

The King bowed his head. 'This brooch came from the bandit?'

'I swear it on my immortal soul.'

The King chewed his bottom lip and Elene could see why her brothers-in-law predicted that he would be far too indecisive in battle. 'I've no idea what to think.'

'If that is the case, my husband deserves the right to defend himself.'

He gave a little smile. 'In a trial? Pybba has demanded that he chose the jury. He wants good and true Mercians.'

Elene rolled her eyes. 'Heaven forfend that a man should face an impartial jury.'

Two bright spots appeared on the King's cheeks. 'Sarcasm is unbecoming, my lady.'

Elene made a little curtsey and apologised. 'This needs to be settled once and for all time or there will be no peace in this kingdom. Lord Pybba has been trying to pick a quarrel with Hafual. He knows that Hafual is one of the reasons you are secure on your throne. Ask yourself—who has done the most to keep your borders with the Hwicce safe? Who has attempted to restore the fortunes of the kingdom through establishing a wool trade with Frankia? Peace brings prosperity.'

Ceolwulf turned the brooch over and over in his hand. 'I dislike my nobles in conflict. I have asked them to make peace in the past.'

'If it comes out that you punished a loyal follower, why should other men give you their allegiance? How long until Wessex takes advantage of such a thing?'

'Then what should I do?'

Elene took a deep breath. She knew what Hafual would want her to ask for, but she hated saying the words. He was not ready for any sort of battle. She needed to find another way. 'Listen to my husband. See if what he asks for is unreasonable. You can see that Lord Pybba tried to poison your mind.'

The King closed his fist about the brooch. 'You speak persuasively, my lady. I will give your husband a chance to make his case.'

'Without retainers. Between you and I, we may be able to broker a peace.'

'Hafual chose well when he married you.'

Elene made a curtsey. 'I prefer to think I chose well when I married him.'

At the sound of the lock turning, Hafual lifted his head. Silhouetted in the light was Elene. Without a word or sign, he knew her. He groaned and hoped that she was mirage. She had no business being here, putting herself in danger.

'Your time is limited,' his gaoler said.

'What I have to say will not take long.'

He could guess why she'd come—to give him the plans Brother Palni had made for escape. He knew the man well enough to know that the monk would have some scheme, except he refused to run.

'I won't escape,' he said before she uttered another word. 'I refuse to spend my life on the run. I'm innocent.'

Elene bristled like an angry cat. 'Did you think I would ask that of you? Give me some credit for knowing how stubborn you are. We are going to fight, and we are going to win. Pybba will rue the day he tangled with me.'

She wasn't coming here with a hare-brained scheme of Palni's. She wanted to fight for him. His wife, the woman he loved, was willing to fight for him. He was not alone. He had Elene by his side, and he knew he didn't deserve her, but he was very pleased she was there.

He raised his chained wrists. 'I've little idea about what you will think.'

She demanded that the chains be taken from his

hands and feet. The gaoler reluctantly shuffled in and undid the chains. At Elene's gesture he left the room. The blood flowed back into his limbs.

Only then did Hafual take her into his arms and hold her tight. He wanted to whisper so many things; instead he rested his cheek against the top of her head and held her until the trembling stopped. She leant back against his arms and gave a smile which warmed him down to his toes.

'It is good to see you. Brother Palni predicted that I wouldn't be able to do it. He has kept working on an alternative.'

He dropped his arms and stepped away from her.

'What is going on? What sort of game are you playing? What have you offered the King?' He shook his head. Elene rarely played games. 'I will not run like a dog, Elene, even for you. Being rescued is not what I require.'

'Are you always this stubborn?'

'When it comes to doing what is right, yes.'

'Circumstances have altered.' Elene rapidly explained about the brooch and the King.

Hafual stared at his wife. 'The brooch was the device of someone whom Pybba hated? How does that help us?'

'The King saw cause to doubt Pybba's sworn oath. Pybba would never have allowed anyone who pledged their allegiance to him to openly wear such a brooch.'

'Pybba will have the excuse ready.' Hafual shook his head. 'This feud will only be solved when one of us is dead. I refuse to leave Mercia, Elene, and start over.'

'No one is asking you to.' Elene gestured to the door.

'Ceolwulf agrees that you and Pybba need to solve

this. A court divided against itself will be rife with intrigue. He knows how the last king's rule weakened when the court gave way to civil war. Some people even said that it allowed the Northmen and the Danes to attack.'

Hafual tried to keep the hope from growing in his breast. 'He has agreed to a duel between Pybba and me? I've been trying for this for months. Every time, Ceolwulf finds an excuse. He sides with Pybba.'

'He cannot have you making accusations against each other. We agreed that a jury trial will not work as Pybba will bribe the jury. You two are to talk in the King's room. I am to take you there.'

'How does that help me?' Hafual ran a hand through his hair. Elene was trying to help, but she was an innocent and putting herself in grave danger. 'Pybba will twist my words.'

'I suspect Pybba will suggest a duel. He knows about your injury.' Elene tilted her chin upwards. 'All I ask is you allow me to speak. I know how to get under Pybba's skin. I've done it before.'

Hafual put a hand on her shoulder. 'King Ceolwulf has already decided the victor. Pybba has a silver tongue.'

Elene retrieved a jar of ointment from the pouch on her belt. Her smile lit up the dark room. 'I believe in you, Hafual—try believing in me.'

Try believing in her. He knew suddenly it was what he had not done. He had forgotten to show her how much he trusted her and her judgement. Every time she'd been right.

'Believing in you is something I do as naturally as breathing.'

Her smile made his heart turn over. Silently he promised himself that should by some miracle they get out of this, he would ensure that Elene knew the depth of his abiding love for her. 'What happens next?'

'We go to see Ceolwulf, but it won't come to a fight. Pybba will show that he is the disloyal one when we meet him. I have faith.'

He caught her hand. His throat closed up. Elene was trying. She'd done more than he could have dreamt possible. She'd given him a second chance. 'Elene—'

She put two fingers over his mouth. 'Hush. Let's solve this mess before you make any declaration. You need to hear the full plan.'

'There's more?'

'We both know about Pybba's temper when he is thwarted. It is about getting him to lose his temper. He did it with my father. He will do it again, and this time you will be able to act.'

'You want me to make him lose his temper?'

She shook her head. 'I'm going to do that. I know how to do it.'

He kissed her fingertips. He was unworthy of such a woman as a wife. Although he doubted that she would be able to do it, it was worth a try. 'I'm pleased I married you. You are truly the bravest of all the sisters.'

Her eyes became large in the dim light. 'If I'm brave it is because I'm fighting for something I believe in. You.'

Hafual's throat closed. He wanted to ask her to give him the opportunity to erase Nerian from her heart and to see if their marriage could truly work. But the words wouldn't come. Her belief in him would be enough for now.

* * *

Elene attempted to ignore the butterflies which were busily dancing in her stomach. Bravest of all the sisters? Her older sisters would have done something completely different. But this was her plan, and she was determined to make it work. Undoubtedly everyone would call her foolish, but this had to be the best way.

Pybba scowled when he saw who was in the King's chamber.

'Why is this traitor here?' he asked, pointing at Hafual.

'Why do you say he is a traitor?' Elene shot back before Hafual could answer. 'What evidence do you have beyond innuendo?'

'The treasure. The Abbot is sending it.'

'No doubt it will mysteriously disappear before it arrives,' Elene said, crossing her arms.

'Women should hold their tongue when men are discussing important matters.' Pybba snapped his fingers. 'Hafual, control your bride.'

A dimple flashed in and out of Hafual's cheek. 'One thing I find impossible to do is controlling my bride's tongue. I enjoy hearing her voice.'

Pybba turned to the King. 'You see the disrespect he gives me?'

'I see the disrespect you give Lady Elene.' The King stroked his beard. 'The lady has done nothing except tell the truth. Her words are thoughtful and pertinent to the matter at hand.'

Pybba's scowl increased further. 'You were always soft on a pretty face.'

Elene kept her gaze straight ahead. If she dared look at Hafual, she knew she'd dissolve into peals of laughter. Pybba was doing an excellent job of digging a mighty hole. The muscles in her neck eased slightly.

'Lady Elene is a very pretty woman. I believe my ealdorman did well to choose her,' King Ceolwulf remarked. 'The match is one I should have advocated for long ago.'

'She attempts to beguile you. Make you believe that her husband is innocent when his black heart is there for all who care to see.'

Elene fluttered her lashes. 'What is my husband guilty of? He acted to save his wife and child from bandits who demanded our treasure and who had severely wounded one of his warriors.'

'He is a Northman. All Northmen are untrustworthy villains. He conspired with the Hwicce on our western border to make me look bad this summer. I complained time and again of this and you did nothing, sire. Nothing. And he has killed my man. I demand my vengeance.'

Out of the corner of her eye, she saw Hafual stiffen and silently prayed that he would keep his temper. Pybba was close to another temper tantrum, if she simply prodded a little more. Hafual gave a slight nod to urge her onward.

'This Northman saved King Ceolwulf's life.'

Pybba stamped his foot. 'Lucky.'

'It was a plot by followers of the old king,' Hafual remarked. 'I believe they also murdered your father and brother, Pybba.'

'What of it?'

'Followers who wore this sort of badge?' Elene took out the badge the bandit had worn. 'Do you recognise it, Lord Pybba?'

Pybba went red and took a step closer to her. He shook his fist. 'I know what that badge is. Don't you dare try to say that any of my followers would ever wear such a thing! My father died because of men who wore that badge!'

'And yet one was,' Elene said in a measured voice. At Hafual's small gesture she moved closer to Ceolwulf. 'The man whom Hafual killed was wearing this badge. Hafual gave it to his son to wear which is why the abbot never had it. I give it to you, sire, for safekeeping.'

Pybba's mouth dropped open and then closed shut, rapidly, several times in quick succession.

'Is there an explanation, Pybba?' the King asked, taking the brooch from her outstretched hand. 'Would anyone in your employ wear such an infamous thing?'

Pybba roared and charged towards her and the King, his sword drawn. 'You lie! You are nothing but a lover of the North. All your family is like that.'

Hafual stepped in front of them. 'No one threatens my wife.'

He lowered his good shoulder and barged into Pybba, getting him off balance. Pybba dropped the sword which Hafual retrieved before his enemy had a chance to pick it up. Pybba drew out his knife and lunged towards him again. Hafual deflected the knife, brought the sword forward and connected with the man's belly.

'He stabbed me.' Pybba wrapped his hands about his middle and blood dripped from his mouth. 'I want it known that the Northman stabbed me. I demand vengeance. He broke our agreement. You must banish him.'

He fell to his knees, gave one gasp, and then collapsed. Dead.

'I wanted to keep him from attacking my wife. Then he attacked me.'

The King mopped his brow. 'I saw what happened, Hafual. It would appear you saved my life once again. That man was going to kill me.'

Hafual bowed his head. 'I accept your apology, sire.'

'You are a true Mercian, Lord Hafual.' King Ceolwulf banged his fist on the arm of his throne. 'A true Mercian. You risked your life for your king. That man would have me off the throne. I should have listened to you earlier.'

'I am going to take my wife back to the lodgings now. I'd appreciate it if my men were released.'

The King gulped twice. 'Of course, of course.'

He sent for one of his servants, who scampered away.

'Are you unhurt?' Hafual asked when they were out of the King's chamber. 'I worried there.'

'King Ceolwulf is convinced you went to save him.' Elene smiled. 'I think that would be good to allow him his mistake.'

'Not him, you.' Hafual put his hands on her upper arms. 'When Pybba went towards you, I had to save you. It did not matter that I was unarmed. My life wouldn't be worth living without you in it.'

Elene's heart skipped a beat. 'You care about me?'

'I started caring about you when you fell at my feet when you were trying to escape the betrothal. Something within me stirred and for the first time since before Svala died, I felt like my life had colour again, instead of being shades of never-ending grey.' He looked down at her with eyes like a warm summer's day. 'Will you give me the chance to make you forget Nerian? To allow me a small place in your life?'

'You know very little about me if you think I have any feelings for a man like him.'

His eyes widened. 'You don't have any feelings for Nerian?'

'A girlish fancy which failed to stand the test of time. Yes, he hurt me when he married another, but I don't think he ever really captured my heart, as I never knew him. My heart whispered the doubts before, but I really discovered the truth when he cajoled me into coupling with him and then told me it was my fault.' She pressed her fingers against his mouth, stopping his words. She knew what was coming, as he had said, but she had to say the words or otherwise she'd always regret it. She refused to hide. 'I grew up, Hafual, and as a woman I discovered that I need a steadfast man who can withstand the storms of life. I believe you are that man.'

'Elene—' he said against her fingers.

'I know how Svala hurt you and how you tried to do your best by staying with her,' she said, plunging onwards. 'I know how loyal and true you are. It is part of the reason why I love you. Yes, love, even though you never wanted it from me. I couldn't help it but that is the way love is. My heart decided who to love and that person is you, Hafual.

'Are you going to let me speak?'

'I've said my piece.'

He gathered her hands in his. His eyes turned deep blue, the sort she could look at for ever and not discern all the colours. She wondered that she'd ever thought his eyes cold and unyielding. 'When Svala died, a mixture of grief and relief caused my heart to shrivel away to nothingness. I was relieved because I was not going to have to face her demands which I could not meet ever again, and I grieved that I'd failed to be the husband she wanted. My heart had frozen, and I couldn't see away to unfreeze it. I took little pleasure in life and in my son. Then you challenged me, asking for help. You refused to take my excuses. You made me see the love my son bore for me. You showed me life was there to be lived. My poor frozen heart utterly melted. You don't have a tiny part, Elene, but you hold my whole heart in your hands.'

Elene shook her head to get rid of the buzzing noise. She had Hafual's heart? 'You married me because my father insisted.'

He softly laughed. 'Since when have I ever done anything because of your father? Even if my brain refused to admit it at the time, my heart knew I married you for one reason only—I required you in my life.'

Elene laid her head against his chest and listened to the steady sound of his heartbeat. He stroked her hair as she listened to the steady thump of his heart, the heart she knew beat for her. 'Shall we go home?'

'There is nowhere I'd rather be than there.

Epilogue

July 876, Baelle Heale

The water meadow a little way from the great hall shimmered in a heat haze with clouds of butterflies rising. In the distance the song of a song thrush trilled. And the sky was a particularly dark blue. Elene stared up and made a memory.

Her sisters and their families had travelled to Baelle Heale to be here for the christening of Elene's first child. The men had stayed up at the hall to thrash out formally the questions of inheritance and what to do about the growing enmity between the Five Boroughs, Mercia and Wessex. In this land, someone always seemed to be causing trouble.

'Peace personified,' Ansithe said from where she sat under the old oak with her eldest son resting on her knee, clearly tired from having tried to keep up with Cynehild's oldest, Wulfgar. 'To think that this is where it all started—where I first spied the Northmen who would change our lives. When I saw them, I thought we would never have peace here again.'

'Thanks to your quick thinking, we defeated them,' Elene said, ready to give praise where it was due.

'We all made a difference that day,' Ansithe said, holding her hands out to her sisters. 'It does my heart good to see you both. My sisters.'

'I'm far too hot to move or I'd hug you,' Cynehild said, wiping the sweat from her brow and motioning for Wulfgar to come sit with her. Narfi, who worshiped him, quickly followed. 'Being pregnant in the summer is less than fun. Kal is hoping for a girl this time.'

'I am beginning to think there is going to be a dearth of women in the next generation,' Ansithe said with a laugh. 'I'd been so sure that my latest was going to be a girl, but we had another boy. Moir is determined to create his own comitatus of sons, a band of brothers.'

Elene cradled her soundly sleeping six-week-old son in her arms. Every day, she was amazed that Hafual and she had created such a perfect being. Hafual had taken such pride in her. After consulting with Father Oswald, they had named him Harold which was fairly close to Hafual but had a Mercian ring to it. 'Thankfully, there is very little for us to do today except enjoy the christening.'

'I can't believe Father married Asida,' Cynehild said.

'They appear well-matched and Asida is enjoying running Baelle Heale while I have my hands full with Wulfhere's Clearing and the house in Ludenwic,' Elene said.

At Asida's suggestion with the three sisters gathered for the christening, it had been decided that Harold would inherit Baelle Heale and Narfi Wulfhere's Clearing. Cynehild's husband had formally adopted Wulfgar and plans were afoot for him to inherit his father's lands. Cynehild and Ansithe would receive payment for their share of the inheritance when their father died.

'They seem to be happy and Asida appears to be a very wise woman,' Ansithe said, her brow wrinkling. 'How did it happen? It was not a union I would have predicted.'

'I believe Asida was determined,' Elene said with a laugh. 'They play *tafl* and she manages the estate now that Ecgbert and his wife have left the area.'

'Did you ever find out if Ecgbert was bribed?' Ansithe asked.

'He admitted it when Hafual and I returned from Ludenwic. Hafual confronted him and explained Pybba's treachery.'

'Where is he now?' Cynehild asked.

'Thankfully, Ecgbert agreed the best course of action was to leave the neighbourhood and never return. He and his wife packed their things and went that very day. Our father did not even protest that they should be given a second chance.'

'I wondered if Asida had any influence over our father with that decision,' Cynehild said.

'I wouldn't like to say, but when we returned, everyone did mention how much they enjoyed playing *tafl* together.'

'Oh, I know all about *tafl*. It is a very different game from the one our father played. Moir taught me the finer points,' Ansithe said.

'Kal would agree,' Cynehild said.

'I really do not want to think about our father in that fashion,' Elene said. 'Some things are best kept private.'

The sisters laughingly agreed.

'What is this about Brother Palni and Father Oswald? Are they really going on pilgrimage together?' Cynehild asked from where she sat. 'Kal mentioned something about it earlier, but I told him that he must be mistaken. Father Oswald hates travelling.'

'Rome. There is some talk of Brother Palni taking holy orders. But Palni says he wants to ensure Father Oswald gets to see Rome and returns safely,' Ansithe said with a confident tilt of her head. 'They are apparently *anam-cara*, soul-friends, now.'

'Soul-friends. That is a wonderful way of putting it. I believe Kal is mine,' Cynehild said.

'And Moir mine.'

Elene hugged her sleeping baby closer to her chest. She would certainly call Hafual her *anam-cara*. One of her favourite times of the day was the evening time when they shared with each other what the other had been doing. It was a partnership in the truest sense of the word. 'We can all agree that our respective husbands are our soul-friends. We three have managed to find the right men for us.'

Although he still had things to do at court, Hafual tried hard to keep the time away to a minimum. He wanted to be there watching his children grow and teaching them. Already, Narfi showed signs of becoming a good warrior.

'I can see our husbands,' Cynehild said, standing up and waving her arm. 'Asida and our father are not far behind.'

The three Northman strode shoulder to shoulder into the meadow. Vibrant and alive but at peace with the world. Each went to his wife and greeted her with a kiss.

'All settled?' Elene murmured against Hafual's mouth.

'All settled. Both Kal and Moir will be pleased to send their wool to Ludenwic. I foresee the town becoming a major port in due course, bringing peace and prosperity to all who use her.' Hafual put his arm about her shoulders.

Elene looked towards her sisters, who were occupied with their offspring and respective husbands. Even her father appeared content as he leaned on Asida's arm. 'Peace and prosperity is all anyone can ask for.'

* * * * *

If you enjoyed this story,
be sure to read the other books in
Michelle Styles' Vows and Vikings miniseries

A Deal with Her Rebel Viking
Betrothed to the Enemy Viking

And why not check out
Michelle Styles' other great reads

The Warrior's Viking Bride
Sent as the Viking's Bride
Conveniently Wed to the Viking

Author Note

While it is tempting to think that history is static and unchanging, this is untrue—particularly in the case of the Vikings. There is much we do not know, and some of the things we think we know might prove to be false or misinterpreted when more archaeological evidence is uncovered. Sometimes it can help to look through a different lens rather the more familiar primary sources' lenses.

Recently I read Neil Price's masterful *The Children of Ash and Elm: A History of the Vikings*—Penguin Books, 2020—which looks at some of the latest research on the Vikings, and I found that I had to readjust a few things. In 2014, for example, a figurine was discovered that changed the perception of how people dressed in the Viking period. People living in that age knew how they dressed. It was only people in later ages—such as the Hollywood golden age—who came up with strange and varied ideas.

Other recent research into the bread made in the period shows that hard tack—including the familiar round hole—and other breads such as pretzels, which are still eaten today, were made and enjoyed in the Viking period. When I was growing up, my maternal grandmother used to give me hard tack as a treat. For people in the UK, hard tack is a kind of crisp rye bread.

The interiors of Viking halls are now thought to have included pieces of stamped gold and silver foil affixed to wooden columns. They were used almost like calling cards to create a brightness. To the Viking, the stamps would have had instant meaning and context, but to twenty-first-century eyes, the best that can be hoped for is a vague understanding of the embossed figures.

I had never really considered how much time it takes to weave a sail such as the ones the Vikings used on their long ships—but it is the equivalent of four years of one person's hard labour simply to weave a sail which would last about five years or so. To equip the average-sized long boat with sails, clothes, rugs, tents and ropes would take a thirty-person team about a year, from spinning to final completion.

When you consider some of the fleets which attacked the coasts of Normandy—upwards of two hundred ships—that is a lot of wool. This increased need for wool helps to explain why the UK, and in particular Middle England, became so prosperous during this period. The name of Woolwich in London—established approximately 918—means literally a place where wool is traded.

You can learn something similar about wood. Different types of timber were required for building and maintaining the ships, as well as for creating shields and indeed everyday items such as bowls. Again, England in particular was well suited for this sort of trade, and the Vikings took advantage of it.

It can be far too easy to think only about the sea piracy, and not about the supplies needed to ensure that sort of life continued, and about what sort of trade routes did exist in the Viking Age. Because of recent finds it has become clear that the Silk Road was operational, even if people only tended to travel part of the way, and many trades had to take place in order for a bead fashioned in China to end up in the grave of a Viking buried in England.

You may notice that London is called Ludenwic instead of Londinium—the Roman name—or Lundenbergh—the Wessex version. Ludenwic was the Mercian name. A *wic* meant a proto-market.

As ever all mistakes, including the inadvertent ones caused by my not studying the latest archaeological reports, are mine.

If you are interested in this time period, I can recommend the following books in addition to the Neil Price one.

Adams, Max. (2017.) *Aelfred's Britain: War and Peace in the Viking Age.* Head of Zeus Ltd.

Adams, Max (2021.) *The First Kingdom.* Head of Zeus Ltd.

Adams, Max. (2013.) *In the Land of Giants: Journeys through the Dark Ages.* Head of Zeus Ltd.

Ferguson, Robert. (2010.) *The Hammer and the Cross: A New History of the Vikings.* Penguin Books.

Jesch, Judith. (1991.) *Women in the Viking Age*. The Boydell Press.

Magnusson, Magnus. (2003.) *The Vikings*. Tempus Publishing.

Oliver, Neil. (2012.) *Vikings: A History*. Orion Books.

Parker, Philip. (2014.) *The Northmen's Fury: A History of the Viking World*. Jonathan Cape.

Williams, Gareth, ed. (2014.) *Vikings: Life and Legend*. British Museum Press.

Williams, Thomas. (2017.) *Viking Britain: A History*. William Collins.